The Sad Case
of Harpo Higgins

Also by Eugene McEldowney

A Kind of Homecoming
A Stone of the Heart

Eugene McEldowney

The Sad Case
of Harpo Higgins

HEINEMANN : LONDON

First published in Great Britain 1996
by William Heinemann Ltd
an imprint of Reed International Books Ltd
Michelin House, 81 Fulham Road, London SW3 6RB
and Auckland, Melbourne, Singapore and Toronto

A CIP catalogue record for this title
is available from the British Library
ISBN 0 434 00358 1

Typeset by Deltatype Ltd, Ellesmere Port, Cheshire
Printed and bound in Great Britain
by Clays Ltd, St. Ives plc

For Gavin

Book One

1

'Get yer hand off my leg.'

'What did you say?'

'You heard me. Get yer bleedin' hand off my leg.'

'My hand's not on yer leg.'

'Oh yeah. What's that then? A bleedin' eliphent's trunk?'

There was the sound of a smack and giggling, a muffled cry. Then silence.

The taxi driver glanced quickly into the mirror. The boy had his arm round the girl's shoulder and was trying to bite her ear. She had her head laid across his chest, her hair shining and dark like a raven's wing. Her skirt had ridden up above her knees and he could see the white flash of underwear.

The driver coughed loudly to show his disapproval. The sound filled the little space. But they took no notice. The driver turned his face away and tried to concentrate on the road ahead.

They were travelling by the quays, the river cold and menacing, the lights of the city twinkling before them. He could see Liberty Hall up ahead, the Custom House, shining white in the artificial light. There were ships moored along the quayside, cranes, gantries, containers and pallets stacked in neat formation by the river's edge. He could see the waves tossing on the water, smell the strong, salt smell of the sea.

From the back seat he heard a low humming sound like a moan or a cry of pain. Then he realised that the boy was serenading her now, singing her a pop song, something he had heard earlier at the concert. The driver's head filled with remembered noise, the crashing of drums, the roar of the amplifiers. Call that music? The driver made a tutting sound with his tongue. Young people. No respect. No morality.

The headlights swept the empty road. Now and then a car passed, going the other way towards the Point, the sound of its engine echoing across the water. They passed boarded shop-fronts, cold, grey warehouses, the grim façades of dockside pubs.

They were approaching the city. It was getting brighter. He saw a builders' yard, a lorry parked outside, pale shadows fluttering in a doorway as they went past. He heard a loud report like a car exhaust backfiring. The sound shattered the silence of the quays. A flock of seagulls started up from the wall and spread out across the river. He could hear the beating of their wings. He thought he heard another sound, like running footsteps, clip-clopping across the wet cobblestones, but he could see nothing.

The driver pulled the taxi in and stopped. There was a man lying on the roadway. He was wearing a dirty blue anorak and jeans. There was a puddle round his head. It looked like red paint.

The driver felt a sickness rise in his stomach. The man was lying on his back, his arm flung wide above his head. There was blood everywhere. It seemed to be pumping from a hole in the man's face, like oil spilling from a can.

'Holy Jesus,' the driver said. He knelt down on the wet road. He could feel the damp seep into his trouser legs. He began to pray. 'Oh my God, I am heartily sorry . . .'

The young couple had wound down the window of the car and were leaning out.

'What's the matter?' the young fella said. 'Did somebody get hurt?'

2

Superintendent Megarry walked along the path below Howth Head and gazed out over the sea. He looked north, past Ireland's Eye and Lambay island, up along the coast where the waves were tossing white and grey upon the sand. There was a smell of heather and gorse from the cliffs and it filled the air. He could hear the cry of gulls. It was the only sound apart from the soft lapping of the sea on the rocks below.

This is peace, he thought. This is what they have all told me I should seek. Doctor Henry, Kathleen, Drysdale, all those people who have fussed over me in the last few weeks. Peace, rest, relaxation. No pressure. There was a stone seat covered in moss and he sat down on it and searched in his pockets for his cigarettes.

In the distance, shimmering in the mist, way past Malahide and Balbriggan, he could just make out the outline of a mountain range, purple and blue in the thin morning light. The Mournes. The outpost of the Northern land. The Northern people.

He sighed and rattled a matchbox in his hand. The breeze from the sea cooled his face. He took out his cigarettes and paused. He wasn't supposed to smoke, not since the mild heart attack he had suffered in Spain, but he had found it impossible

5

to stop. Instead he had compromised with Kathleen and tried to cut down.

He remembered how it had happened. A heavy lunch in the little restaurant beside the beach. He had eaten a steak with potatoes fried in oil and garlic. They'd had a table outside in the shade. He remembered that it was hot. Ninety degrees someone had said. The wine had tasted tepid and afterwards a large brandy. He had just lit a cigarette, just like now, when he felt the pain burn across his chest, the dizziness, and then falling across the table. He remembered hearing the crash of plates and glasses, Kathleen's scream. He remembered thinking, *I mustn't make a fool of myself. I mustn't make a scene.* And then oblivion.

He had wakened in the hospital. His first impression was how bright everything was, shining white, the bedclothes, the curtains, the walls of the private room, the starched habits of the nursing sisters, the white coat of the doctor who had come to talk to him and explain, in his broken English, precisely what had happened.

'Señor Megarry,' the doctor had begun. 'You are not a young man.' It had sounded exactly like Kathleen, the same song she had been singing all these years. 'You are not a fit man. Look at you.'

The doctor had prodded his stomach and smiled. 'You have too much weight. Also you smoke cigarettes.'

'How do you know that?' Megarry had asked.

'Your wife.'

'Ah.'

'You have had a heart attack. But not serious.' The doctor had rushed to dispel alarm. 'Nevertheless it is a warning for you. You must change your life. No more cigarettes. Also eat less. Get more exercise. Look at you,' the doctor had said once more and prodded his stomach again and laughed.

He'd spent a week in the hospital while they carried out tests. They had checked his cholesterol level, his blood pressure. They'd X-rayed him, attached wires to his chest while they examined his heart. One of the nursing sisters, an elderly nun with a huge crucifix draped across her bosom, could speak

6

English. She'd made a point of coming to see him every evening about seven o'clock, just as it was beginning to get dark. She'd sat with him and talked about Ireland, the troubles. She'd given him the news. Once she'd got hold of three consecutive issues of the *Daily Telegraph* and presented them proudly to him like it was some secret treasure.

When they finally released him, Kathleen had suggested that they come here to Howth to convalesce.

'But there is nothing wrong with me,' he'd protested. 'They've given me a clean bill of health.'

'It will do you good,' she had said sternly. 'You need to relax. I don't want you dying on me.'

He'd looked at her and seen the concern in her eyes. She has had a tough time, he'd thought. While I was in hospital it was no picnic for her. So he'd relented and they'd come to stay with Kathleen's sister and her husband.

It had proved to be restful. He had settled into a routine. There was tranquillity here, order. Breakfast at nine o'clock and then a leisurely walk along the cliffs to the village. A pint in the Royal Hotel and a rustle through the *Irish Times*. Dr Henry had said that alcohol was all right but in moderation.

'What is moderation?' Megarry had inquired.

Dr Henry had sighed. He'd had the look of a man who was much put upon. 'Just don't overdo it,' he had said.

In the afternoon, Megarry sometimes played golf or borrowed a fishing rod and went angling for dogfish from the rocks off Balscadden bay. Today he was meeting Inspector Mulqueen for lunch.

He lit his cigarette and ground the match underfoot. He hadn't seen Mulqueen for how long? Five, six, seven years? He tried to fix the date with reference to a conference on cross-border security at a quiet hotel in County Louth, civil servants and policemen from North and South talking about terrorism.

He smiled at the innocence of it all. Those conferences never really achieved anything. There was too much waffle and the paramilitaries were too clever. Anything worthwhile was done on the ground, between individual police officers. He had kept in touch with Mulqueen with phone calls and cards at Christmas.

From his seat on the cliff path, Megarry watched a cormorant swoop from a rock and dive deep into the water, surfacing out in the sea with a fish in its beak. He became aware of the gentle chug-chug sound of an engine and then a boat came into view. It stopped beneath him and he saw a man in yellow oilskins begin to pull up lobster pots, the water dripping from the rope like silver drops of rain.

He started walking again. It was all downhill now, the hard work of climbing over, yet he found a light film of perspiration begin to dampen his brow and his breath come in laboured gasps. Weight, he thought. I must get my weight down. I must do all those things they have told me to do. Shed a few stone, change my diet, get more exercise. And yet I feel as fit as ever. I have enough energy. I'm alert.

He rounded a turn in the path and the village lay before him, smoke curling from chimneys, the spires of the churches, the marina with the sun sparkling off the bright paintwork on the yachts. He thought of his boss, Chief Superintendent Drysdale, of the peace that had suddenly come over the North. What would the Security Committee talk about now? What would they discuss? And those mysterious men in grey suits from the Northern Ireland Office who had made his life a misery at conference after conference? What would they find to do if the peace held? There would be no more work for them.

Or for me, he thought. It was an idea he had toyed with from time to time. Superintendent of Special Branch. If the peace held, he could become redundant. That might solve a lot of problems, he thought and a smile puckered the corner of his mouth. Kathleen would welcome it. She had been at him for a long time to give it up, to take early retirement.

At the bottom of the hill he met a man with a dog on a lead. They exchanged greetings and Megarry continued past the car-park and the pumping station and into the village. He thought about the afternoon. What would he do when the lunch was finished? Mulqueen would go back to work. But what would he do? Another round of golf, a stroll along the pier, the library?

Kathleen was going shopping with her sister, but he hated shopping, the crowds, the crush, the noise.

He suddenly realised that something was bothering him. It had been bothering him for days, like an itch or a stone in his shoe. A slow drip drip of discomfort. As he turned off the road and saw the sign for the Pier House Inn come into view, he realised what it was.

He was bored.

The lounge of the Royal Hotel was half empty when he arrived. He checked his watch and saw that he was early. He had told Mulqueen one o'clock. It was now twenty minutes to one. He ordered a pint of Guinness at the bar and went off to the restaurant to confirm the lunch appointment. He had made the reservation by phone and he knew from experience the way these things sometimes went astray. But there was no mistake. The plump little *maître d'hôtel* quickly consulted the book and pointed to a quiet table in a window alcove overlooking the street. There were flowers in a vase and a sparkling white table-cloth and knives and forks laid out in a tidy row.

'Whenever Mr Megarry is ready,' the man said with a smile and a little bow.

'My guest hasn't arrived. I'll have a drink first,' Megarry said. 'And then I'll come back.'

'As you wish, sir.'

Megarry returned to the bar where he found the pint waiting for him, the white head like a parson's collar along the rim of the glass. There was another man standing at the bar, a tall, well-built man with a slight paunch and a fading suntan. He was dressed like a businessman, in a finely tailored suit, well-polished shoes. Megarry lifted the glass and the man spoke.

'Grand m-morning out there. Grand m-morning for a walk.'

'Yes,' Megarry said. 'That's just what I've been doing.'

'Oh.' The man suddenly took an interest. 'Where did you go?'

'Along the cliffs. From the Summit down along the cliff path to the village.'

'That's a grand walk all right,' the man said. 'That's one of the b-best walks in Howth. Great views. Grand sea air.'

Megarry sipped his pint and spread out the paper he had bought earlier. For a minute he read in silence. Then he heard the man's voice again. 'P-pardon me,' the man said. 'You're a visitor. Am I right?'

'Yes.'

'From the North? You're from the North somewhere?'

Something warned Megarry to take care, some long-assimilated caution when faced by strangers asking questions. But he was here in Howth, well away from Northern Ireland. And anyway, the war was over.

'Yes. That's right.'

'I knew it. I caught it in your voice.' The man smiled. 'I like the North. I like Northerners. Solid G-god-fearing people.'

Megarry bent his ear forward. Was he hearing things? Did the man have a slight stammer?

'I do a lot of b-business in the North. I've a lot of good customers there. And I'll tell you one thing.' The man raised his glass to his mouth and took a drink. 'They p-pay on the nail. There's never any messing when it comes to paying their bills. I wish I could say the same for the rest of the people I do b-business with.'

God-fearing, Megarry thought. That's what he thinks of us. Yet we're no different from anyone else. He remembered some of the people he had known who wouldn't have recognised God if He had come in here and sat down beside them.

At that moment the door opened and Inspector Mulqueen came in and stood for a moment blinking round the bar. He was dressed in civilian clothes but Megarry recognised him, despite the long years since they had met. Megarry lifted his newspaper and waved, and the policeman came bustling over, rubbing his hands together in anticipation.

'Am I late?' he asked apologetically. 'I drove out. The traffic at Fairview was diabolical. I should have put my feet up and taken the train.' He took Megarry's hand and pumped it. 'Cecil. You're looking good. Jesus, you don't look a day older. How long is it since I saw you last?'

Megarry studied the other man. His hair was thinning and there were dark circles forming beneath his eyes. They would turn into wrinkles eventually, crow's feet. But there was something else about him, a weariness that came from responsibility, and Megarry noticed it at once. He remembered a bright young detective sitting beside him at a conference and yawning as some idiot in a suit tried to lecture them about counter-intelligence.

'It's seven years, Dan.'

'Is it begod? That long? Jesus, Cecil, how time flies when you're enjoying yourself.'

He stretched his neck and laughed at his own joke and Megarry saw the thick barrier of hair sprouting like grass in the dark nostrils. He gestured towards the bar with its bank of gleaming bottles. 'A snort, Dan? For old times' sake?'

The other man hesitated, then shook his head. 'I better not,' he said. 'I've got a case pending.'

'What is it?'

'Murder, by the looks of it. They found a guy this morning shot in the back of the head down along the river. I've got the post-mortem at two thirty.'

Megarry nodded.

'You've no idea, Cecil. This town is falling apart. The criminals aren't afraid of the police any more. No respect. And to make matters worse, I've a dog of a superintendent on my back who expects me to solve crimes before the blood has had a chance to dry.'

He sighed and fidgeted with his hands. 'I'm sorry. You didn't come here to talk about my problems. I expect you've got your own.'

'No,' Megarry said. 'I don't mind listening. I went through it myself. I understand.'

'The truth is, since I took promotion, I've had nothing but pressure, pressure, pressure. They expect instant decisions, instant solutions. I'm run ragged. And I'm relying on other people to help me out. They can let you down, Cecil.'

'I know.'

Mulqueen lowered his voice. 'To be honest, I'm not sure that I did the right thing taking promotion. The pay, you know. Okay, so they gave me an increase. But it hardly compensates for all the extra responsibility, all the hassle I've now got to put up with.'

'You can only do your best,' Megarry said firmly. 'That's all anyone can reasonably expect. Superintendent or no superintendent.'

He took Mulqueen's arm and guided him away from the bar towards the restaurant. It was beginning to fill up. They took their seats at the window and Megarry passed a menu across the table.

'How are Marie and the kids?'

'They're fine. At least they seem to be okay whenever I get the chance to see them, which is not a lot these days.'

'The steak is good here,' Megarry said softly. 'So is the fish. They get it fresh every day from the boats. I can recommend it.'

'You've eaten here before?'

'The other evening. Kathleen and I had dinner.'

Mulqueen put down the menu. 'My God, I'm sorry, Cecil. My damned manners. I forgot all about her. How is she?'

'She's first-class. Fussing over me like a mother hen. I told you I had a little touch.' He pointed to his chest.

'But you're fine now. You look fit. It was nothing serious?'

'No. It wasn't serious. But I've been told to take it easy. Kathleen wants me to pack it in. She wants me to take early retirement.'

'And how do you feel about it?'

'I don't know.'

A waiter came and took their order, and on impulse Megarry asked for a half-litre of the house wine. What did it matter? He had no case to worry about, no appointments to keep, no superiors breathing down his neck like poor Mulqueen.

He glanced across the table at the other man, cutting meticulously at his plate. Probably he had kept this lunch appointment out of a sense of politeness, out of a fear of giving offence. Megarry suspected that if he hadn't agreed to see him, he would probably have eaten lunch at his desk out of a brown paper bag, ordered from the canteen. He knew policemen.

12

They were the same everywhere. They had bad breath from indigestion, and wind and constipation. They never sat still long enough to do anything properly.

He lifted the carafe and poured some wine, then gestured towards Mulqueen's empty glass. 'You're sure, Dan? Just a drop?'

Mulqueen smiled and pushed the glass across. 'What the hell?' he said.

'Tell me about this case.'

The other man put down his knife and wiped his mouth. 'There's nothing much to tell so far. Guy gets nutted down by the river. Taxi-man found him on his way back from some concert at the Point Theatre. The technical people have been down there all morning. I'll get a report later. They've moved the body to the morgue.'

'Motive?'

'Hey, Cecil. C'mon. There doesn't have to be a motive any more. People get killed in this town over a six-pack of cider.'

Megarry gazed away across the street. There was a dog sleeping in a doorway, a breeze rustling the leaves of the sycamore trees outside the church.

He thought of his own town, Belfast. People getting gunned down on street corners, in bars, on lonely roads. Women getting blown to pieces on a Saturday afternoon in a fish shop.

'There's always a motive, Dan. Even the most senseless killing has some reason behind it.'

Megarry lifted his glass and drained it, then set it down squarely in the centre of the table beside the empty carafe.

An idea had struck him, a wild, irrational notion. It might have been the wine. 'What time did you say the post-mortem was?'

Mulqueen chewed for a moment before replying. 'Two thirty.'

Megarry looked at the clock on the wall above the door. It was an old-fashioned clock like the kind he remembered from his days at school. The hands showed five minutes to two. 'Do me a favour,' he said. 'Let me come with you.'

3

The city morgue was a squat building behind a redbricked façade at the back of the bus station. They drove in along the coast road, past Dollymount strand and the smoking stacks of the Pigeon House. Across the bay, the Dublin mountains brooded in the pale afternoon light.

Megarry shifted in his seat. 'Who's likely to be there?'

'The pathologist. His name is McNamara. A bit fussy, but basically okay. Then there'll be Mulligan and Kelly.'

'Who are they?'

'The officers I've assigned to the case.'

'Will anyone object to me coming along?'

Mulqueen shrugged. 'I don't see why. I'll say you're a visiting dignitary. Hell Cecil, this is the era of cross-border co-operation. We're all supposed to be on the same side now.'

Megarry said no more, just sat back and watched as the city flashed by, streets, houses, factories, cinemas. They left the car in a parking space reserved for morgue officials and walked the remaining few yards to the main door.

It was opened by a uniformed attendant who showed them into a corridor smelling of disinfectant. He was a small, deferential man with a light coating of reddish hair on his upper lip. He seemed to know Mulqueen.

14

'This is a terrible business, Inspector.' The man made a tutting sound. 'Poor divil's in an awful mess. Half his face is shot away.'

He led them along the grey corridor towards a room where they could see lights burning. They stopped outside a frosted-glass door with a little plastic plaque which read: AUTOPSY ROOM.

The attendant rapped with his fingers on the glass and a voice said: 'Come in.'

There were three men inside. They were grouped round a table. As the door opened they looked up and stared. One of the men wore a white laboratory coat and had a pair of metal tweezers in his hand. He took off his glasses and nodded towards Mulqueen. 'We've just started,' he said. He motioned with his free hand for them to join him.

Megarry slowly approached the table. There was a bright arclight overhead and it shone down on the pale corpse beneath. The man on the table was in his early thirties, thin, clearly undernourished. His legs were like poles, the toenails grotesque and overgrown. Megarry could see the bones of the rib-cage protruding through the skin. It seemed to him, in the bright light from the lamp, as if the body was covered in a fine coating of down, like some scrawny bird, newly hatched from a bloody egg.

As he got closer, the figure in the white coat turned away and pulled his surgical gloves further up his arms. He was a youngish man with a dark, receding hairline. With one hand he rotated the head of the corpse in a slow professional manner.

No attempt had been made to bandage it. Megarry could see a mass of ruptured flesh and torn skin, the eye hanging like a marble from its gory socket. There was blood everywhere. It soaked the man's blond hair and left a dirty trail across the plastic pillow on the table.

'It's straightforward,' the pathologist said with emphasis. 'Haemorrhage of the brain. Gunshot wound. Here.'

He pointed with the tweezers towards a small hole at the back of the head below the ear, where the skin had been swabbed.

'Entrance wound. Exit wound at the front. Tore away part of the face, dislocated the eyeball. Death would have been instantaneous.'

'Only one wound?' Mulqueen asked.

'Yes. Heavy-calibre revolver I'd say. Look.'

He adjusted the light so that they could see a small piece of metal imbedded deep within the entrance wound. Megarry recognised it but said nothing.

'Cartridge fragment?' Mulqueen asked.

'That's right. I'll take it out. Your forensic people can examine it.'

'Any signs of struggle?'

'Slight bruising of the upper forearm and chest. Abrasion of the skin on the neck.' The man pointed again with the tweezers. 'It's consistent with pressure having been applied. As if someone had him in an arm-lock. There's something else.'

He spoke with a smug satisfaction and pointed once more towards the small hole in the man's neck. The pale skin around the edges was beginning to turn blue. 'Look at the direction.'

Mulqueen peered closer.

'It's not straight,' the pathologist said. 'It's angled upwards.'

'What are you suggesting?'

'Shooting upwards was almost certain to kill him. The bullet would travel through the brain. Your average gurrier wouldn't know that. Either the person who did this was an expert or . . .'

'Or what?' Mulqueen said sharply.

'It was an accident.'

'An accident?'

'The result of a struggle. I'm assuming that this man didn't stay still.' He indicated the corpse. 'He'd try to escape. He'd fight. He'd try to run away. You hold a gun like this.' The pathologist gripped the tweezers in his right hand. 'The natural position is pointing upwards. If there was a struggle and the gun went off, it's a ten-to-one chance that the bullet would travel upwards.'

Mulqueen grunted. 'That's all speculation,' he said dismissively. 'I just want facts. You pull a gun on a man, the object is to kill him. You've no proof this was an accident. We're investigating a murder.'

He turned to the two detectives who had so far remained silent.

'What about his clothes?' he said to a surly-looking man in a faded tweed jacket. Megarry looked at him. He had a sad face, like someone who has grown weary with the world.

'They're being examined,' the man said.

'Any buttons ripped, any tears, stains? Anything like that?'

'Not that I'm aware of.'

'Anything found at the scene? Who's looking after that?'

'The Technical Bureau. I spoke to them before we came here. They say they'll try to get a report over to you by this afternoon.'

'Try?' Mulqueen said in an exasperated voice. 'They better do more than try. They better have that damned report on my desk by the time I get back there or somebody's ass'll be in a sling.'

'Have you got a name for him?' Megarry said softly. It was the first time he had spoken. He was aware of their eyes turning to examine him, wondering who he was, what he was doing here. 'Have you identified him yet?'

The two detectives looked towards Mulqueen for guidance.

'It's all right,' Mulqueen said and waved his hand. 'I should have introduced you. This is Superintendent Megarry. RUC. He's down here on a familiarisation course. He's working with me.'

The men looked again at Megarry with renewed interest.

'His name was Higgins,' the second detective said. He was a young man, early thirties, bright, intense face. 'He had a wallet. Social insurance card, some bits and pieces.'

'Money?'

'Fifteen pounds.'

'Well that rules out robbery,' Mulqueen said emphatically.

'Where is it?' Megarry said. 'His wallet and stuff? Do you have it with you?'

'It's back at the station.'

'Anything else?'

'A couple of letters.'

'I'd like to go through it with you,' Megarry said and smiled. 'If that's all right.'

He saw the two men exchange glances. He caught the resentment in their eyes. They regard me as an intruder, he thought, butting in, poking my nose into their business. Maybe I should just shut up.

The pathologist was beginning to wash the dead man's face. He had taken out a roll of bandages and a large pair of scissors.

'Have you finished?' Mulqueen asked.

'For the time being. We'll probably want to conduct further tests.' The pathologist spoke politely but formally as if setting out for the superintendent the demarcation lines between their functions.

'What will you do with him now?'

'Clean him up a bit. Stick him in the freezer till his relatives claim him.'

Megarry looked once more at the pale corpse, the thin, neglected body. The life gone out of it. He had an empty feeling, the way he often did in the presence of death. This is someone's son, he thought, someone's husband, brother, lover.

As he turned away, his eye caught sight of something. He lifted the dead man's arm. The flesh felt cold. Rigor mortis was beginning to set in. The skin was already turning an ashen grey. In the crook of the arm there were a couple of small puncture marks, little blue-black holes the size of pin-pricks.

He lifted the other arm and there they were again. A handful of tiny needle marks.

The pathologist saw them too. He pushed the glasses hard against his nose. 'I didn't notice that,' he said apologetically.

'What is it?' Mulqueen asked. 'Something else?'

'Puncture marks,' Megarry said. 'This man was injecting something.' He spoke to the pathologist. 'It might be no harm to run a blood test and maybe an analysis of his stomach contents. See what's in there.'

The pathologist sniffed, clearly discomfited. 'I was going to do that anyway. It's routine.'

Megarry took Mulqueen aside and lowered his voiec. 'Can I make a suggestion?'

'Sure.'

'Ask the Press Office to withhold the cause of death. Don't say it was gunshot wounds.'

'Why not?'

'It's for the best. Believe me. The less information in the public domain the better.'

4

Megarry decided to ring Kathleen from the station to let her know where he was. She would have returned by now from her shopping trip to Dublin and found him absent.

The station was half a mile away across the river. It was an old building of white stone, an imperial relic left behind by the British. It had recently been sandblasted and now the exterior gleamed white in the afternoon sun. Mulqueen's office was in the back, in a modern extension of steel and glass that towered over the surrounding shops and offices.

They went up in the lift and watched silently as the city slipped into view; the spire of Christchurch Cathedral, the Custom House, the cranes along the docks where the river snaked into the sea.

The lift shuddered to a halt and they got out. The older man, Mulligan, had gone home. He had been on the early shift. It was he who had first received news of the murder and alerted the technical squad. The younger detective, Kelly, had taken over from him.

Mulqueen bustled along the corridor and opened his office with a key and showed them in. He had a grim set to his jaw.

'You wanted to use the phone, Cecil?'

'If you don't mind.'

'Sure. Help yourself.'

Mulqueen pulled out a chair and gestured to a battery of instruments on a desk. It was in disorder. It reminded Megarry of Harvey's desk back in his own station in Belfast, books and papers and files abandoned in a heap.

'What do I do?'

'Dial Nine and you'll get an outside line.'

Megarry sat down and fumbled with the machine. He pressed the instrument close to his ear and waited till Kathleen's sister answered. He exchanged pleasantries, then his wife came on.

'Where are you?'

'I'm in town. I told you I was having lunch with Mulqueen. He brought me in to show me his new office.'

'Did you have a nice lunch?'

'Yes. It wasn't bad.'

'Nothing too heavy?'

He hastened to reassure her. 'No. It was all very healthy. Plaice and boiled potatoes and a green side salad. How did you get on?'

'So-so.' Kathleen said. 'I bought a few things. I got some presents for Jennifer. A dress and shoes. I know what she wants.'

'She'll like that.'

There was a pause and then she said: 'Will you be home soon?'

'Well, that's just the point,' Megarry said quickly. 'I might be delayed.'

'*Delayed*?'

Across the room, he could see the others watching him. He rushed ahead, determined to see the matter through. 'Mulqueen's got this case. He's asked for my advice. I'm in his office now, going over it with him. It might be some time.'

'*Cecillll* . . .'

He heard her begin to argue, but she was too late. 'I have to go now,' he said cheerfully. 'Don't wait up for me.'

He put the phone back carefully on its cradle. Mulqueen had turned away and was talking furiously on another line.

20

Megarry sat for a while staring out the window. Then he spoke to Kelly.

'You said you had some things belonging to the dead man. Could I have a look at them?'

The young detective hesitated. Megarry could see him struggling to make up his mind, trying to decide how much resistance he could safely offer. Then, with a great show of reluctance, he pulled open a drawer and withdrew a plastic bag. He sighed and handed it over without speaking.

Megarry emptied the contents on to the desk. They had all been carefully tagged. There was a pen, a comb with fair hairs caught in the teeth, a soiled handkerchief, a folded ten-pound note, some coins, a roll of peppermints, a couple of keys on a ring, the wallet which Kelly had already mentioned and two letters still in their crumpled envelopes.

'No watch?' Megarry asked.

'No.'

'And his clothes are with the Technical Bureau?'

'That's right.'

Megarry took the letters and studied the envelopes. One was handwritten, the other typed. They both had Dublin post-marks. He noticed something else. The addresses were different. He took out the letters and spread them on the desk. From the corner of his eye he could see that Mulqueen was still busy on the phone. He spoke again to Kelly. 'You've already read these?'

'Yes.'

'Anything interesting?'

'Depends what you're looking for.'

The young detective was making no effort to conceal his hostility.

'Let's see,' Megarry said.

The first letter had been sent to an address in Ballymoss. It was neatly typed on office stationery. The heading read: Dempsey Engineering Co., Clontarf, Dublin. It had been sent about six months earlier.

The letter was short and to the point. It read: 'Dear Mr Higgins, I have to inform you that your failure to supply sickness certificates for your recent absences from work necessitates that you present yourself at this office on next Monday at nine thirty for examination by the company doctor. Failure to attend will result in the termination of your contract of employment with this company.' It was signed. N. Costello. Personnel Manager.

Megarry put the letter back inside its envelope and opened the second one, the one with the handwritten address. It was a barely legible scrawl.

'Need to see you urgently. Tried ringing but no one in. The Quare Fella is very annoyed with you. Get in touch. Soon.' The last word had been written in capital letters and underlined. It was signed E.B. The sender had failed to put his own address on the note and there was no date or telephone number.

Megarry turned over the envelope and noted the address: 44 St Martin's Gardens, Dublin. 'Where is that?' he said to Kelly.

Kelly shrugged. 'I'm not sure. Ringsend, I think. You'd need to check it in the street directory.'

Megarry put the letters aside and opened the wallet. There wasn't much. A lottery ticket, a death notice cut from a newspaper, a Saint Christopher medal, a piece of paper with a few scribbled phone numbers. He withdrew a small printed card with a picture of the Virgin Mary and the legend in blue writing: I Prayed for You at Knock.

He passed it to the younger man. 'What is that?'

'It's a prayer card. Someone he knew made a pilgrimage to Knock. It's a shrine in County Mayo to the Virgin Mary.'

'And whoever gave him this card had prayed for him?'

'That's right.'

'Well,' Megarry said and tried a joke. 'Didn't help him much. Did it?'

Kelly didn't respond, just sat with a cold look of resentment on his face.

Megarry examined the rest of the contents. There was a social security card with the printed name: James Anthony Higgins and a number. There was another card in a plastic cover. It carried the information, 'In Case of Emergency, Contact Mrs

Annie Nolan.' It gave an address in Ballymoss. It was the same address as the letter from Dempsey Engineering Co.

He closed the wallet and put it with the letters on the desk.

Mulqueen had finished on the phone. He came across and lowered himself wearily beside them. His lip was trembling.

'I've just been talking to the superintendent. He's in a foul mood. Those bastards over in Forensic haven't even completed the preliminary report yet. I asked for assistance and they tell me there's no one to spare. That I'll just have to make do with what I've got.' He waved his hands in a hopeless gesture. 'Now you know what I have to put up with, Cecil. I ask you. Is this any way to run an army?'

'Have they identified the weapon yet?' Megarry asked.

'.375 Magnum.'

'That's a heavy-calibre weapon,' Megarry said. 'Where I come from, it's fairly common. Guaranteed to inflict a lot of damage.'

He saw Kelly shift in his seat.

'I was thinking what the pathologist said about the entrance wound and the fact that the weapon was pointed upwards. Whoever did this certainly meant to kill him.'

'Of course they meant to kill him,' Mulqueen said. 'Don't listen to McNamara. That bullshit about an accident. He doesn't know what he's talking about.'

'What bothers me is the motive,' Megarry said. 'It wasn't robbery. His wallet wasn't taken and he doesn't look like the type of man who would have had much money.'

'Fifteen pounds,' Kelly reminded him. 'I've counted it.'

'It could be revenge. It could be anything,' Mulqueen said. 'He could have been screwing somebody's wife.' He gritted his teeth. 'How the hell am I supposed to deal with these things when they won't even give me support?'

'Somebody killed him and they had a reason,' Megarry said. He reached into his pocket and took out a packet of cigarettes. He saw Mulqueen glance at him. 'Do you mind?'

Mulqueen waved his hand.

Megarry paused and then spoke from behind a cloud of

smoke. 'You have to get a formal identification. There's a woman's name in his wallet and an address. Ballymoss.'

'Kelly can do that,' Mulqueen said sharply. 'He can go out there.'

'It's a dirty job. Nobody likes being the bearer of bad news.'

Mulqueen stared. 'Are you kidding? This is police work, Cecil. This isn't the Band of Hope.'

'I'll go with him.'

Mulqueen started to protest. He glared at the young detective. 'He's a copper, Cecil. He's not an altar boy. He's got to get used to this sort of thing.'

'It's all right,' Megarry said calmly. 'I don't mind. It's on my way home.'

They went in Kelly's car to Ballymoss. On the way, they saw the sky darken, heavy with black clouds coming in from the sea. Soon it was raining, big, round drops hurling themselves at the windscreen and running in streams along the windows.

Megarry tried to start up a conversation. 'How long are you in this game?'

'Nine years,' Kelly said.

'And how long have you been a sergeant?'

'Three.'

Megarry pursed his lips. 'Any family?'

'I've a little boy. Jamie. He's eight. We've also got a baby.'

'Eight is a good age,' Megarry said.

The conversation trailed off. Kelly kept his eyes on the road ahead.

'You don't like me, do you?' Megarry said.

'It's not personal.'

'You think I'm interfering?'

'Yes.'

'I'm only trying to help.'

'We don't need your help,' Kelly said coldly. 'We're quite capable of handling this ourselves.'

'That's not what Mulqueen was saying. He's complaining that he doesn't have sufficient resources.'

'Mulqueen always complains. We can handle it.'

24

'You think so?'

'Of course.' Kelly gripped the steering wheel tightly. 'We don't need people like you butting in, trying to tell us how to run our show. You stick to your patch. We'll stick to ours. Keep your nose out of our business.'

'Stop the car,' Megarry said abruptly.

Kelly looked at him in confusion, then pulled over to the side.

Megarry unbuckled his seat-belt. 'Do you know who you're talking to?' he said.

The young detective didn't reply.

'If you worked for me and you spoke like that I'd slap your face. I'm offering to help because Mulqueen is a friend of mine. I don't need your say-so. I certainly don't need your insolence. As long as I'm involved in this case I'll thank you to keep a civil tongue in your head. Do you understand?'

Kelly looked away.

'I asked you a question,' Megarry said.

'Yes.'

'Yes what?'

'Yes. I understand.'

'You've a lot to learn,' Megarry said with contempt. 'Three years a sergeant. You're only a greenhorn. I'll tell you something. When the heat comes on, and the superintendent starts screaming for results, you'll be glad of my help. Or anyone else's for that matter.'

He put his belt back on. Kelly's face was burning scarlet.

'Drive,' Megarry said. 'And keep your mouth shut until you're spoken to again.'

They drove the rest of the way in silence.

Ballymoss shopping centre was deserted when they arrived. On every side the housing blocks stood like giant sentry posts, great porridge-coloured buildings poking up to a leaden sky. There was a scattering of gloomy shops, a newsagent's, a chemist's, a bookmaker's with racing results posted on a board. The smell of cooked chicken wafted out from a nearby butcher's.

The whole place had an air of poverty and dereliction. They parked outside a pub, a stark, custom-built hulk with green

25

pictures of the Irish soccer team in the windows and blue ones of the Dublin GAA squad. Megarry got out of the car, pushed open the doors of the pub and went inside. Kelly followed him to the counter.

A barman was waiting, a tall, angular man in a white shirt and neat bow-tie.

'What are you drinking?' Megarry said to the detective.

Kelly hesitated.

'Give him a pint,' Megarry said to the barman. 'And one for me. And a large Bushmills whiskey.'

He waited till the drinks were poured, then took them to a table at the back of the room where he could watch the door. Kelly trotted behind him.

'Have you ever done this before?'

'No.'

Megarry grunted and swallowed the whiskey. It burnt his throat and chest. He thought of the last time he had brought news of a death. It had been a sectarian assassination in Belfast. A young man. He left a wife and family. He remembered the look on her face as he told her. The way the colour drained away, the struggle to comprehend. And afterwards, the tears, the anguish. It was a dirty business. There was no easy way.

His hands found the matches in his pocket. He lit a cigarette. A thought came to him. Why am I doing this? What am I trying to prove? That the heart attack hasn't diminished me? That I'm still as good as I ever was? Is that what it is? Pride?

He sat for a long time watching as the grey smoke drifted slowly towards the ceiling. At last he finished his drink and stood up. 'I'll go alone,' he said. 'You wait here and have another pint.'

'I can't let you do that,' Kelly protested.

'I said I'll go alone.' He spoke firmly and then he softened his tone. 'It's all right. I've done it before. I know what to say.'

Annie Nolan lived in Michael Davitt Tower, one of the grim housing blocks that squatted on the fringes of the square. The rain had stopped when he left the pub. He could see the roof-tops of the houses, like so many little boxes stretching away towards Santry, the green hump of Howth Head rising in the mist.

The lift wasn't working so he began a weary climb up the cold concrete stairs. There was a smell of urine. At each landing he paused for breath, trying to read the graffiti that defaced the walls. At last he came to the flat.

The door was opened by a thin woman with a pale face. She peered nervously at him from the doorway. A couple of children clutched at her dress. Behind them he could see the flickering images of a video.

'Mrs Nolan?'

'Yes.'

'I'm inquiring about James Anthony Higgins.'

The woman stared at him. He could see that she was frightened. She knew that he was police. It was his voice, his manner, his clothes. The way that he had used all the man's names. Only a policeman would do that.

'Harpo?'

'I beg your pardon.'

'Is it Harpo you're looking for?'

'I think so.'

'He's not here,' she said quickly.

'I know that.'

Something in his voice alerted her. He saw it in her eyes.

'Can I come in?' Megarry said. He tried to speak gently. 'I need to talk to you somewhere.' He waved his hand. 'Somewhere more private.'

She backed away and he entered the flat. It was a tiny shell. His overwhelming impression was how small it was and how cold. It was like a prison.

'What's he done?' the woman asked. 'Is he in trouble?'

He had tried to fortify himself for this. He could still feel the sweet whiskey taste on his tongue. But it was difficult. The words, when he spoke them, seemed to be coming from someone else. 'I think he might be dead. We need you to come to the morgue. We need an identification. He had your name on a card in his wallet. What is your relationship?'

'I'm his sister.'

'Ahh.'

He was about to ask about a wife, a family, when the youngest child started to cry, clutching tightly at her mother's skirt, urging her to retreat into the cold certainty of their little world, to expel this strange man and the trouble he was bringing into their lives.

'I've got a car,' Megarry said. 'It won't take long. I can drop you back again.'

He thought of the comforting words he had planned to say to ease her grief, but the woman simply averted her eyes and reached for a coat from behind the door.

He had expected her to weep, to show some emotion. Her reaction scared him. Do the poor not feel pain, he thought? Are their lives so stripped of comfort, so filled with petty tragedy that they have no feeling left for the big events like death?

'I'll have to get someone to mind the kids. Give me a few minutes. I'll see you downstairs.'

She made to close the door, then as if remembering something she stopped. 'What happened to him? Was it an overdose?'

'Why do you say that?'

'He was an addict. I thought you knew.'

'No,' Megarry lied. 'I didn't know.'

'What was it then?'

He lowered his eyes. 'He was shot.'

5

'Have another scone, Cecil,' Nancy said. 'I baked them myself.'

They were sitting at the breakfast table, just the three of them, Megarry, his wife and her sister. He smiled and tried to wave away the plate.

'Ah, go on. Sure aren't you on your holidays? A little of what you fancy does you good, I always say.'

He glanced nervously towards his wife and then reluctantly reached out a hand to take the scone.

'And some butter and jam.' His sister-in-law began to push little dishes across the table towards him. 'I've got clotted cream in the fridge, if you'd prefer?'

'*Good God*, no,' Megarry said and slit the scone open with a knife, making sure that the crumbs spilled carefully on to the plate. 'I'm supposed to be on a diet. I'm supposed to be watching my weight.'

'Nonsense,' Nancy said. 'There's nothing wrong with your weight. It suits you.'

'That's not what my doctor says. He's told me to lose several stone. There's a whole range of things I'm not supposed to eat. Butter is one of them. Clotted cream is another. It's absolutely crawling with cholesterol.'

He raised the teacup to his mouth and watched Kathleen from the side of his eye. So far she had said little, just the normal polite formalities over breakfast. But there was a tension in the air. She was annoyed with him about last night.

He'd got back around eleven o'clock after taking Mrs Nolan to the morgue to identify her brother's body. She'd signed the relevant papers, slowly and mechanically as if she was in a daze, as if the full import of what had happened hadn't yet sunk in.

Kelly had tried to interview her, probing her with questions about the dead man. She had answered in a frightened voice, as if she felt intimidated, and after a few minutes Megarry had been forced to put an end to it by taking her gently by the sleeve out into the cold night air to where the car was waiting.

When he got home, at last, all the lights were out and everyone had gone to bed. He had undressed in the dark, the street-lamps casting pale shadows into the room, and when he finally got into bed beside Kathleen she had turned her back to him and pretended to be asleep. That's when he'd known there was going to be trouble.

He pushed his plate into the centre of the table and wiped his mouth with his napkin. 'How's Andrew?' he asked, keeping up the small talk. 'Did he get off to the office all right this morning?'

He saw Kathleen cast a glance at him and knew at once that he had said the wrong thing.

'He waited up for you last night,' Nancy said. 'He thought maybe you'd want to go down to the Anchor Bar for a game of darts. But in the end he had to go to bed. You know he has an early start?'

'I know,' Megarry said and forced an uneasy smile. His brother-in-law worked in an insurance firm in town. He was a senior executive and his job was very important to him. On the handful of occasions when he had accompanied him to one of the local pubs, Andrew had strictly limited himself to two glasses of beer and insisted that they be back at the house by half past ten. They had not been rollicking evenings.

'What *did* delay you, Cecil?'

It was Kathleen. She was staring at him from her seat near the window. There was a laburnum tree in the garden outside and

30

it was coming into leaf, the buds unfolding in a bright-yellow rush of colour.

Megarry swallowed hard.

'We thought you were just going for lunch. We certainly didn't expect that you'd be gone all day. *And* most of the night.'

She sat forward with her chin resting in her fists and Megarry realised that the inquisition had begun.

'*Wellll,*' he said and tried to clear his throat. 'It started simply enough. Mulqueen insisted that I accompany him into town to see his new office. He's got promoted, you know. He's an inspector now and they've given him this new place. He's very proud of it. And then . . .'

He felt his face begin to flush as the lies poured out. I am a practised liar, he thought. It's part of my job. But Kathleen can tell every time.

'He's got this case he's working on. A murder case. A man got shot dead the other evening. Mulqueen wanted my advice. So I thought since I wasn't doing anything else and you and Nancy had gone shopping for the afternoon . . .' He smiled across at his sister-in-law who smiled back. 'I thought there'd be no harm in going in and giving him a hand. He's short-staffed. I'm afraid it's the same story down here as it is back home. No resources and too much work to do.'

'But that shouldn't have taken you all day, Cecil.'

'No, well. There were er . . . complications.'

'*Complications?*'

'The dead man had to be formally identified. I volunteered to go out and talk to his sister. She lives in Ballymoss. Out in the tower blocks.'

'Poor woman,' Nancy said. 'How did she take it, Cecil?'

'Badly,' Megarry said, glad of the interruption. 'She seemed to be in a state of shock. She didn't have much to say for herself.'

Nancy shook her head. 'That's a terrible thing. A policeman coming to the door like that.'

Kathleen spoke again. 'I'm sure they appreciated your assistance, Cecil. But this isn't really your business.'

'I was just helping out,' he said deprecatingly. 'Everybody

31

can appreciate a help-out every now and then. I was just being a good Samaritan.'

He tried to get up from the table, to escape to the sanctuary of the garden, somewhere quiet, but just then the phone rang out in the hall. Nancy rose quickly and went to answer it.

Kathleen leaned across and hissed at him, 'Andrew was furious. He thought he had an arrangement with you to play darts.'

'I'd no arrangement,' Megarry said innocently. 'He must have imagined it.'

'It's bad manners apart from anything else. We're guests here. You can't just go gallivanting all over the place as if you were at home.'

'But I simply looked up an old friend,' he said, trying to keep his voice low. 'Jesus Christ. This place isn't a concentration camp.'

He saw her frown.

'I'm concerned about you. You're supposed to be taking it easy. Remember what the doctor said.'

He reached out and gently patted her arm. 'Don't worry.'

At that moment the door opened and his sister-in-law was back. 'It's for you,' she said, a puzzled look on her face.

'For me?'

He got up quickly and went out into the hall, with its bright mirrors and pictures on the walls of little sea views. The phone was lying neatly on a stand near the front door.

'Hello,' he said and pressed the instrument close to his ear.

It was Mulqueen. 'I'm just ringing to thank you for your help last night. It was much appreciated. Kelly's never done that sort of thing before. It was generous of you to volunteer.'

'That's all right. How is the case going?'

He heard Mulqueen sigh.

'Not great. I got the forensic report this morning. It doesn't advance things very much.'

'What about the house in St Martin's Gardens? Anybody try there?'

'I sent a man round. The house was empty. He couldn't get in.'

'But there was a bunch of keys in Higgins's belongings.'

'I know that,' Mulqueen said wearily. 'None of them fitted.'

'That's odd.'

'Well, there you are.'

'And what about the neighbours? Did they have anything to say?'

'That's another odd thing. Hardly anyone wanted to talk. As if they were afraid. Normally in a situation like this we get inundated with information. You know, all the amateur sleuths coming out of the woodwork anxious to help. But on this occasion, practically nothing.'

'When was Higgins last seen at the house?'

'About a week ago. One neighbour said she saw him leaving early one morning with a suitcase and getting into a taxi. He seemed to be in a hurry.'

'I'm sorry,' Megarry said at last. 'But keep at it. Something's bound to turn up. It always does.'

'I've only got a handful of men, Cecil. They can only do so much. And the superintendent is pawing the carpet.'

'Hump him,' Megarry said.

He returned to the kitchen and took his jacket from the back of a chair.

'Going out?' Kathleen said. She was helping her sister to clear the table.

Megarry looked from the window at the view over the harbour. The sun was out and the boats in the marina were tossing in the breeze. 'I thought I'd take a different route this morning. Through the Castle grounds and up to the rhododendron gardens. There's a dolmen up there. An ancient Celtic burial ground. Somebody recommended it.'

'And when will we see you again?'

'For God's sake, Kathleen. Let go of the leash.'

'I *know* you,' she said to his departing back. 'I know you too well.'

St Martin's Gardens turned out to be a dreary row of artisans' dwellings at the back of the greyhound stadium at Ringsend. It had a shabby-genteel appearance, like a scuffed shoe or a darned sock. The street had once been pretty, but it had fallen into disrepair and despite the sturdy efforts of some of the residents to brighten the houses with garden plants and paint, it retained the battered look of a place that has seen better days.

Megarry had taken the DART train into town and looked up the location on a street map in the General Post Office. Then he had got a bus and alighted at a stop near the bridge and walked the rest of the way. When he arrived, the street was dozing in the morning sun. There were a few cars parked here and there but no sign of life, no children playing, no noise except for the low hum of traffic from the main road.

He made his way carefully along the street, watching for anything unusual, prying eyes, busybodies, good neighbours who might take it upon themselves to ring the police if they saw a strange man at number forty-four. When he came to the house, he paused and quickly glanced around. There was no one in sight. He placed his hand firmly on the iron gate and tried to open it.

It was hanging off its hinges and stiff with rust and he had to push hard to get it to budge. The garden was overgrown, the grass sprouting in clumps after the recent rain, and monstrous weeds encroached along the path. The house itself looked dark and forbidding. Torn curtains covered the downstairs windows while on the upper level an old blanket had been draped across the panes to keep out the light.

He stood close against the door and pressed the bell, listening as the sound echoed along the hall. But there was no response, no hurrying footsteps, no voice calling out for him to wait. He bent down and peered in through the letter-box. There was some mail lying on the bare floorboards, flyers and bills, and a child's bicycle abandoned against a wall. He could see two doors but they were closed and there was no sign of life.

He decided to try the back. He made his way through the garden, stepping carefully over the small dark mounds of dogshit that cluttered the grass. There was a paved yard and another small garden, untended like the first, with a couple of sprawling apple trees coming into leaf. There was a sagging clothesline with a solitary plastic peg, and an old lawn-mower, rusting in the sun.

The back windows had no curtains and he was able to see into the house. The first window gave on to a bedroom, with an unmade bed and an old wardrobe stuck drunkenly in a corner as if no one could think of a better place to put it. There were some clothes lying on the back of a chair and a bundle of fading newspapers stacked in a pile near the door.

He moved to the next window and found himself looking into a kitchen. There was a sink with a dripping tap and further back a table and chairs and a cooker with a clutter of greasy pots and pans. Megarry rapped on the pane. He heard the sound rattling around the kitchen and out into the hall but no one came. The door of the kitchen stayed firmly closed. It was obvious now that the house was empty.

He crept along by the wall till he came to another door. He tried it and found it locked. He went back to the kitchen window and attempted to lift it up, but it remained obstinately stuck. When he looked closer, he saw a stout snib fastening it into place. It seemed that there was no possibility of gaining entry without breaking the window.

He moved along to the bedroom, tried the window there and met with more resistance. He stretched his neck to look and this time he saw that the snib was loose. With a bit of luck he might get it to open. He took off his jacket and folded it neatly on the sill and tried again, huffing and puffing from the exertion. The window shifted slightly, but still held fast. He applied more pressure and heard a creaking sound as the window began to shift. He pushed once more and then suddenly, with a jolt, it gave way.

He stood for a moment to catch his breath. He felt a weakness in his legs and a familiar dizziness that he hadn't experienced since that time in Spain. But it quickly passed. A sweat had broken on his brow. He looked around to make sure that he hadn't been seen, then he took his jacket and climbed up on the sill, cursing softly. Carefully, he lowered himself into the bedroom.

His first impression was of a damp, musty smell. It seemed to hang everywhere in the room as if the windows had been closed for a long time and no air had got in.

He stood for a moment listening to the sound of his own breathing. He felt a strange sensation, as if he was a thief or a burglar, as if at any moment a voice would cry out or a door would open and an angry face would demand to know what he was doing there. But the house was silent. Nothing stirred. He pulled the window closed and locked it and then turned to examine the room.

It was in disarray. The bed was unmade, sheets and blankets tossed carelessly aside. There was a chest, its drawers hanging open, contents flung in abandon. He rifled through them, socks, underwear, a faded white brassière. There was a dressing-table and a mirror with a long black crack running down the centre like a scar. Its drawers too had been pulled open. It occurred to Megarry that someone had been here before him, someone in a hurry, possibly looking for something.

He moved to the wardrobe in the corner of the room. An old suit hung crookedly from a wire hanger. He tried the pockets but found only a couple of coins. He examined the clothes on the back of the chair. There was nothing. He took a final look around the room, then grasped the door handle and pulled it open.

He was out in the hall. From the glass panes above the fanlight on the door the sun came filtering in. The air was filled with dust, little particles floating in and out of the sunlight like grains of sand. He turned right and entered the kitchen.

There was a different smell here, the odour of stale food, of long-forgotten meals. He opened a cupboard and found a half-eaten loaf, green and blue with mould around the edges. There were a few tins, spaghetti and peas, and a box of cornflakes. On the table was a milk bottle with a coating of crusted cream and three plates with the remains of a meal, knives and forks and cups abandoned.

In the sink some unwashed dishes had been left, and on the cooker a pot with what looked like a stew. He sniffed the contents and recoiled quickly from the putrid smell. He stood for a moment to survey the kitchen.

There was something strange, something unnatural. He realised that the silence in the house was all-pervading, not even the sound of a ticking clock or a buzzing fly. On the road outside he heard a car pass by, its engine gently humming; then it came to a stop and he heard the sound of the engine dying away and the silence returned. He closed the kitchen door and went back out into the hall.

There was another door and it gave entry to a larger room. The curtains on the windows cast a yellow pall. He turned on a light and saw that he was in a living-room. It had a fireplace with dead coals and an old settee and a couple of armchairs. There was a set of prints on the walls, rural scenes of sporting ploughboys at a village inn. They seemed so inappropriate; the scenes of jollification so out of place in this damp, dreary room where no daylight penetrated.

There was a photograph on the mantelpiece. He lifted it and saw a man with a little boy. He seemed young and carefree, laughing into the camera as he held the child up to the sun. In the background he could see the striped awning of a tent and the painted outline of a merry-go-round. The picture had been taken at a fairground and it was immediately obvious to Megarry who the man was. It was Harpo Higgins.

But it was a different Higgins from the one he had seen only twenty-four hours earlier on the mortuary slab. There he had seen an emaciated body, undernourished, the bones of the rib-cage almost thrusting through the pale yellow skin. This was a fit man, healthy, robust, full of life, obviously enjoying himself on a day out somewhere with his son.

The contrast was so striking that it caused Megarry to pause. He looked at the photograph again and thought of the wasted life, the promise, the days that must have stretched before Higgins then, filled with opportunity. And the reality of his end on a lonely quayside beside the dark waters of the river. He sighed and slipped the photograph into the pocket of his coat. As he did so, his eye caught something else.

At first he thought it was a pencil, but as he moved closer he saw that it was a syringe. It was clotted with a reddish brown substance that looked like dried blood. Beside it was a spoon, the underside burnt black, and a piece of leather strap that had been tied in a noose. Megarry immediately recognised the paraphernalia of drug abuse.

He felt his gorge rise. He thought again of the smiling young man in the photograph and the pale corpse in the pathology room and the litany of drug addiction that linked them like a chain. He took out a handkerchief and wrapped it round the syringe and carefully put it in his pocket.

He began a search of the room. There was hardly anything of value. On a little table was a pile of children's books and toys, a racing car, a plastic action man. Beside the settee was a small locker. He opened it and found several magazines and a cigarette lighter and a pack of playing cards. He moved to a sideboard. The first drawer was empty, but in the second he saw a couple of music tapes and a pocket diary. He took it out and flicked it open.

It was a cheap plastic diary and here and there across its pages messages had been scrawled in a spidery hand: *Meet Bosco, Meet Fransy, Meet Ger*. He turned to the first month and began a careful examination.

It seemed that the owner had used the diary to keep a list of engagements. Most of these were at weekends, and as Megarry turned the pages the number of entries increased. One name seemed to predominate: *Meet the Fat Man*, or *Fat Man called* or *Have to see the Fat Man*. He turned quickly to the night of Higgins's death but the page was blank. He turned to the previous day and there it was again in the same uncertain hand: *Ring Fat Man*.

He felt his heart beat faster. He slipped the diary into his pocket along with the photograph and syringe and looked once more around the room. Then he moved to the door and prepared to search upstairs. As he did so, he heard something that made him stop.

He had grown accustomed to the silence all around him, but now he could hear the unmistakable sound of footsteps. They seemed to be outside the house. He heard the scraping of the gate and the footsteps approach along the path. They paused at the door and then he heard a key being inserted into the lock.

38

His first thought was to put out the light, but before he could do anything the front door had opened and someone had entered the hall.

He was overwhelmed with the same feeling he had when he first came into the house. It was as if he was a thief or an intruder, as if he had no right to be here and was now about to be found out. He looked around desperately for somewhere to hide, but the bare room gave no cover. He heard the front door close and the footsteps start along the hall.

He looked up, and a young woman was standing in the doorway.

6

The woman in the doorway was about twenty-seven. She was tall, dark and very attractive, and Megarry's first impression was that he had seen her somewhere before, on television or on the cover of a magazine. For a brief moment she seemed as shocked as he was. She stared at Megarry's plump, dishevelled figure, then quickly regained her composure. 'Who the hell are you?' she said. 'How did you get in here?'

'I'm a police officer.'

The woman's expression didn't change. She folded her arms, advanced into the room and looked around as if she wasn't convinced. 'No doubt you can prove that. Or do I have to ring for the guards to come and take you away?'

It occurred to Megarry that the woman was very confident. For all she knew he could be a burglar or a rapist. He could be armed and could do her harm here in this empty house and no one would ever know. He put his hand into a pocket and withdrew his identity card.

The woman glanced at it and gave it back. 'RUC?' She looked surprised. 'You've no authority down here. This is a separate jurisdiction.'

'I'm helping the gardai with an investigation.'

'Are you now? So you don't mind telling me what you're doing here?'

40

Megarry found that he was sweating again. He took out a handkerchief and wiped his brow. 'I was looking for the occupant.'

'Harpo?'

'Yes, Harpo.'

The woman seemed to relax a little. 'Is he here?'

'It doesn't look like it.'

She looked around again, as if she expected to find something missing from the bare, sparsely furnished room. 'He's rarely here,' she said with a toss of her head. She looked into Megarry's face and he was struck again by how beautiful she was. Such a woman was totally out of place in this house. What could she possibly have in common with the poor, undernourished addict he had seen in the morgue?

'How did you get in?' she asked.

'I used the bedroom window.'

'That's breaking and entering.'

'Technically, yes. But I have a warrant.' He kept a straight face as he told the lie.

She shrugged and he saw a smile in the corner of her mouth. 'What did you expect to find here? It's just a dump as you can see. Just a doss-house really.'

Megarry paused. It was obvious from her demeanour that she didn't know about Higgins's death. He would have to tell her. 'Do you mind if *I* stop answering your questions, and *you* answer some of mine?'

'Like what?'

'Like, who *you* are and what *you* are doing here?'

The woman didn't hesitate. 'My name is Dee Dee Clarke,' she said. 'I'm a friend of Harpo's.'

'Dee Dee?' Megarry asked.

'It's a nickname. It's short for Deirdre.'

'And you let yourself in?'

'Yes. I've got a key.'

'And what's *your* business here?'

'Hey,' the woman suddenly said. '*You're* the intruder.'

'I'm also a police officer.'

'I just told you. I'm a friend of Harpo's. I was paying him a social call.'

'But you said yourself that he's rarely here.'

For the first time he thought she looked confused. But it passed quickly and she was talking again in her firm, confident voice.

'I came on spec. I was going to leave him a note. Get him to call me.'

She opened her handbag and took out a pen and pad. Without looking up, she said: 'Is he in some kind of trouble?'

Megarry took a deep breath. 'You could say that.'

She finished the note and folded it and looked into the policeman's face. 'What's happened?'

'He's dead.'

For a moment there was no response. Megarry became aware again of the stillness in the house, not even the ticking of a clock. The woman's face seemed to go pale and then she was clutching wildly at his arm.

'What did you say?'

'He's dead.'

'But he can't be. I saw him only a few days ago.'

She was screaming now, shaking her head violently from side to side. Megarry put his arm around her shoulder and led her to the settee. He spoke soothingly, the way he would speak to a child. 'I'm sorry to break it to you like this. We found him yesterday morning.'

'No,' the woman said. 'I don't believe this.'

She was staring at him, a wild look in her eyes. Suddenly she bent her head against his chest and began to sob.

He sat beside her and stroked her hair. He found himself contrasting this woman's reaction to the calm, almost cold response of Higgins's sister. Who is she? he thought. Why should his death cause her so much grief?

He heard a car pass by on the road outside and then another. He wished that he could find something useful to say, but nothing came. He sat beside her on the shabby settee and after a while she began to compose herself. She looked up and he saw that her eyes were red with tears.

'What happened?' she said. 'Was it an overdose?'

This was the second time that he had been asked that very same question. And then he realised it was the obvious response. Most addicts, when they went suddenly, went that way.

'No,' he said. 'He was murdered.'

He saw her shoulders shake and the tears start again, tumbling down her face like drops of rain. 'Jesus,' she said. 'Not that. Not murdered.'

He gave her a handkerchief and she gripped it tightly in her hands.

'Who would do that? Poor Harpo. He was such a lovely guy. He wouldn't have harmed a fly. Who would want to do a thing like that?'

'That's what we're trying to find out,' Megarry said. 'That's why I'm here. I'm trying to trace his movements. Maybe you can help.'

She looked up quickly. 'No,' she said. 'I wouldn't know anything like that.'

'You knew he was an addict?'

'Of course.'

'Tell me about it.'

'What is there to tell? He was just a poor junkie.'

'When did it start?'

'I don't know. About ten years ago. It was only messing at first. Small stuff. Blow mainly. Everybody smoked at that time. Then Harpo started to buy skag at the weekends. He was always a daredevil. He never thought he'd get hooked.'

She started weeping again, silently this time. 'He was such a lovely guy. You should have known him. He would have done anything for anyone. And to die like that. Like a dog in a ditch.'

She took out a packet of cigarettes. Megarry took one and fumbled in his pocket for matches. She bent her head into the flame.

'I can't believe this. When you told me just now, I thought you were making it up.'

'When did he develop a habit?'

43

'God knows. He'd been shooting up for a while. Skin-popping at first and then mainlining.'

'How bad was it?'

'Pretty bad.'

'Like how much?'

'Twenty or thirty pounds a day.'

'Where did he get the money?'

'Where they all get it. Robbed, stole. Sold what he could. Look at this place.' She waved her arm around the room. 'This used to be a lovely house, but he sold everything to stick it in his arm.'

Megarry tapped ash from his cigarette into the empty fireplace. 'Was he dealing?'

'Now and then.'

'Much?'

'Just a little on the side. Just to support his habit. He wasn't a bad guy. He wasn't out trying to get schoolkids hooked on drugs. None of that bullshit that you read in the papers. He only sold to other addicts.'

'How well did you know him?'

She hesitated for a moment. 'Pretty well.'

'Tell me something else. Was he married?'

'No. Harpo wasn't married.'

'But he had a child.'

She stared.

'Harpo had a child.' Megarry repeated. He was about to take the photograph from his pocket, but some instinct made him stop.

She suddenly crushed out the cigarette. 'Who told you that?'

'It doesn't matter. Do you know where the child is now? Do you know who would have him?'

'No,' she said and he could see that she was angry. 'You bloody cops are all the same. One damned question after another. I don't know Harpo's whole bloody life story.'

'Do you know anyone called Bosco?'

She looked confused.

'Fransy?'

'No.'

'The Fat Man?'

'Who?'

'The Fat Man. Do you know him?'

'No,' she said dismissively. 'I don't know any Fat Man. Why do you think I would know these people? I didn't know all Harpo's friends. They're probably junkies, just like him.'

'Or dealers?'

'Yes,' she said. 'They could be dealers. What makes you think I would know them?'

'What about someone called the Quare Fella?'

She had taken out a little compact-case and was busy now rearranging her make-up.

She lowered the case and gave Megarry a penetrating look. 'What a silly name,' she said at last. 'Where do you get them?'

'It's just a name I came across. Do you know him?'

'No. I just told you.'

She smiled and it seemed to Megarry that her grief had been short-lived.

'Do you have any idea why Harpo might have been killed? Or who might have done it?'

'Sorry,' she said. 'I wouldn't have a clue.'

She stood up and straightened her skirt. 'If you've finished looking around here, I think I'll lock up.' She walked out into the hall and waited for him to follow.

'There's one last thing,' he said. 'Do you have an address or phone number where I could contact you? Just in case I need to talk to you again.'

She opened her handbag and took out a card. He looked at it. 'Dee Dee Clarke. Bentley's Model Agency' it said. There was an address and a telephone number.

'You're a model?'

She smiled. 'Yes. I'm a model. Don't look so surprised.'

Megarry walked with her to her car. The sun had gone in and dark clouds loured across the sky. He held open the door and she settled into the driving seat.

'If there's anything else you think of, maybe you'd give me a ring. Cecil Megarry. You can leave a message for me at Barrack Street station.'

45

'I got your name the first time,' she said.

She started the engine, then rolled down the window as if she had remembered something. 'When's the funeral?'

'I don't know,' Megarry said. 'His sister's looking after that.'

He watched her drive up the street and turn out towards the main road. He started after her, his shoes clip-clopping on the cracked pavement. He saw that one of his laces had become undone. As he bent to tie it, a thought kept coming back into his head.

Who is she? What was she doing here?

7

George Buchanan woke shortly after twelve o'clock. He woke with a start, as if some subconscious alarm had gone off at a predetermined moment. He rolled over in bed and flung out his arms and, as he did so, he knocked over a half-filled glass of whiskey on the bedside table. George stared, watching the whiskey seep into the sheets, spreading outwards in a widening stain.

For a moment, he sat there and listened to the quiet of the little room. The curtains were pulled but he could see the faint rays of the sun struggling through an occasional gap at the window. George disliked the sun, the bright light that hurt his eyes and dampened his nice white shirt with perspiration. He preferred dark, dim corners, barely lit snugs where people had to struggle to see your face. The sun gave him headaches.

He had a headache now, a dull, throbbing pain at the base of his skull. When he turned his neck the pain bit deeper, sending ripples of shock into his brain. He reached out a hand and righted the whiskey glass. There was a little drop left, about half an inch that hadn't spilled. George raised it to his lips and drank.

He lay back in the sheets and tried to unravel the night. He could see his trousers draped carelessly across a chair, his shoes flung beside the radiator, laces still tied, socks in a ball, shirt stretched like a sail across the door of the wardrobe. George had a regard for his clothes. It wasn't like him to leave them in such disarray.

'I must have been drunk,' he thought as if the headache wasn't sign enough. 'Jesus Christ, I must have been locked.'

He tried to remember how he had got home. It must have been a taxi, although he could recall nothing about it. His last memory was of Jangles night-club up on Leeson Street, bottles of cheap champagne at £30 a go, the hum of the music, the dark, the smell of sweat and aftershave, the camp crowd from the Bunch of Grapes, the excitement of it all.

In the men's toilet, he had come across a tall young man with a ring in his ear snorting a line of coke. He had stared at George, one finger pressed tight against his nostril and at first George thought he was going to start a row. But then the man had slowly smiled and languidly extended the hand that held the mirror.

'Toot?' he had asked and George had nodded and bent his own head over the glass and inhaled the bright white powder, feeling an instant rush of pleasure. That was one of the things that he liked about Jangles. People were very generous with their dope.

He had gone there about ten o'clock in pursuit of Dee Dee. It was a little job he was doing for the Quare Fella. Keeping an eye on her. Making sure she didn't fall in with bad company. Didn't do anything foolish. She'd got herself into one or two small scrapes in the past, principally to do with substance abuse and the Quare Fella didn't like it.

So George had kept an eye on her all day, following her from the time she left her flat in Ranelagh to go to work, following her at lunch-time, following her home again in the evening. He knew he would pick her up at Jangles. It was her favourite place, herself and that snobby crowd she hung around with, models and photographers and poncey hairdressers.

That was George's main line of business, keeping an eye on people. That and trading pieces of information, little bits of gossip that he picked up here and there. He regarded himself as a sort of journalist, although he had never been very good in the writing department. He had left school at fifteen. But he had often heard the Quare Fella say that information was money. Information was power. There was always someone, somewhere, willing to pay for the right kind of gossip. George made a living keeping his eyes and ears open.

He had heard something last night in a darkened alcove at Jangles Club. Pinky Somerdale had been buying. He had a wallet stuffed with money, purple twenty-pound notes that he fished out at regular intervals to order more champagne. Pinky had declined to say where it was coming from, but George had got the impression that he was after pulling off some kind of a deal. George never inquired into these matters. Some things were best left unsaid.

'Harpo Higgins is dead.'

Pinky Somerdale lifted his champagne glass and finished it off, then took a dark bottle from the silver ice bucket and poured again, topping up George's glass as he went.

'What?'

'Harpo Higgins. You remember Harpo? Used to be the roadie with the Dancing Queens.'

There was a racket coming from the amplifiers but George didn't mind. There was a pleasant buzz in his head from the line of coke and a good-looking woman with a minidress up around her ass was smiling at him from a table nearby. George was happy. He was at that stage of intoxication where the world was at peace. He raised his champagne glass to his lips and smiled back.

'What happened?'

'He was murdered. Geezer I met today told me. Down along the quays somewhere.'

George examined Pinky through a haze of cigarette smoke. He was wearing a smart new suit, button-down shirt, nice silk tie. And he'd had his hair styled. Where *was* he getting the money, George wondered?

'Poor ould Harpo,' Pinky said. 'Wasn't the worst. Decent guy in his day, though I thought he'd gone to the dogs recently. He had a bad habit, you know. Bleedin' skag did him in.'

'What happened to him?' George said again. There was a

warm feeling spreading along the edges of his brain. The woman was getting up from the table and was coming towards him.

'I just told you. He was murdered.'

'When?'

'Night before last, I think.'

Something inside George's head clicked and he felt a little worm of fear. 'Night before last? What night was that?'

'Monday.'

George remembered Monday night. He had been in Brannigan's Bar, just hanging out, keeping his eyes and ears open. The place had been full of journalists and plain-clothes cops and hangers on. You wouldn't know who you might be talking to. He had seen something and the memory of the event scared him a little.

The woman passed by the alcove and ran her fingers along his cheek. 'Nice buns,' she whispered.

George smiled and straightened his tie. He bent closer and peered into Pinky's face. 'Murdered, did you say?'

Pinky nodded and finished his glass.

'Jesus,' George said. 'That's a bit bleedin' thick. What do you think it was?'

Pinky shrugged. 'Drugs, I would say. He was doing a little dealing on the side. Yes, I'd say it was definitely something to do with drugs.' And he raised his hand and waved to the barman for more champagne.

George knew now he had a hangover. He groped under the bed with an unsteady hand till he found the neck of the whiskey bottle. Then he took the glass from the bedside table and poured a large measure. He felt it warming his chest and stomach. Give it a few minutes, George thought, till it does its work.

He got out of bed and searched the pockets of his suit till he found his sun-glasses and put them on. The pain in his head was sharper now that he was standing up and he noticed that his fingers weren't co-ordinating the way they should. He plugged in the kettle for coffee, then went into the bathroom and ran the shower.

He got under the stream and turned up the heat as high as it could go. He felt the jets of water like needles on his skin. He stood beneath the scalding shower till he could take no more. Then he abruptly turned the switch to cold and waited till his ears and face and scalp began to go numb. George had a formula for dealing with hangovers. It was based on the principle of a greater pain driving out a lesser one.

He stepped out of the shower and began rubbing himself vigorously with a towel. By now his arms and legs were trembling and goose pimples as big as mosquito bites stood up on his pale skin. He glanced in the mirror and his blue face stared back. George poured hot water into a mug and spooned in coffee.

He tried to get his thoughts in order. He recalled the conversation in Jangles. Harpo Higgins murdered. And what he had seen in Brannigan's Bar. That information must be worth money to somebody. But who? And how would he handle it? He felt the fear return. It was dangerous information, the sort that could get you into trouble. Maybe it would be better to forget all about it, put it out of his mind as if it had never happened.

Gradually, with the whiskey and the coffee and the shower, George began to feel a kind of normality return. He checked his watch. It was twelve thirty-five. Dee Dee was on a job over in Ballsbridge doing a television advert for chocolate bars. He could be there in forty-five minutes if he ordered a taxi right now. He took his wallet from the dressing-table and counted six twenty-pound notes. He was getting low. All this running around after Dee Dee was eating a hole in his budget. He'd have to touch base soon with the Quare Fella for a top-up of expenses.

He lifted the phone and rang the taxi firm, giving precise directions. In George's experience most taxi drivers were dozy, forever getting lost or not turning up.

'This is urgent,' he barked into the receiver. 'Make sure he gets here.'

He went to the wardrobe and selected a nice charcoal-grey suit with turn-ups in the trousers. It was his very best suit. Four hundred quid he had paid for it. He picked a white shirt and dark tie and laid them carefully on the bed. George knew the importance of appearance. He started the serious business of getting dressed.

Normally this was something that he liked to spend some time on, making sure that the creases in the trousers were straight, that there were no stray hairs on the shoulders of the jacket, that the knot in the tie was just right. But there was a rush on if he was going to get over to Ballsbridge before Dee Dee broke up for lunch.

He smoothed down his shirt and gave his jacket a little tug so that it fitted neatly about his waist. Then he bent and gave his shoes a quick wipe with a paper napkin till they shone in the filtered light from the window. As he straightened up again, he heard the buzzer on the door start to go, telling him that the taxi had arrived. He reached for the door handle and as he did so, the phone rang.

Without thinking, George took it. It was his mother.

'I thought I'd better ring you,' she said. 'Just to remind you.'

'What?'

George realised that his head was still giving him trouble.

'Remind you,' his mother said. Her voice seemed to be coming from somewhere far away, muffled as if she was in a cave.

'Remind me of what, Ma?'

'The Mass, of course. Your father's anniversary.'

George took a deep breath. 'Oh,' he said. 'Right.'

'You hadn't forgotten?'

'No,' George lied. 'Of course not.'

'You're coming?'

This was an annual ritual organised by his mother and her sisters. Mass for the repose of the soul of George Buchanan Senior.

'Don't you think he's in heaven now, Ma? All these prayers. Don't you think they're sort of wasted?'

'Not at all,' his mother said. 'Prayer is never wasted. It's not like worldly goods. It never goes stale. Think of it as a bank. You're building up a deposit. Some day you might need to make a withdrawal.'

She paused.

'It's the same place, by the way. Church of the Holy Sepulchre. Two o'clock.'

'Right,' George said.

'Are you okay?' his mother asked.

'I'm fine.'

'You don't sound fine. You sound as if you've got a cold or something.'

The buzzer went once more. If he didn't answer the door, the taxi driver would think he'd got the wrong address and would go away.

'I have to go, Ma. I've got a taxi waiting.'

'A taxi?'

George snapped, 'A taxi, Ma. You know, those things with four wheels that take you from place to place.'

'There's no need to be cheeky,' his mother said. 'Where are you off to in a taxi at this time of the day?'

'I have to meet a client.'

'A what?'

'Goodbye, Ma.'

George put the phone back and ran down the stairs to the front door and the waiting cab. He adjusted his sun-glasses and got into the back seat while the driver started the engine. George hoped he wasn't going to talk. He wasn't in the mood for silly chatter from taxi drivers.

'Where to?' the man asked.

'Ballsbridge.'

George settled into the upholstery. He liked riding in taxis. He liked sitting in the back. It gave him a feeling of power.

'Not a bad ould day,' the man said, testing George for conversation.

'No,' George said tartly and stared out of the window at the houses flashing by.

'More like the kind of weather we should be getting this time

53

of year. Weather's a funny thing. Mind you some people like it. I had a couple of American tourists once . . .'

George sat silent in the back seat and let the man ramble on.

They went in by Clontarf, past the yacht club. George closed his eyes and tried to think. The hangover was still there. It was proving hard to shake. When he opened his eyes again, they were almost at the river.

I need another drink, George thought, somewhere quiet to sit and work things out. He glanced at his watch. It was almost one o'clock. Dee Dee would be breaking up for lunch soon.

George thought of the long hours hanging about in doorways or walking discreetly through crowds or jumping into passing cabs. What the hell, he thought, I can pick her up again in the afternoon.

He leaned forward and tapped the driver on the shoulder. 'I've changed my mind,' he said. 'Forget Ballsbridge. Drop me at Brannigan's Bar.'

8

Megarry was at the premises of Dempsey Engineering for half past three, after travelling on the bus along the coast road past Fairview, gazing out of the window at unfamiliar streets. In his pocket he had the letter which had been sent to Harpo Higgins threatening him with dismissal if he didn't turn up for a medical check. He had phoned earlier and made an appointment with Mr Costello, the personnel manager who had signed the letter.

He got off at the corner of Verdon Avenue and started to walk. The weather was changing. The bright morning sun had dimmed and now the sky was angry, dark clouds heavy with rain. Already the sea beyond the Bull Island was heaving, slate-grey waves flecked with white.

He recognised the place at once, a modern industrial complex, rows of low-level buildings giving off a satisfying hum of industry. He stopped at the gate and told the man his business, and was directed to the administration block, a shiny building of smoked-glass windows and steel.

There was a forecourt with spaces marked in white paint for half a dozen cars: Managing Director, Chief Executive, Company Secretary. He noticed that all the spaces were filled with cars that exuded wealth, polished bodywork, leather upholstery, car phones resting on the dashboards.

He made his way up the steps and the doors slid open to

greet him. He entered a wide hall with potted plants. There was a scent of lavender. Immediately in front of him was a security desk. A man in uniform stood up as he came in.

'Megarry is my name. I have an appointment to see Mr Costello.'

The security guard pressed some buttons on a console while Megarry waited. He let his eye travel round the hall. It had been tastefully decorated in bright pastel shades. On the walls were prints. He recognised one or two. Renoirs. Paris café society. In the corner of the hall was a lift. The doors opened and a small man came bustling towards him.

'Mr Megarry?'

'That's me.'

'Costello.' He put out his hand and the policeman grabbed it. 'We're upstairs.' He pointed towards the door. 'Nasty weather. It's going to rain.'

'Yes,' Megarry said. 'I think you're right. And I haven't brought a coat.'

Mr Costello's office was on the third floor. There was another man waiting for them, younger, with blond hair and a pale face.

'This is Mr Byrne.'

The younger man nodded a greeting and Costello sat down.

'What do you make here?' Megarry asked.

'Farm machinery. Tools. Heating equipment. We have a large export business. Mr Dempsey is very energetic. He will make anything if the price is right.'

'I've no doubt.'

Costello pushed his glasses tight against his nose. 'Now,' he said. 'You wanted to know about James Higgins.' He took a pink folder from the desk. Mr Costello was efficient. He had already dug out the file on Higgins in preparation for the visit.

'Is he in some kind of trouble?' the young man asked.

They were both watching him now. Was it possible that they didn't know?

'He's dead.'

For a moment there was silence.

'*Dead*?' Costello said.

'He was murdered.'

'Dear God.'

'I heard something on the radio,' Byrne said quickly. 'Was it down along the quays somewhere?'

'That's right.'

He shook his head. 'Poor old Higgins. I didn't connect the name. You know the way sometimes you listen to the radio with only half an ear.'

'Yes,' Megarry said. 'It's a very messy business.'

'Do you know what it was all about?'

'There's no apparent motive.'

Costello made a tsk tsk sound with his tongue. 'And you wanted us to provide you with some information about him? Is that the idea?'

'If you don't mind.'

'No. Not at all.' He opened the file and began to read. 'Higgins worked with us from February 1993 till November 1995. General operative. It was a fairly basic job. He more or less stood at a conveyor belt all day. He wasn't a very steady employee.' He looked at Megarry over the top of his glasses. 'Lot of absenteeism, I'm afraid.'

'He was an addict,' Megarry said.

'I beg your pardon?'

'A drug addict.'

He saw the two men exchange glances.

'I didn't know that,' Costello said.

'He was. Maybe that might account for his absences from work.'

'Of course.'

'What happened in November?'

'We had to let him go.'

'He didn't turn up for his medical?'

Costello glanced quickly at the file and then at Megarry. 'That's right. How did you know that?'

'You sent him a letter. He had it in his pocket.'

Costello sighed. 'That's what happened. We have a company policy here. Ten days' uncertificated sick-leave in any twelve-month period. It's very generous. Much more generous than most companies. But Higgins was disappearing for weeks on end. When he didn't attend for his medical we had no option but to let him go. Effectively, he fired himself.'

Megarry got the impression that he was apologising. Now that he knew that Higgins was dead he was trying to distance himself from any responsibility.

'How did he get employment here in the first place?'

'He applied in the normal course.'

'And was interviewed?'

'That's right.'

'By you?'

'Well maybe not by me personally. It's so long ago now that I can't remember. But somebody would have interviewed him. It's company policy.'

'And he appeared normal?'

'Naturally. Otherwise we wouldn't have hired him.'

'Had he any experience in this work?'

'No, but that doesn't matter. It's fairly low-skilled work. And we have a training programme.'

'And what was he doing before he joined the company?'

'He was unemployed for a period. Before that he worked in the music business. Public relations.'

'When did this pattern of absenteeism begin?'

Costello consulted the file once more. 'Shortly after he commenced with us. He began to take days off. Nothing that would get him into trouble. It got worse after that. In the end, he was hardly showing up for work at all.'

Costello gave the policeman a look that said: What else could we do?

'What address did he give when he started work with you?'

'Forty-four St Martin's Gardens.'

'But the letter you sent was addressed to Michael Davitt Tower in Ballymoss.'

'That's right. He moved.'

'Did he give any reason?'

Costello shook his head. 'He didn't have to. Where he lived was his own business.'

'Do you know if he was married?'

Costello peered at the file and Megarry saw a frown pass

over his face. He glanced quickly towards Byrne who was sitting quietly watching him and then the two men bent their heads together and conferred.

'It doesn't say.'

'Isn't it something you would normally ask a prospective employee?'

'Normally yes. He'd have had to fill in an application form. It's a standard question. Not that it makes any difference, you understand. But.'

'Yes?' Megarry pressed.

'His application form is missing from his file.'

The policeman took a deep breath and watched the other man's discomfort.

Costello's face turned red. He rustled through some papers in the folder, then looked once more at Megarry. 'No,' he said. 'No application form.'

Megarry pushed back his chair and stood up. 'Is there anything else you can tell me about him?'

Costello closed the file and spread his hands. 'Afraid not. I'm sorry the poor devil is dead. When is the funeral?'

'I don't know. Why do you ask?'

'We'll have to send a wreath. We always do. Company policy.'

Byrne followed him out into the corridor.

'Thanks for your help,' Megarry said. 'I can make my own way down.'

The young man coughed gently into his fist. The policeman noticed the blueness of his eyes, like the sky or the sea, he thought.

'Have you got a moment to spare?' Byrne said.

'Of course.'

'Mr Dempsey would like to see you.'

'Mr Dempsey?'

'The managing director. He's waiting for you now in his office.'

'He wants to see *me*?'

'Yes,' Byrne said and smiled.

Megarry looked puzzled. 'Well then,' he said. 'Let's not keep him waiting.'

They walked to the end of the hall and took the lift. Byrne stood politely beside the door as the carriage ascended. There was a jolt and the lift slid open. They stepped out into a corridor similar to the one they had left except that this one was carpeted and the walls were panelled in brown wood and from the window there was the most spectacular view that Megarry had ever seen.

It gave out over the whole city, the spires and chimneys, the river tumbling into the bay, the broad expanse of ocean, dark and grey now in the dull afternoon light. There was a handful of ships like toy boats passing up the channel. And further away, the outline of the Sugar Loaf and Bray Head and the Wicklow hills hunched in the distance.

Byrne saw the admiraton on Megarry's face. He moved forward and stood beside him. 'Some sight, eh?'

'Yes, indeed. It must be breathtaking on a clear day.'

Byrne seemed pleased. He had an air of confidence about him. A young man on the way up, Megarry decided. Keen, ambitious. He was probably scrupulously efficient.

'Mr Dempsey had his office built specially to take advantage of the view. Any time we have foreign visitors he always brings them up here and shows it to them. Mr Dempsey is a Dublin man. He's very proud of this city.'

'Well he has much to be proud of,' Megarry said.

They walked to the end of the corridor and Byrne knocked on a door, then pushed it open. A young blonde woman looked up from her keyboard.

'Mr D?' Byrne said and raised his eyebrows.

'He's waiting,' the woman said and indicated yet another door. Byrne politely leaned across and pushed the door open for the policeman.

They were in a sumptuous office, the walls panelled, like the corridor, in dark wood and lined with certificates and photographs. The windows on two sides gave out over the same magnificent view. There was a large oak desk dominating the centre of the room. It was bare except for a writing pad and a telephone. Behind it a tall man was sitting. He had a plump, weatherbeaten face.

Megarry had seen him before.

The man rose as they came into the room. Megarry saw the look of surprise as he struggled for recognition.

'The Royal Hotel,' Megarry said quickly. 'You were in the bar.'

The man's face spread in a broad smile. 'You had just f-finished your walk.'

Once again, Megarry caught the stammer in the man's voice.

'That's right. It's part of my routine. Walking the hills of Howth. It's supposed to keep me fit.'

The man came out from behind the desk and held out his hand. 'Harry Dempsey.'

'Cecil Megarry.'

'This is a coincidence,' Dempsey said. 'Can I g-get you a drink?' He gestured towards a large cabinet in the corner of the room. It was lined with bottles and glasses that shone in the light.

Megarry considered. He was parched. He would enjoy nothing more than a large whiskey. And since he had no car, he didn't have to worry about driving.

'I'll have a Bushmills, please. Do you have it?'

'Of course.' Dempsey said. 'I've got everything. You Northern p-people are great men for the B-bushmills. It's a grand whiskey. I drink it myself.'

Without being told, Byrne slipped behind the desk and took out two glasses. He lifted a bottle and held it up for the policeman. 'Ice, water?'

'Both.'

Byrne charged the glasses and brought them back to the two men. He hesitated for a moment, then quietly left the room.

Dempsey raised his drink. 'Slainte.'

'Good luck,' Megarry said and sipped at the whiskey.

'You're a p-policeman?'

'That's right.'

'And you're living out in Howth? I mistook you for a visitor the day we talked.'

'I *am* a visitor,' Megarry said. 'I'm an RUC officer. I'm on secondment down here. I'm staying with friends.'

'Ah, so that explains it.' Dempsey raised his glass and took a long drink. He put it down on the desk and wiped his mouth with a gleaming handkerchief. 'God's little acre,' he said.

'I beg your pardon?'

'It's my n-name for Howth. God's little acre. I love the place. It's got everything. Sea, hills, green fields. Do you realise that wherever you live in Howth you are within f-five minutes of the sea? It's a peninsula.'

'Ahh.' Megarry felt a warm glow settle over him from the whiskey. 'I'm helping with the murder of James Higgins,' he said. 'He used to work for you.'

A grave look came over Dempsey's face. 'I heard. Byrne just told me. It's a terrible b-business. Poor devil.'

'Did you know him?'

Dempsey shook his head. 'Not p-personally. I employ over two hundred people here. I don't know them all. I might have seen him around the place from time to time.'

He drained his whiskey and gestured towards Megarry's glass. 'One more?'

He stood with a coaxing smile on his face. 'Why not?' he said. 'A b-bird never flew on one wing.'

Megarry finished his drink and gave over the empty glass. There was something about Dempsey. A disarming quality. He had expected someone formal. A stuffed shirt. But this man was open and relaxed. He had no airs.

He came back from the cabinet and gave Megarry a fresh drink. 'I b-built this place up myself, you know. From nothing. When I started, I had a garage in Glasnevin and a second-hand van. That's all I had. I was up to my neck in debt to the bloody b-banks. Me and my wife Claire lived in a mobile home.' There was a proud note in his voice. 'I came from nowhere. My father was a c-cooper in Guinness's brewery. There were thirteen of us. All living in a little house in the Liberties.'

'That's a big achievement.'

'You've no idea,' Dempsey said. 'I had to fight every inch of the way. It wasn't easy. The established firms tried to put me out of b-business. Oh, I could tell you stories. But do you know what the secret is?' He held up a finger. 'Control. I always maintained control. I took every decision myself. Oh, I listen to people. I take advice. But when it comes down to making decisions, I do that myself.'

At that moment the phone on the desk rang.

'Excuse me,' Dempsey said and bent to lift the instrument. Megarry used the opportunity to look around the room. Along a wall was a glass cabinet. It was lined with trophies; cups and medals and shields mounted on wooden plaques. Megarry noticed the ornaments, pieces of marble and onyx, souvenirs, delicate pieces of china and glass.

'I can't see him now,' Dempsey was saying. 'You d-deal with him.' He paused to listen. Then he was speaking again. 'He shouldn't call like this without an appointment. Tell him I said that.'

He put down the phone and turned back to Megarry. 'People have so little consideration,' he said. 'They expect to be able to walk in off the street and see me. That was a c-customer. It's amazing. They think I've got nothing b-better to do. They expect me just to drop everything and come running.'

Megarry waited. 'What did you want to see me about?' he asked.

Dempsey stared as if he had lost his run of thought. 'Ah, yes,' he said. 'I wanted to tell you that we will help you in any w-way with your investigation. Anything we can do, don't hesitate to ask.'

'I've already spoken to Mr Costello. He was very helpful.'

'Don't hesitate,' Dempsey said firmly. 'I mean that.'

He finished his drink and put it down. 'Will you be in Howth long?'

'Until the case is finished.'

'And how long will that be?'

'Who knows? I'll stick with it till the end.'

Dempsey seemed to consider. 'Do you play g-golf?' he said suddenly.

'Badly.'

'Sail?'

Megarry shook his head.

'I was going to suggest you might like to come out on my b-boat.'

'No,' Megarry said quickly. 'I'm not a sailor. I'd only get seasick.'

'Well then,' Dempsey said. He walked with Megarry to the door. 'Maybe I'll see you in the Royal some day. We might have a p-pint.'

Megarry went down in the lift. The whiskey was warming his chest and stomach. He felt a little light-headed. He realised he hadn't eaten anything since breakfast.

There was a shudder and the doors of the lift slid open. He headed for the main entrance. He could see that the rain had started, gusts blowing against the windows, running in little streams along the panes. He had no overcoat or umbrella. He was going to get soaked.

As he reached the front door, he heard a voice call his name. He turned quickly to see Byrne's pale face staring at him.

'Superintendent,' he said. 'There's something I wanted to tell you.'

'Yes.'

Byrne glanced around, then lowered his voice. 'Costello wasn't quite accurate earlier. Higgins *did* have a wife,' he said.

Megarry blinked.

'Well maybe not a proper wife. A woman that he lived with. I'm not sure that they were legally married.'

'Really?'

'Her name is Marie O'Gorman.'

'How do you know this?'

'She called here for him. Several times. I used to deal with her.'

'And where would I be able to find her?'

'I'm not sure,' Byrne said. 'But I know where her parents live.'

'Where's that?'

'O'Casey Villas in Crumlin.'

9

The following morning Megarry went in to see Mulqueen. He wanted to bring him up to date on progress so far, his visit to St Martin's Gardens and his interview with Costello. He found Kelly already there, sitting across the desk from Mulqueen and looking unhappy.

'Sit down, Cecil.' Mulqueen gestured to a battered chair with the stuffing poking out from one side. 'I've just been running over the inquiry with Kelly here. It seems as if we're getting nowhere fast.'

He drummed his fingers on the desktop. Megarry noticed the red in his cheeks. It spread upwards to his temples in a crimson tide. The conduct of the case was certainly doing nothing to improve the inspector's blood pressure. He shuffled some papers about and spoke gruffly to the young detective. 'The way I see it we've got no motive, no suspect, no witnesses, no murder weapon, no evidence worth talking about. Correct me if I'm wrong. But we have no bloody case.'

'We have a number of angles,' Kelly said weakly.

'Angles? What are angles?'

'Lines of inquiry.'

'Lines of inquiry? That's just bullshit. Have you made any arrests yet? No. Have you got an idea at all why this man was murdered? No. Have you any idea of his movements before he was killed? No. All you have is supposition and I can tell you this.' Mulqueen leaned forward and stared across the desk. 'It doesn't convince me. It certainly doesn't convince the superintendent. I had him on to me just half an hour ago wanting to know when we were going to make a breakthrough. And do you know what I had to tell him? I had to tell him that I didn't know.'

He leaned back and sighed. 'Isn't that a pretty state of affairs when I have to admit to the superintendent that I don't know how the case is going? And why? Because I've handed it over to a pair of incompetents. Kelly and Mulligan. Laurel and Hardy. By the way, I've taken Mulligan off. He's a waste of time. Maybe I should take you off too?'

Megarry looked away. He hated sitting in on scenes like this, watching someone getting a dressing down. He wished he could excuse himself, get up and leave the room and let the pair of them sort it out between them.

He felt in his pocket for his cigarettes and then decided against it. He saw the young detective glance in his direction, clearly embarrassed that he was witnessing his discomfiture. An ugly thought came hurtling into his head. Maybe this will teach you to look a gift-horse in the mouth when you get an offer of help.

Mulqueen was speaking again. 'What about this drug aspect? Cecil here says he was an addict.'

'I'm working on it,' Kelly said feebly.

'Working on it? Who have you talked to?'

'Nobody yet.'

'*Nobody*?' There was a note of incredulity in the inspector's voice.

'I've been busy with other things.' Kelly looked exasperated. He began a recitation of the people he had interviewed, the places he had visited in the last three days.

'That's all rubbish.' Mulqueen flung his arms out and the crimson tide spread further up his face. 'Jesus Christ. Do I have to show you what to do? It's as plain as daylight that this thing is connected to drugs. A rookie just out of Templemore would see that. And what have you done about it? Nothing.'

It struck Megarry that the interrogation of Kelly had gone

66

beyond the point where it was serving any useful purpose. It had deteriorated into simple abuse. All Mulqueen was succeeding in doing was stoking Kelly's resentment.

'These things take time.' Megarry's voice seemed to fill the room. Mulqueen and Kelly turned to stare. 'I'm sorry, Dan. But you know what I mean. He can't just pull a suspect out of a hat. And as for arrests? What's the point of it, if you have to release the person again? No one will thank you for that.'

Mulqueen blinked, as if unsure what to say. Then he drummed his fingers on the desk once more. 'Get out,' he said to Kelly and waved his arms in a shooing motion. 'Go on. Get out of my sight. Go and do some bloody work.'

Kelly rose quickly and left the room. For a moment there was silence as the two men regarded each other.

'I'm sorry. I shouldn't have done that. I shouldn't have butted in.'

'No. You shouldn't.'

'But I think he *is* doing his best. He's young. He doesn't have our experience. You know yourself how difficult some cases can be. Sometimes you just need a lucky break.'

Mulqueen's voice had regained its authority. 'There's something you have to realise, Cecil. This is my case. I call the shots. If I want to chew out one of my staff, that's my business. I don't expect you to put your oar in.'

'I'm sorry,' Megarry said again. He took out the diary and the photograph and the syringe and put them on the desk. 'I found those in St Martin's Gardens.'

'You got in there?'

'Yes. There was a window that was loose.'

Mulqueen stretched his neck.

'The place was deserted. I don't think anyone has been living there for some time. I also talked to Higgins's employers. He worked for an engineering company called Dempsey Engineering. They're out in Clontarf.'

He began to recount the activities of the previous day.

Mulqueen fidgeted in his chair. Suddenly he got up and walked to the window and stood with his back to the room gazing out on the street. 'I'm not happy,' he said.

'Why not?'

'I'm not sure that you can go on like this. It's highly irregular. A policeman from one jurisdiction interfering in another.'

'*Interfering*? I thought I was helping you.'

'That's not what I mean. And I do appreciate your assistance so far. But I've been thinking. If the superintendent got to hear about this he might not be pleased.'

'He doesn't have to know,' Megarry said in a disappointed voice. 'You're short-staffed.'

Mulqueen turned to face the room again. 'Nevertheless . . .'

'Don't worry about the superintendent,' Megarry said and prepared to leave. 'I know superintendents. At the end of the day they're only interested in results.'

Kelly was waiting for him in the corridor outside. He sidled towards him and shifted awkwardly from one foot to the other. 'I want to thank you.'

Megarry examined him. There was an innocence, a naivety. He really was a greenhorn. The world had not yet made him cynical.

'I was also rude to you the other day. I want to apologise for that too.'

'Oh, for Christ's sake,' Megarry said roughly. 'Forget all about it.' He began to walk towards the lift. 'Mulqueen is right. This drugs angle. It's the obvious one. What have you done about it?'

Kelly started to explain once more. 'I just didn't have time.'

'Well make time, for God's sake. Where's the Drugs Squad located?'

'Eighth floor.'

'Why don't we go and talk to them?'

Inspector O'Toole was in charge of the squad. He was a tall, athletic man in his mid-thirties, well dressed in a smart leather jacket and roll-neck sweater. Too young to be a police chief, Megarry thought as he took a seat in his office.

Kelly began. 'The man we're interested in is called Higgins. James Anthony Higgins. He went by the nickname Harpo.'

'He's the guy who was murdered?'

'That's right. He was shot. Down along the quays.'

'And what do you want from me?'

'Anything you've got. We're trying to check his background. You know, people he might have consorted with, contacts, suppliers. He was an addict.'

'I'd need to check the files,' O'Toole said and swung his long legs up on the desk. 'You think this murder was drug-related?'

'We're looking at all the possibilities.'

Megarry took out a large handkerchief and sneezed.

'Are you okay?' Inspector O'Toole said and looked concerned.

'I'll be all right.' Megarry blew his nose. His eyes had started to water and he felt a soreness in his throat. He knew what was wrong with him. He was getting a cold.

He thought of the previous evening, the long walk to the bus-stop in the rain. By the time he had arrived in Howth his clothes were soaked, the rain streaking his hair across his skull like strips of thread.

Kathleen met him at the door.

'Andrew is waiting for you,' she whispered. 'He's sitting now in the parlour reading the paper. He wants to play darts.'

'Jeeesus,' Megarry said. 'Look at me. I'm drowned.'

'Run upstairs and get dried,' she said. 'You can't let him down, not two nights in a row.'

'But I don't want to play darts. I want to put my feet up by the fire and have a glass of whiskey.'

'You're a visitor. You have certain responsibilities.'

'I just want to relax.'

'You can do that down in the Anchor,' she said and pushed him urgently along the hall and up the stairs.

Andrew drove the half-mile to the pub. He was in cheery mood, babbling in the car about sporting developments, rugby, soccer, darts. He talked chiefly about darts.

Megarry hadn't played the game since he was a teenager, but he persevered for his companion's sake, taking off his jacket and rolling up his sleeves and sighting nervously along the dart's plastic flight while he prayed that he would at least hit the board.

It might have been a pleasant night, if Andrew hadn't clung obstinately to his determination to restrict himself to two half-pints of beer. Megarry had tried coaxing him, but to no avail. In the end he had contented himself with a succession of hot whiskies which he excused on medicinal grounds. By the time they left the Anchor at half past ten he realised that he was drunk.

'Do you know how many addicts there are out there?' O'Toole asked and waved a hand towards the window.

'No,' Kelly said.

'There's thousands of them. And more coming along every week. Heroin is cheap now. The city is flooded with it. We can't keep tabs on them all.'

'Maybe he had a record.'

'Well if he had a record we'd certainly know about him.'

O'Toole picked a paperweight off the desk and examined it. He showed no urgency about Kelly's request. Megarry thought he could detect a touch of arrogance. He remembered what someone had told him once about the Drugs Squad. They're prima donnas. They think they're in the movies.

'How soon do you think you could check your files?' Megarry asked.

The drugs chief turned and stared. 'That accent?' he said. 'Where are you from?'

'Belfast.'

He saw O'Toole's eyebrow rise.

'And what's your interest in this case?'

'I'm with the RUC. I'm here on secondment. I'm assisting Inspector Mulqueen.'

'Secondment?' O'Toole said.

Megarry stared back. 'Secondment.'

O'Toole swung his legs off the desk and sat up straight. 'I'll get somebody to check the records,' he said at last. 'But it'll take some time. He might not have been using his real name. They do that. Some of these guys have half a dozen aliases. What do you know about him?'

70

'I've got two addresses.' Megarry took out a piece of paper he'd prepared earlier and passed it across the desk. 'I've also got a mugshot we took in the morgue. I can let you have his fingerprints too, if it's any use.'

'Give me everything you've got,' O'Toole said.

Megarry opened his briefcase and took out the material.

'How long will it take?' Kelly asked.

'I've got a case conference going on right now. I'll get somebody working on it as soon as they're free. If we've anything on him I'll send it over to Mulqueen.'

He put his feet back up on the desk. Megarry noticed the soft leather of the shoes, the bright shine.

'So you think this murder might be drug related?'

'We don't know,' Kelly said. 'We have an open mind.'

'Mostly they die of overdoses or AIDS. They never live to old age. On the other hand if he was a dealer, he might have crossed somebody. Maybe he owed money. Maybe he was moving in on somebody's patch. These suppliers are ruthless. There's big money in this business.'

Megarry snapped the lock on his briefcase and prepared to go.

'It's a scourge,' O'Toole said and Megarry thought he could detect a softness in his voice. 'It's devastating whole communities. Kids as young as twelve and thirteen hooked on heroin. Can you imagine what life they have? Half the crime in this city is related to drugs. We picked up a fourteen-year-old kid last week touting for prostitution up at the Park. He was doped up to the eyeballs.'

He walked with them to the door.

'Thanks for your time,' Megarry said. 'You've been very helpful.'

'It's all right,' O'Toole said. Now that the ice had been broken he seemed reluctant to let them go. 'I could tell you a hundred stories about this business. People wouldn't believe the half of it. The misery, the pain these people go through. It's an awful existence. Sometimes it's hard not to feel sorry for them.'

He stopped at the corridor. 'Do you have any drug problems in Belfast?'

'Not like here,' Megarry said. 'But it's starting.'

71

He got out his handkerchief just in time to contain a violent sneeze.

'Are you sure you're okay?' O'Toole asked.

'What do we do now?' Kelly asked, once they had left O'Toole's office.

'We go and talk to Marie O'Gorman.'

'Who's she?'

'Higgins's common-law wife.'

'Do you know where we can find her?'

'I've got an address,' Megarry said.

They drove west in Kelly's car, along the dark waters of the canal. Megarry watched the young detective as he drove. He reminded him of Nelson, his colleague from Belfast. He had the same shyness. It was not a quality that you would normally associate with a policeman and yet Nelson had turned out fine. He was meticulous, energetic, dogged in pursuit of a case. He had learnt well at Megarry's side.

'Do you like this work?' Megarry asked.

'Most of the time.'

'I'll bet your wife complains. What's her name?'

'Sinead.'

'They all complain,' Megarry said. 'Those who haven't given up. This job is destructive of marriages and family life. You should watch that. Make time for your family.'

'That's easy to say.'

'Do it,' Megarry commanded. 'Your little boy, Jamie. He's at an age when he thinks the sun shines on you. He thinks there's no one like his father. There'll come a time when he'll grow away from you. He'll have his own friends. He might even think you old-fashioned.'

He remembered his own father, the trips to rural bowling matches on warm summer nights, the drives in the car along winding country roads, the scent of new-cut hay. He had thought then that there was no man living who could match his father. He remembered the grief he had felt when he had learnt of his death, blown apart in a car bomb meant for Megarry himself. The inconsolable pain, the void, the emptiness that stretched dark as night.

'Jamie. What does he like?'

'Football mainly.'

'Does he play?'

'Yes,' Kelly said with a hint of pride. 'He's on the school team.'

'He must be good.'

Kelly smiled. 'He's all right.'

'Spend time with them,' Megarry said. 'Don't let the job consume you. Don't be an old man with regrets.'

He thought of the lonely months of separation from Kathleen, the grimy flat with the fading wallpaper and the stains on the ceiling, the nights of riotous drunkenness in the Montrose hotel after hours. He was about to say, 'Don't make the same mistakes that I did. Don't neglect your wife and children.'

An image of Jennifer came flashing into his mind, curled like a waif in her hospital bed, pushing away the food, refusing to eat, clinging like a limpet to her anorexia. He had always blamed himself for that. He had neglected her. He had been a bad father.

He looked from the window, out over the grey streets of the city passing by in the dull light. He felt a pain tighten his chest. I'm a hypocrite, he thought. Who am I to patronise this young man?

'It's easier said than done,' he heard Kelly say. 'You should know that.'

'Just try to make time,' Megarry said.

As they turned the car at Dolphin's Barn, the rain started; big, ugly drops hurling themselves at the glass in a fury of wind. O'Casey Villas stood at the back of an abandoned cinema. It was a street he had seen a hundred times, neat corporation houses, black-slated roofs, tiny patches of garden looking miserable in the pouring rain. They saw a delivery van and Kelly stopped the car and asked the driver where the O'Gormans lived. The man pointed to a house at the end of the street.

They parked outside. Megarry pulled his coat tight around

his chest as Kelly struggled with the gate. The house had a slightly shabby look, paint peeling off the window frames and a gutter-pipe leaking water down the wall. But at least it was occupied, unlike the last such house Megarry had visited, for as they approached the door he could hear the sound of a television set booming out from the front room.

They stood in the porch to escape the rain. Kelly grasped the knocker. There was a loud rattle. The television was turned down and footsteps approached. There was a shudder as the door was pulled open and a surly-looking man in shirt-sleeves and braces was looking at them from the hallway.

Megarry stared. The man must have weighed eighteen stone, massive head and arms and a belly that hung in rippling folds above his trousers.

'Mr O'Gorman?' Kelly asked.

The man didn't reply. Megarry observed him. He was unshaven and carried with him a smell of cigarette smoke and beer. He stood in the doorway and examined the policemen from behind a pair of thick spectacles.

'Who's looking for him?' he said at last.

'We're detectives,' Kelly said. 'We'd like to talk to Marie.'

At the mention of the name the man's face clouded over. 'She doesn't live here.'

'We thought . . .'

'No. She hasn't lived here for a long time. She moved out.'

'Do you know where we could find her?'

'What's she done?'

'She hasn't done anything. We just want to talk to her.'

Megarry could hear the rain beating a tattoo on the paving stones of the path. He felt its cold grip on the collar of his shirt.

'She doesn't live here any more,' the man said again. 'I haven't seen her for months.'

'And you don't know where she is?'

'Afraid not. She doesn't keep in touch with us.'

'Look,' Kelly appealed. 'Could we discuss this with you inside?'

'There's nothing to discuss.'

Mr O'Gorman prepared to close the door but Megarry

74

moved quickly and blocked it with his foot. The man glared at him and raised his fist.

'You're not being very co-operative,' Megarry said.

'Why should I be?'

'Because we could make things difficult for you. Bring you down to the station. We could hold you for forty-eight hours. You'd be co-operative then all right.'

The man looked from one face to the other. Reluctantly he turned back into the hall and gestured for the detectives to follow. He pushed open the door into the front room and bent to turn off the television.

It was a small, neatly furnished room with a fake leather settee and a cabinet with ornaments and holiday souvenirs. Above the fireplace was a cheap print of birds in flight, their great wings a splash of purple and gold. On the mantelpiece Megarry noticed a pair of drinking mugs decorated with stars and stripes and World Cup '94 painted in green letters.

'Are you alone?' Megarry asked. 'Where's the missus?'

'She's gone to the shops.'

The man lowered himself into an armchair with difficulty. His great chest heaved as he glowered across the room. 'Marie's in trouble,' he said. 'That's what this is all about.'

'No,' Kelly said.

'She's always in bleedin' trouble,' the man said and the two policemen exchanged glances.

'What do you mean?'

'Since she took up with that bastard Higgins. She was a lovely girl till she took up with him.'

'Who's Higgins?' Megarry said quickly before Kelly could speak.

'The miserable bastard she's living with. A bleedin' junkie. That's what she took up with. A bleedin' drug addict.'

'We didn't know that,' Megarry said.

'Well it's true. And I'll tell you something else.' The man stabbed a beefy finger in the air. 'He's got her on drugs as well. He's destroyed her. She was a lovely girl till she met up with him.' He shook his head. 'I never liked him from the first time I set eyes on him. There was something about him. I said to myself this guy's a messer. But you know what kids are like nowadays. You can't tell them nothing. She was only twenty-one. You couldn't talk to her.'

'What happened?' Megarry said.

'They started going out together. She was very taken with him. He was older than her, about twenty-six, I'd say. He had a motor bike in them days and he used to come here and take her for rides down to Wicklow. I never liked that motor bike either. Then before we knew it, she had moved in with him.'

He sniffed and sat back in his chair.

'Is that the house in St Martin's Gardens?'

'That's it. Have you seen it? A bleedin' pigsty. That's where he took her to live. Away from her nice home where she had everything she wanted. Her own room, come and go as she pleased.'

Megarry watched the man. His round face had grown dark with anger as he talked.

'Before long she was coming back to us with black eyes and bruises. The bastard was beating her up. One time he even broke her arm.'

'Did you report it?' Kelly asked.

'No,' the man said in disgust. 'She wouldn't let us. I threatened to go to the guards loads of times, but she kept pleading with us to give him another chance. I don't know what kind of a hold he had over her, but she always went back to him. In the end we just gave up. I told her it was him or us. If she wanted to stay with him, that was the end of it as far as we were concerned. I thought it would bring her to her senses, you see. But I was wrong. She went back to him and we heard no more about her except bits and pieces of gossip we'd pick up from time to time. It broke her mother's heart, I can tell you.'

'You said she was using drugs,' Megarry said. 'How did you find out?'

'The hospital. She was taken in with an overdose. They got in touch with us. I suppose they must have found our address in her handbag or something.'

'And how long did she stay?'

'Till she was well enough to sign herself out. They wanted

her to undergo a treatment programme, but she wouldn't hear tell of it. As soon as she was able to walk, she got out and went straight back to him.'

The man took off his glasses and wiped his eyes with the back of his hand.

'And you have no contact with her at all?'

'None.'

'What about Higgins?'

The man's lip curled. 'He knows better than to show his face round here. When he started to beat her, I ran him out of it. Me and a couple of my mates. I told him I'd break his fucking neck if he ever came round here again.'

He put his glasses back on and looked away towards the fireplace. 'You don't know the pain that bastard caused us. She was a lovely kid. Here . . .' He got up slowly and took a photograph from the dresser and pressed it on Megarry. It showed a young girl in a white communion dress, her small hands clasped tight round a rosary. There was an air of innocence, of simplicity. 'That was Marie before that bastard got his hands on her.'

Megarry gave back the picture. 'She has a child, doesn't she?'

'*A child*?' The man started to laugh. 'No, Marie has no child, thanks be to Jaysus.'

Megarry thought of another picture he had seen, a young boy at a fairground with his father. 'But I thought . . .'

'*He* has a child.'

'Higgins?'

'Yes. Higgins.'

'I don't understand.'

'He was married before. Oh, years ago. Long before he took up with Marie.'

Megarry felt a little shiver of surprise. He'd been told that Higgins wasn't married. Now it turned out that he was. 'Where is she now? His wife, I mean?'

'God knows,' the man said. 'I suppose she hopped it. I suppose he was beating her too, only she'd more sense than to put up with it.'

'And she left him with the child?'

77

'That's right. Marie is rearing him. Can you imagine that? She can hardly look after herself.'

'Would you know any of his friends?'

'Are you kidding? I wouldn't give them the time of day.'

Despite Mr O'Gorman's protestations, Megarry took a piece of paper from his pocket and started to read from it.

'Bosco?'

'Never heard of him.'

'Fransy?'

'No.'

'Ger?'

'Who are they?'

'Just some names I picked up.'

'I just told you. I wouldn't have anything to do with Higgins or his pals.'

'I don't suppose you'd know anyone called the Fat Man?'

There was a pause. O'Gorman's face grew dark. Megarry watched the huge chest rise and fall.

'Well? Do you know him?'

'I should think so.'

Megarry smiled. 'I thought you would,' he said. 'It's . . .'

'Eddie Butcher,' Mr O'Gorman said suddenly. 'That's who it is. The Fat Man. It's his nickname. That's what they call him.'

'Eddie Butcher?' Megarry gasped.

'He's a gangster,' the man said dismissively. 'He's into everything. Robbin', thievin'. Him and Higgins is well matched. He used to bring him round here from time to time before I cottoned on to who he was.'

'You're sure?' Megarry said. 'I thought . . .'

'You thought it was me?' O'Gorman threw back his head and laughed. 'You thought I was the Fat Man?'

Megarry blushed.

'Would he be into drugs?' Kelly asked.

'Sure. Anything to make money. He's one bad bastard. And violent with it. I saw him and Higgins have a row one night. Over money, I suppose. He pulled a knife. I think he would have used it too.'

'Where would we find him?'

'He used to live out by Finglas somewhere. Some estate with flowers in the name. Bluebells or tulips. Something like that.'

Megarry sat back in his chair and examined O'Gorman. There was no doubting the sheer hatred he felt for Higgins, and the anger. It wouldn't take much for that anger to flare into violence.

There was a silence for a moment and then Kelly spoke again. 'We're sorry,' the young policeman said. 'This whole thing is a terrible mess.'

A sullen smile puckered the corners of the man's mouth. 'You can say that again. Only it's my mess, not yours. When you walk out that door, you walk away from it, but it stays right here with me. I'll tell you something.' The smile drained away and the scowl returned. 'I curse the day she ever took up with him.'

'He's dead,' Megarry said softly.

He waited for the man's reaction, a flicker of surprise, some sign of emotion. But there was nothing.

'*Dead*?'

'Yes. He was murdered.'

'He got what he deserved,' the man said. 'A bastard like him always makes enemies.'

'You're not sorry?' Kelly said. 'You feel no grief?'

The great chest was heaving and the smile was back, an ugly, vicious grin. 'No,' the man said. 'To tell you the truth, I feel like going out and gettin' pissed.'

The car was cold and damp. Kelly put on the heater and Megarry sunk deeper into his overcoat for warmth. He was feeling miserable. The soreness in his throat had got worse. There was a dull, throbbing pain in his head and a thickness in his nose that made it difficult to breathe. Outside, he could hear the rain hammering on the roof of the car. It was blanketing the street, a dull grey curtain of mist.

As they were driving out of the estate, he said: 'I need a drink. Can you stop somewhere?'

'A drink?' Kelly looked surprised.

'Yes,' Megarry said. 'You know the stuff they sell in public houses. One of those. That's what I need.' Immediately he regretted the outburst. 'Just find me a pub,' he said. 'I feel like I'm going to die.'

He ordered a large hot whiskey and a shandy for Kelly and they settled into a snug near the door. Megarry had got hold of a phone book and began leafing through it. A couple of men played dominoes beside the bar but paid them no attention. Megarry sipped at his whiskey and felt it warm his chest. He took out his handkerchief and blew his nose.

'He could have done it,' Kelly said. 'What do you think? He obviously hated Higgins.'

'That fact hadn't escaped me.'

'He's the first person we've interviewed who has a clear motive.'

'Yes,' Megarry said.

'If he didn't do it himself, he could have paid someone. There's a lot of that nowadays. People hiring contract killers. You can have someone murdered for a couple of thousand pounds.'

Megarry ran his finger along the list of Butchers in the book. 'Edward,' he said with a whoop of satisfaction. 'Daffodil Grove. Finglas.'

He put the directory down on the table and sipped his whiskey.

'It could be him.'

Kelly's impetuosity was beginning to irritate him. 'You're going too fast, Peter. We've hardly begun. There's lots of people we have to talk to yet.'

'But you heard Mulqueen.'

'I heard him. Don't let him rush you. It's not a simple matter of bringing charges against someone. You have to make them stand up in court.'

He felt a sneeze coming on and took out his handkerchief again.

'You're definitely coming down with something,' the young man said.

'It's just a cold.'

'Vitamin C. That's good for colds.'

'I'll remember that.'

80

He fumbled in his pockets till he found his cigarettes. As he struck a match he heard Kelly say: 'You smoke too much.' And then immediately, 'I'm sorry.'

But it was too late. Megarry gave a roar. The men playing dominoes turned to stare. 'Jesus Christ. Stop persecuting me. You sound like my bloody doctor.'

Daffodil Grove was a street of corporation houses just beyond Finglas village. The rain had stopped when they got there, but the afternoon sky remained dull and overcast and it seemed to Megarry as he stepped from the car that it had suddenly grown colder.

Eddie Butcher's house was the middle one in a block, just where the street turned off into another with similar houses stretching away into the distance. Kelly parked the car at the footpath and the men started towards the gate.

The house looked smarter than its neighbours. It had a tacky exuberance that was out of place. There were flowers in the garden, a well-kept lawn and a couple of freshly painted gnomes beside a garden pond. Part of the lawn had been paved with concrete and just outside the front door stood a brand new Volvo. Megarry ran his hand along the bonnet as Kelly stepped up to the door and pressed the bell.

The door was opened by a large woman in slacks and a white blouse. She folded her arms in the doorway and looked down her nose at them.

'Could we speak to Eddie Butcher?' Kelly began.

Megarry shivered in his damp overcoat.

'He's not here,' the woman said.

It was the usual reaction. Prevarication, evasion, lies.

'We're police, Mrs Butcher,' Kelly said. 'We can get a warrant.'

The woman's face turned up in a sneer. 'Well, if you're police you should know where he is,' she said. 'Your people came and took him away an hour ago.'

10

Mulqueen met them at the door of his office. He was smiling for a change. It was a smile of satisfaction, as if he had just pulled off some spectacular coup. 'I have Butcher in the interview room,' he said and rubbed his hands together in excitement. 'We pulled him in a while ago. I've already grilled him.'

He gave Kelly a look that said: I knew I'd have to show you how it is done.

'Has he said anything?' Megarry asked coldly.

'He's a tough nut. Denies any knowledge. Just keeps sticking to his story.'

'How did you find him?'

'I went to O'Toole.'

He opened a drawer and took out the pocket diary that Megarry had found in St Martin's Gardens.

'His name's all over it. There's a reference to him just a few days before Higgins got done. I figured the Drugs Squad should be able to tell me who the Fat Man was. Edward Butcher. He's got a record as long as your arm. They know everything about him.'

Megarry felt a weariness settle over him. He felt foolish. He took out a handkerchief and sneezed violently into it. 'What about Higgins? What did O'Toole turn up on him?'

'Nothing.'

'No record?'

'Apparently not.'

'I'm surprised. He was a full-blown addict. Don't you think he would have come to the attention of the Drugs Squad somewhere along the way?'

Mulqueen shrugged. 'I don't doubt it. But they've no record. There you are.'

Megarry felt a strange disappointment. He had felt it the whole way in from Daffodil Grove. He had been too cocky. Too sure of himself. Maybe even too patronising to Mulqueen and his team.

'You did good work,' he said at last.

Mulqueen smiled. 'It was just a break, just a bit of luck. What you said yourself. Sometimes that's what you need.'

'No. Don't put yourself down. Take credit where it's due.' He went to the percolator and poured some coffee. 'What did Butcher say?'

'Not a lot. He admits to knowing Higgins, but denies anything to do with his murder. He says he has an alibi.'

'Of course he has. He was expecting the police to get on to him.'

There was just an edge in his voice. He tried to rein it in.

Mulqueen took a folder from his desk. 'That's his record. Have a look.'

Megarry opened the file and ran his eye down the long list of offences. It was mainly drugs: possession, possession with intent to supply. One item caught his attention.

'He did eighteen months for grievous bodily harm in 1993.'

'That's right. Stitched a man up in a pub fight. Broken bottle.'

Megarry put the file back on the desk.

Mulqueen was smiling again. It was a smile of triumph. 'This could be our man, Cecil. It's got everything. Drugs, violence.'

'Motive?' Megarry asked, remembering what Kelly had said in the pub just half an hour ago.

'We'll find a motive,' Mulqueen said.

The Fat Man turned out to be an exceedingly thin man, one of the thinnest men that Megarry had ever seen, almost as thin as

Higgins when he had observed him stretched out on the pathology slab in the morgue.

He sat hunched at the end of a table in the sparse interview room, his shirt collar several times too big for him and his expensive jacket draped in folds across his miserable frame. Megarry calculated that he was about fifty years old. He was grey and balding and sat now in a plastic chair smoking a cigarette. There was an arrogant glint in his eye, a cockiness that Megarry had witnessed before in men who had too often seen the inside of a police station.

He looked up as they came trooping into the room and the policeman saw him shake his head.

'Three of yis now,' he said. 'Jesus Christ. Three bleedin' rozzers to question one innocent man. Where's the civil liberties in this bleedin' country? That's what I want to know. Where's the bleedin' rights of the accused?'

Mulqueen said nothing. He sat at the end of the table and opened a folder.

Megarry sat down beside him. He could see that Butcher was observing him, trying to calculate who he might be.

'Edward Butcher?' Mulqueen opened the file and pretended to read.

Megarry recognised the technique. It was an old police trick designed to give the impression that Mulqueen knew more than he really did.

'You asked me that already,' Butcher said.

'I'm asking you again.'

'Well then, you know the bleedin' answer. What's the point of going over it ad infibleedin'itum?'

'You know why you're here?'

Mulqueen kept his eyes fixed on the file and didn't look up. Butcher grunted.

'You knew James Anthony Higgins?'

'Harpo? Of course I knew him.'

At the back of the room, Megarry saw Kelly switch on a tape-recorder.

'I should advise you that this is a formal interview. Anything that you might say . . .'

Butcher stubbed out his cigarette and grunted once more. 'Cut the crap and get on with it,' he said.

Megarry heard Mulqueen sigh.

'Can you account for your movements on the night of 8 April?'

'Sure, I can. I was at home till ten o'clock. Then I went down to the boozer.'

'Where would that be?'

'The Old Shebeen.'

'What time did you leave there?'

'Ten to twelve.'

'And where did you go then?'

'I went to the chipper and got some burgers. Then I went home.'

'And you'd have witnesses to all of this?'

'Sure I have. How many would you like?' Butcher sniggered.

Mulqueen put down the file and Megarry saw the strain on his face, the dark circles beneath his eyes that he had noticed the first time they had met in the Royal Hotel in Howth.

'You find this funny?' Mulqueen said. 'A man's been murdered and you find it funny?'

'I didn't say it was funny. I liked Harpo. He was an old mate. I'd a lot of time for him.'

'Then why did you laugh?'

'Who was laughin'?' Butcher said. 'I just . . .'

He didn't finish the sentence. Instead he reached once more for the cigarette packet which sat before him on the table. Mulqueen stretched out a hand and took it from him.

'I'd prefer if you didn't smoke. I don't like people who smoke.'

'What the hell?' Butcher said. He pointed across the table at Megarry who had taken out his cigarettes and was quietly lighting up. 'What about him?'

'He's different. He works here.'

Butcher's face clouded and he stuck out his chin. It was round and smooth like a baby's. I'd love to punch it, Megarry thought. See how he'd react to that.

'Now then,' Mulqueen began again. 'Tell us what you know about James Higgins.'

'I don't have to tell you anything,' Butcher said defiantly and he sat back and folded his arms. 'I know my rights.'

'That's true. You have the right to silence. But if you want to get out of here and back home to your wife, I'd advise you to talk.'

Butcher glanced quickly from one policeman to the other and seemed to make up his mind. 'He was a junkie.'

'Where was he getting his drugs?'

'Jeeeesus. How would I know? He could have been getting them anywhere.'

'Were you supplying him with drugs?'

'Me? No way. I've finished with that racket.'

'So where was he getting them?'

Butcher smiled. 'Are you for real?' he said. 'There's no problem gettin' gear in Dublin.'

'Did he owe you money?'

'A few quid.'

'How much precisely?'

'Five hundred.'

'What for?'

'For nuthin'. I just lent it to him.'

'You just loaned him five hundred pounds? A junkie? A guy who didn't work? Who had no means of paying you back? I'm surprised at you. That doesn't sound to me like very good business practice.'

'He was stuck. I felt sorry for him.'

'You felt sorry for him? Do you make a habit of going around lending money to people who can't pay you back?'

'I just told you. He was an old mate. He would have paid me back eventually.'

Mulqueen suddenly sat forward and stared into Butcher's face. 'I don't think you loaned him the money,' he said. 'I think it was money for drugs. He was dealing. You were supplying him. When he didn't pay you back, you killed him. Isn't that what happened?'

86

'You're out of your tree,' Butcher said. 'Why would I want to kill him? Now I'll never get my money back.'

'Maybe you did it as a warning to others.'

'Rubbish,' Butcher said and his face assumed a look of innocence. 'I wouldn't lay a finger on anyone. I'm a pacifist.'

'A pacifist. Don't make me laugh.' Mulqueen lifted the file and opened it. 'You've a conviction for grievous bodily harm. You did eighteen months for slashing a man's face.'

'That was different. He provoked me.'

'Provoked you?'

'Yeah. He called my wife a slut. What would you do?'

Mulqueen banged the folder on the table. It was obvious to Megarry that the interview was going nowhere. Butcher was too clever. They were going to have to let him go.

He tried to breathe but found his nose stuffed up. 'You threatened Higgins,' he said quietly.

Butcher turned quickly to look at him. 'No I didn't.'

'I have a witness.'

'Who's that?'

'Come now,' Megarry said.

'He's lying.'

'No,' Megarry said. 'You're lying. You've been lying since you came in here. Everything you've told Inspector Mulqueen is a lie.'

He was conscious of his Northern accent, how out of tune it was with the other accents in the room.

'Wellll,' Butcher said and shifted in his seat. 'Maybe we had words from time to time. But that happens with the best of friendships. It doesn't mean that I killed him.'

'Do you carry a knife?'

'A knife?' Butcher watched Megarry warily. The disdain he had shown for Mulqueen had been replaced with something closer to respect.

'You know what a knife is, don't you? It's a sharp instrument with a blade. It's used for cutting things. Or people.'

'No. I don't carry a knife.' Butcher held up his arms, inviting the policeman to search him. 'Anyway, he was shot, wasn't he?'

There was silence in the room. Megarry was aware that the others were watching him.

'How do you know that?'

'I read it in the paper.'

Megarry suddenly leaned forward and stared into the other man's face. 'But it wasn't in the paper. We deliberately withheld that information.'

'I heard it somewhere. Somebody told me.'

'How did you know?'

Butcher wriggled in his seat. 'I can't remember.'

'How did you know?' Megarry pressed.

Butcher started to get up out of the chair. 'I've had enough of this,' he said. 'I'm not answering any more questions till I get a solicitor.'

Megarry stretched out his arm and pushed him firmly back into the seat. 'How did you know?' His voice was rising. He realised that it sounded rasping and hoarse.

'I . . . I . . .'

'Let's all calm down.'

Megarry turned quickly.

It was Mulqueen. He had his hands raised as if appealing for restraint. 'We're all getting a little excited. There's no point losing our tempers.' He took the packet of cigarettes and pushed them back across the table towards Butcher. 'Have a smoke,' he said.

11

George Buchanan peered into the gloom of Brannigan's Bar. He smelt a rush of porter and meat pies. It was quiet and still, not like the madhouse it would become later in the evening when people in the surrounding offices got out from work. Then it would be four deep at the counter and fellas bumping into you and spilling drink and women shrieking and barmen running about like blue-arsed flies.

Now it was quiet and gloomy, the only light the shaft of sunshine that poured in from the door behind him. That's what George liked about the place. The gloom. He let the door swing closed and walked quickly to the bar.

'Pint and a large one,' George said, reaching into his pocket for the ten-pound note he had left after paying the taxi-man. The fare had been seven pounds and in a wild moment of generosity George had tipped him three. He liked grand gestures. It reinforced his feeling of superiority over taxi drivers. But now he had a sneaking feeling of regret.

He took off his sun-glasses and looked around the bar. There were a couple of ould fellas further along the counter and a man in a peaked cap at a table reading a morning paper.

He heard a voice coming from somewhere nearby. 'Jesus, I don't believe it. It's George.'

There was a high-pitched, tinny laugh, a woman's laugh. He

spun round and saw a small bird-like figure waving to him from the snug.

'Hello Jacinta,' George said.

He paid the barman and walked across the room with the drinks. Jacinta Moore was tucked up in a corner of the snug with a friend. They were both dressed in black. Black blouses and skirts and black stockings, George noticed as Jacinta unfolded her legs. Like a pair of blackbirds, he thought as he leaned against the door and smiled to show his nice white teeth.

'Who's your man?' Jacinta's friend said and the two women started to giggle into their vodkas and tonics.

George smiled again to show that he didn't mind them laughing at his expense. He understood women. He knew that it was only nervousness. 'Mind if I join you?'

'Why not?' Jacinta said. 'It's a free country.'

She moved aside on the faded leather seat and made room for George to sit down. He took out a handkerchief and wiped the seat and pulled up his trousers a little bit at the knees, then settled himself beside her.

'This here is Rosemary,' Jacinta said, indicating her friend.

'Game ball,' George said.

The other woman smiled and George smiled back. She was a small, thin woman of about twenty-six with a pointed chin and dark-blue eyes.

'You're early,' George said.

'You're early yourself.'

'Well,' George said and sucked the froth off the top of his pint. 'I had a late night. Feeling a bit fragile. You know how it is.'

'Ohhh,' the women said and Jacinta added: 'Where were you? Anywhere exciting?'

'Leeson Street,' George said and smoothed down his hair with the palm of his hand and stretched his fingernails to examine them. 'I was up at the clubs.'

'Ohhh,' the women said again and George could see they were impressed. He took another sup of his pint. Women like Jacinta and Rosemary were easily impressed.

'I haven't been up at the clubs for a long time,' Jacinta said.

'All them ould fellas trying to get you drunk and gropin' you under the table.'

She made a face and Rosemary giggled.

'But they've got money,' George said pointedly. 'You need money for the clubs.'

'Doesn't matter. What do you think I am?'

'Don't be so touchy,' George said. 'I only made an observation.'

'Bleedin' observation. What's that when it's at home?'

'Jesus. What's wrong with you?' George snapped. He took another sip of his drink. 'Anyway, depends where you go. There's clubs and clubs.'

'And where were you?'

'Jangles.'

'See anybody interestin'?'

'Loads of people. Dee Dee Clarke. You know her, the model?'

Jacinta turned down her lip. 'That cow.'

George sat forward in his seat. 'Why do you say that?'

'Because it's true.'

'She's not a cow.'

'Yes, she is. She's a bleedin' junkie.'

'Oh,' George said and took a sip of his whiskey. He felt it burn his stomach. The hangover was fading fast. He was beginning to feel normal again.

'We saw her one night. Didn't we Rose? She was out of her tree.'

Jacinta leaned across to lift her glass and George saw the strap of her bra like a black mark against her skin.

'She was drunk,' George said.

'No she wasn't. She was doped up to the eyeballs. You couldn't get like that on drink.'

'Like what?'

'You know. Falling around the gaff. Laughin'. Acting the eejit. All that energy. She was flying.'

'Where was this?' George said.

'Different places.'

'Where?' George said with enough emphasis to cause Jacinta to stub out her cigarette.

'What is this? A bleedin' interrogation?'

'I'm sorry,' George said. 'I always thought she was a nice girl. I didn't think she'd be into anything like that.'

'Listen to him,' Jacinta said and nudged Rose. 'Nice girl. You'd be surprised what some of your nice girls get up to. Just because she dresses fancy and gives herself these la-di-da airs. Don't be taken in by that.'

George fell silent. In his line of work, there were times when it was best just to listen, let the other people talk.

'We saw her in Murphy's one night,' Rosemary said. 'She was stoned.'

'And then there was the time we saw her in that new place up in Baggot Street. You know where all the actors go.'

'The Boutique,' Jacinta said.

'Yeah, the bleedin' Boutique. She was with that poncey hairdresser fella.'

'David,' Jacinta said.

'She was legless. They had to put her in a taxi.'

'She's a slut,' Jacinta said. 'Just because she's a model, get's her picture in the papers, doesn't mean she's got nice morals. I know that bleedin' crowd. They're no better than the rest of us.'

'Worse,' Rose said.

'Yeah, worse. At least we're not junkies.'

'Alcoholics maybe. But not junkies.'

'You're right, Rose,' Jacinta said and laughed so that her small breasts bounced against the thin fabric of her blouse like billiard balls in a bag.

'Where would she be getting it?' George asked casually.

'Gettin' what?'

'Gear, where would she be getting it?'

The women stared.

'Did you come down in the last shower, George?' Jacinta said. 'Sure she could be gettin' it anywhere. The town's flooded with it. Sure she'd only have to go to the corner of O'Connell Street.'

'Naw,' George said and shook his head. 'Not Dee Dee. I can't see her out scoring on the street. She's too grand. Somebody must be supplying her.'

'Grand my arse. There you go again.'

'Who was she with? The times you saw her.'

'Different people.'

'Yeah, but who?'

'You ask an awful lot of questions, George,' Jacinta said suddenly. She rubbed her eyes, so that the mascara got smudged. 'Jesus Christ, you'd think you were a bleedin' detective.'

In a sort of a way I am, George thought, and straightened his tie. 'Who was she with?'

'You know that crowd she knocks around with, photographers and newspaper reporters. There's always a gang of them up at the bar, drinkin' their poxy cocktails as if they owned the gaff.'

'A quick screw up against the wall,' Rose said.

'What's that?' George said, taken aback.

'The name of the bleedin' cocktails.' Rose said and spluttered so that some vodka and tonic ran down her chin.

George smiled. Women could be so crude.

'I saw her in the Elephant one night with yer man. What's his name, Rose? Big fella with black hair. Fancies himself a bit.'

'Tommy Bolger.'

'Yeah, Tommy Bolger. You remember him, George? Used to knock around with Harpo Higgins.'

At the mention of the name George felt a tingle of apprehension. The memory came back. The crowd along the bar, the noise, the cigarette smoke. Harpo near the door, shivering in his anorak.

'He's dead,' George said.

Jacinta put down her glass. 'I heard that. Poor ould Harpo. Now there was a good-lookin' guy when he was younger.'

'What happened to him?' Rose said.

'He was murdered.'

'Jesus.'

The two women shook their heads.

'Used to be in a band, didn't he?'

'He was a roadie,' George said. 'With the Dancing Queens.'

'I remember them,' Jacinta said. 'Where are they now?'

George leaned back against the seat and his fingers played with the corner of a cigarette box. There were times when he didn't like his work, when he wished he could do something else.

He saw Jacinta finish her drink and rattle the ice-cubes in the empty glass.

'Be a decent man, George, and get us a refill.'

'Yes,' Rose said.

George felt in his pocket for the folded notes. He looked at his watch and saw that it was almost two o'clock. There was no point wasting time with this pair, all he was getting was tittle-tattle. They didn't know anything important. He'd have one more drink with them and then he'd head off to Ballsbridge to catch up with Dee Dee.

He got up and walked to the bar and gave the order and then with a jolt he remembered that the Mass for his father would be starting soon. His mother and her sisters and all the rest of the family would be expecting him. George shrugged and watched the barman pour the drinks. What the hell, he thought. He couldn't be praying for ever for someone who was dead ten years.

12

Megarry spent the following morning in bed, dozing and waking every so often to find Kathleen fussing over him with hot drinks and medicine which she had got from the chemist in the village. His cold was raging now, his nose streaming so that he needed several handkerchiefs tucked in the pocket of his pyjama top and a box of paper tissues beside the bed.

The curtains had been drawn in the bedroom but he could see that it was bright outside, the sun filtering into the room in a strange subdued light. He found that he was still angry with Mulqueen for the abrupt way he had intervened when he was questioning Butcher. It had destroyed the interview. Butcher had sat with his arms folded and refused to say anything more until they got him a solicitor. In the end they had no option but to let him go.

Mulqueen had apologised to Megarry afterwards. 'I'm sorry,' he had said. 'I just didn't want him getting all legalistic on us. In my experience once that happens you can forget all about getting any information out of them at all.'

'But that's exactly what did happen,' Megarry had said.

'It wasn't my intention.'

'It was the end result. Now any time we bring him in he'll go through the same performance. He knows he's got us in a corner.'

'I can try to have him monitored,' Mulqueen had said

weakly. 'I could ask some men to keep an eye on him, follow him about.'

'I think they'd be wasting their time. He's too clever.'

'You think so?'

'Yes, I do. But it's your case, you make the decisions.'

He had sensed the testiness in his voice and Mulqueen had sensed it too.

'Yes,' Mulqueen had said. 'It's my case.'

He found that his thoughts kept returning to the little house in St Martin's Gardens, the disarray, the drawers in the bedroom pulled open and the contents scattered as if the place had been burgled. He remembered walking into the kitchen and seeing the remains of the meal on the table, the places set for three people, the pot on the stove, the unwashed dishes piling up in the sink. There was something about the place, something unnatural, something that didn't make sense.

He woke around midday and discovered that the sheets were soaked in sweat. He put his feet on the carpet and it felt cold. When he stood up, he found that his legs were weak, as if the strength had drained out of them.

He washed and dressed and went downstairs to find Kathleen and her sister watching a morning soap on the television in the living-room. They both looked shocked at his appearance.

'What are you doing out of bed?' Kathleen said and started to get up.

'Can I have the car keys?' Megarry said.

'*What*? Are you out of your head?'

'I'm going to see a doctor.'

'But we can get Doctor O'Leary to come to *you*,' Nancy said. 'He's only down in the village. His surgery stops at one o'clock. I'll ring him now and ask him to call.'

'There's no need. I'm up now.' He appealed to Kathleen. 'You know me,' he said. 'I can't stay in bed all day.'

He drove along the coast road. The sun was high in the sky now and it shone off the water all the way across to the Bull Island.

There were a couple of windsurfers at Sutton and a ship ploughing up the bay, smoke like threads billowing from its stack. He turned inland at Raheny and in twenty minutes he reached the maze of houses that made up the Daffodil estate.

Butcher's Volvo was still in the driveway. It had been cleaned and polished and it sparkled in the sun. He parked a little way beyond the house and stepped out. From habit, he looked around. Two youths in denims were watching him from the end of the street. Megarry stared and they turned away. He locked the car and marched quickly along the drive to Butcher's front door.

Butcher answered it himself. He was wearing a neat suit. It had obviously been tailor-made for it fitted his thin frame like a glove. He looked at Megarry and his jaw dropped. 'You again. I thought I told you yesterday . . .'

'This is something else.'

'What?'

'I need to talk to you.'

Megarry reached into his inside pocket and took out an envelope. He held it up to Butcher's face. 'Is that your handwriting?'

Butcher blinked. 'What if it is?'

'You wrote this letter to Higgins. You were trying to warn him about something. I want to know what it was.'

'You're jumping to conclusions.'

'No,' the policeman said. 'This time I'm right.'

He took out a large handkerchief and blew his nose. 'Can I come in?' he said.

'What if I say no?'

'I'll bring you down to the station. You can get all the solicitors you like. I'll keep doing it till you talk.'

Butcher shrugged and turned away from the door. Megarry followed. The house was an ordinary corporation dwelling but it had been extensively extended and remodelled in a flashy way. The policeman noticed the garish wallpaper, the mirrors, the chandeliers glittering from the ceiling. Butcher opened a door and they were in a large kitchen overlooking a tiny back garden. There was the inevitable video flashing in a corner. Butcher walked across and turned it off.

97

'I was just watching a movie. Can I get you something?'

His manner seemed to have changed. He opened a cabinet and Megarry saw the phalanx of bottles.

'Tea,' Megarry said. 'Hot tea.'

Butcher fussed with a kettle. It was as if he got some secret pleasure from entertaining the policeman and showing off his house. 'You've got a cold,' he said. 'I noticed that yesterday.'

'Yes.'

'Best thing for a cold is hot whiskey.'

'I've got to drive.'

'But you're a cop. You can do what you want.'

'No,' Megarry said. 'It doesn't work like that. I've got to obey the law like every other citizen. Just like you, for instance.'

Butcher poured the tea into a mug. He took some bottles from the cabinet and filled a glass with gin and tonic.

'Where you from? You're not from here?'

'I'm from the North.'

'The North, eh? Bleedin' rough up there.'

'Yes,' Megarry said.

'Have you been here long?'

'Sometimes I think I've been here too long,' Megarry said cryptically. He looked around the room. 'You've got a lovely home.'

Butcher beamed. 'Margie designed it. She's the missus. She's the one with the taste in this family.'

Megarry allowed himself a smile. He reached out and fingered the lapel of Butcher's suit. 'You're not without some taste yourself.'

'I like to dress well. Appearance is very important. My old da always used to say that. He was a wise old owl, God be good to him. In my line of business, appearance is mega.'

'And what exactly is your line of business?'

'I'm a, what do you call it, an enterpenoor.'

Megarry's eyebrows rose. 'An entrepreneur?'

'Yes. I see opportunities and I sort of move in on them.'

'I see,' Megarry said. He had produced the envelope once more and now took out the letter. 'You wrote this, didn't you? E. B. That's you. Eddie Butcher?'

The other man said nothing.

'Look,' Megarry said suddenly. 'For what it's worth, I don't believe you had anything to do with Harpo's murder. But I want to get to the bottom of this business. Higgins left home in a hurry. I've been to St Martin's Gardens. It's in total disorder, as if Higgins just packed a bag and fled. In fact somebody saw him leaving with a suitcase. Now why did he do that? He must have been afraid.'

'He was afraid,' Butcher said. 'He was bleedin' terrified.'

'Of what?'

'Of what was going to happen to him. And he was right. The bastards got him in the end.'

'Who was it?'

'Some people who were after him.'

'What for?'

Butcher lowered his eyes.

'Was it something to do with drugs?'

Butcher hesitated, then he quickly nodded. 'Yes. That's it. Drugs.'

He swallowed the glass of gin and tonic and got up and made another one.

'Was it someone he owed money to?'

'Yes. He owed money.'

'For drugs?'

'Yes.'

'Someone who was supplying him?'

'That's it. A guy was supplying Harpo and he didn't pay him back.'

Butcher fidgeted in his pockets and pulled out a packet of cigarettes. He held it open and Megarry took one. He noticed that Butcher's hand was trembling. He's afraid, he thought. He knows something and it makes him afraid.

'This letter you wrote. You said that the Quare Fella was very angry with Harpo. Who is the Quare Fella?'

'Just a guy.'

'Was it the man who was threatening him?'

Butcher puffed on his cigarette and the policeman could see him trying to figure out a response. 'Yes.'

Megarry sat back in his chair and studied the other man. 'Do you want to tell me his name?'

'Jesus,' Butcher said. 'Are you mad or something? Do you want me ending up the same way as poor ould Harpo?'

'Poor ould Harpo?' Megarry said. He remembered the woman he had met at St Martin's Gardens. Dee Dee Clarke. She had said that Harpo was a lovely guy. He wouldn't have harmed a fly. Yet Mr O'Gorman had called him a miserable bastard. There were obviously two versions of Harpo Higgins or at least two perceptions of him. 'I've been told that he was vicious, that he used to beat up his girlfriend.'

'That's not true,' Butcher said. 'He was harmless. He was just a poor junkie.'

'Did you know her? His girlfriend?'

'Marie O'Gorman?'

'Yes. Did you know her?'

'Of course.'

'Do you know where I could find her?'

' 'Fraid not,' Butcher said. 'Is she not staying at home? St Martin's Gardens?'

'No. The house is deserted.'

'Well then.' Butcher shrugged.

'Who is the Quare Fella?' Megarry asked again.

'I can't tell you that. Jesus Christ. I've told you enough already. I've told you enough to get myself nutted.'

'It'll go no further. I promise you that.'

'I know your kind of promises. You bluebottles are all the same.'

'No,' Megarry said. 'It'll go no further.'

Butcher sighed. 'His name is Joey Morton.'

'And where does he live?'

'I don't know. The southside somewhere.' Butcher finished his drink and stood up. He was clearly agitated.

'Just a few more things,' Megarry said. 'Marie O'Gorman has the boy with her. The little fella. What's his name?'

It seemed to Megarry that Butcher's face had gone pale, but it could have been the light.

'Henry,' he said.

Megarry smiled. 'Henry Higgins.'

'What's so funny?'

'It's nothing. One last thing. How did you know that Harpo had been shot? We deliberately kept it out of the papers.'

Butcher stubbed out his cigarette. 'His sister. She told me.'

Higgins's sister. He thought of the thin woman in the damp flat in Ballymoss, the children cowering at her skirts. He should go and see her. Go out there again and talk to her.

'Of course.'

Butcher was walking towards the door to indicate that he wanted the policeman to leave. In the hallway, he stopped. 'I've told you a lot,' he said. 'Now you tell me something.'

'Sure,' Megarry said.

'Who informed you that I pulled a knife on Harpo?'

Megarry's face broke in a smile. 'You wouldn't expect me to tell you that, now. Would you?'

Butcher closed the front door firmly. Megarry paused for a moment. Out on the road, his car stood where he had left it, but he noticed that there was something shining on the ground around the wheels. His first thought was that the car was leaking oil and then another thought came to him.

He pulled open the gate and started to run, even though he knew that it was already too late.

The glass was everywhere, scattered like confetti on the seats and the floor, and spilling on to the tarmacadam of the road. The window had been smashed and the radio was gone.

He drove into town in a fury. What was he going to tell Kathleen? How was he going to explain that he had taken the car, not to visit the doctor as he had said, but to interview a Dublin criminal about a murder case and in the process had got the window smashed and the radio stolen? There wasn't even any point reporting the theft. He knew that the chances of recovering the radio were virtually nil.

His head was aching now, filled with the cold, and he realised that he was running a temperature. Despite his better judgement, he stopped at the nearest bar and went in and ordered a large hot Bushmills while he considered what he should do.

He found Mulqueen in his office.

'You look like you've seen a ghost,' he said.

'My car was broken into. The radio was taken.'

'Where?'

'Out in Finglas. I went to interview Eddie Butcher again.'

'You *what*?'

Megarry sat down wearily and took out a handkerchief. 'I talked to Eddie Butcher. There was a letter that he wrote to Higgins warning him that a man was angry with him. I . . .'

Mulqueen interrupted him. 'Before you go any further, the superintendent wants to see you.'

Megarry felt his stomach sink. 'He wants to see me?'

'Yes. I was going to ring you.'

'What's it about?'

'I don't know,' Mulqueen said and looked away.

The superintendent was a tall man with a round baby face and an accent that Megarry had difficulty understanding.

'Sit down,' he said, after they had shaken hands. He leaned forward in his chair and lifted a pencil off the desk. He rolled it gently with his palm. Megarry could sense his disapproval.

'You're from the RUC?'

'That's right.'

'Special Branch?'

Megarry nodded.

'You've had a rough time these last few years. Things have been bad up there.'

Megarry could feel his forehead burn. He felt miserable. He realised that he should have stayed in bed, done as Kathleen had urged. The last thing he wanted to do right now was sit in this office and have a discussion with the superintendent about the troubles in the North.

'Yes,' he said. 'It's been very bad.'

'And you were in the thick of it. Special Branch.'

'We have all been in the thick of it. The terrorists didn't discriminate. I've had many good colleagues murdered.'

'Please God the peace will hold,' the superintendent said.

He sat back in his chair and played with the pencil. 'I

understand that you've been assisting Mulqueen with the murder investigation. This man Higgins.'

'That's right.'

'Did you seek anyone's permission?'

Megarry looked up sharply. 'I didn't think it was necessary. It's not official. I'm actually here on holiday.'

'Don't you think it would have been proper to have sought approval?'

'It didn't occur to me. Mulqueen is understaffed. I volunteered to help.'

He saw the superintendent's nose twitch. Had he caught the whiskey on his breath?

'Every division is understaffed. We've a very heavy crime load in this city. How do you know Mulqueen?'

'I met him once at a security conference. We kept in touch.'

The superintendent rolled the pencil with his hand. Megarry straightened his tie and tucked his shirt in at the waist. He felt like a cigarette but was afraid to ask.

'Why did you want to see me?'

'I've only just heard of this arrangement you have with Mulqueen. It's highly unusual. A member of one police force assisting a murder inquiry in another jurisdiction.'

Megarry said nothing.

'It could cause difficulties, especially since it has not been sanctioned. I'm not sure it can continue.'

'What are you trying to say?'

The superintendent stared at Megarry from across the desk. 'I can't allow it,' he said firmly. 'It's not you personally, you understand. I'm sure you're a good policeman in your own way.'

Megarry felt the insult, the ingratitude. He opened his mouth to speak but no words came.

The superintendent put the pencil down squarely in the centre of the desk. 'You are to cease your investigations immediately. Do you understand? You are to get off this case.'

Book Two

13

'Twelve o'clock. Dalkey village. The train station. Same as yesterday. Have you got that?' her agent said.

'Yes,' Dee Dee said.

'Do you want me to send someone to pick you up?'

'No. I'll get there.'

'All right. Now listen carefully. Be on time. Be together. Leave all your personal baggage at home. This is a big job. Know what I mean?'

'I'm always together.'

'Not always, Dee. You know that. No substances. This is an important client. There's more work here. We have to make a good impression.'

'Just leave that to me.'

'I mean it Dee. Don't let me down. Sorry, I'll rephrase that. Don't let *us* down.'

'Hump you,' she said.

'Hump you too. Be on time. Be together. Remember what I said.'

'I love you,' she said.

'Love you too. Just make it happen. Okay?'

'Goodbyeee.'

She put down the phone. Be together. He had a damned cheek. A little bit of toot now and again to get her going in the morning. A little buzz of energy. It was nothing. A lot of the girls were doing it. You'd think to hear him she was some kind of bloody junkie. Nevertheless, it bothered her. She had a lot bothering her recently.

The man in the bed beside her smiled up at her, a wide, satisfied grin, like an athlete who has just performed some enormous feat, broken some record. She could see the sweat on his brow, his upper lip, the black curls on his chest. His dark hair shone in the light. He made a pouting gesture with his lips.

'Smooch, smooch,' he said. 'Somebody giving you hassle?' He reached out a hand and squeezed her breast.

'My agent.'

'Fuck him.'

She could smell his breath, the rancid taste of tobacco. No, she thought. Fuck you.

He ran a finger along the curve of her ass, paused for a moment and started again.

I'll have to get rid of him, she thought. 'Please Micky,' she said.

'You like it.'

'I *liked* it. Now I have to get ready for work. Girl's got to earn some money. Can't play all day long.'

'C'mon,' he said.

She looked at him. Twenty-two. So full of himself. All choked up on his ego. I should stop this, she thought, picking up young studs on Leeson Street. Start acting my age.

'I have to go to work,' she said and sat up in bed, but he pulled her down.

She felt him sliding into her, the slow motion, jig jig, like a little steam engine, up and down. She felt the pleasure start again. What the hell, she thought, if it keeps him happy.

Afterwards, when she was showering, she thought of Harpo. She had been thinking of him a lot since she'd heard the news from that fat cop in St Martin's Gardens. An RUC man. What was he doing down here?

Harpo's death had presented an opportunity and Dee Dee

had been turning it over in her mind, every spare moment she had.

She could hear Micky humming to himself in the bedroom as he got dressed. La la la. He was stomping around the floor, beating out a tattoo in his stockinged feet. Such an innocent. I love you. Biting her ear. I want to marry you. Twenty-two years of age and already he was thinking with his prick. And then, just at the moment when she was starting to come, that look of triumph on his face.

'Thank you, Micky,' she had said, out of breath, as she pushed him off.

'You're welcome. Any time. Why don't you marry me? Lots of women want to marry me. We'd make a lovely couple. Don't get left behind in the rush.'

He had smiled and she smelt his breath again and it was all she could do not to smash in his beautiful face with her fist.

She thought of Harpo. Poor, decent Harpo who wouldn't have harmed a fly. And some bastard had killed him. When she heard the news at first she had been stunned, she thought the cop had been lying, making it up to trap her or something. And then she had seen the look on his face and she knew he was speaking the truth. Her reaction had been: Maybe it's for the best.

She remembered the last time she had seen Harpo. She had gone to St Martin's Gardens for a little cocaine. He'd spoken to her earlier on the phone. I'm meeting a guy tonight, he had said. He's promising good stuff. Finest Colombian. She remembered how she had smiled as a thought came into her head. Anyone listening to us would think we were talking about coffee beans.

She'd been surprised at his appearance. He'd stood at first behind the door, asking who it was. And when she had told him, he'd slowly pulled open the door. The light had come filtering along the hall. It seemed as if he was caught in a photograph, an old black-and-white, the pale face, the black suit, the little beams of dust dancing in the light.

He was all skin and bone, hardly a pick on him, and the shake in his hands that he could barely control.

'Are you alone?' he'd said.

'Sure I'm alone, Harpo.'

He had glanced nervously up and down the street just to be certain, then closed the door.

'Can't be too sure. I've been getting a lot of trouble lately.'

'What sort of trouble?'

'Oh, the usual. Some people leaning on me.'

'Can I help you?'

She had looked around the dirty house, the sparse furniture, the smell of trapped air.

'I think it has gone too far for that,' he'd said cryptically and she'd felt a little tinge of sorrow, remembering better times.

'Marie's not here?'

He had lowered his eyes. 'She's out right now.' And then he'd said: 'You've still got your key, haven't you?'

'Sure.'

'Well any time I'm not here, you can let yourself in, leave a note or something. I'm on the move a lot at the moment. But I'll get back to you.'

And he'd gone off to the top of the house and come back with a little packet of cocaine wrapped in a plastic bag. He'd stuck the money in a pocket in his jeans and she'd seen the hand tremble again.

What sort of life was that? Scrambling around from pillar to post looking for a fix. Every waking moment dominated with the idea of getting drugs. The drugs had taken over his life in the end, destroyed him. Maybe he was better out of his misery.

That's what had gone through her head as she stood in that little front parlour after hearing the news, although she had kept the thought to herself. And then another thought had come to her as she was driving away from the house, the fat cop with the Northern accent standing in the street and watching her go, so that she felt a creepy feeling as if he suspected her of something. Maybe someone I know killed him?

She had dismissed the idea at once, because she didn't want to think about it. It frightened her. Instead she tried to think of the enemies that Harpo would have made, people in the drug trade that he owed money to. One of them had done it. That's what had happened. But she realised one thing for certain.

Harpo's death had changed everything. It had presented her with an opportunity and she was going to seize it.

She heard the phone ringing again, Micky picking it up, his stupid voice booming along the hallway: 'Are you here?'

'Who is it?'

There was a pause as Micky bent once more to the phone. She stepped out of the shower and began to dry herself.

'Some guy called Paul.'

She caught the note of disappointment in his voice. She wrapped the towel around her and started back towards the bedroom. 'I'll take it,' she said.

Micky sat on the edge of the bed and watched her as she talked. There was a sullen look on his face. He had lit one of her cigarettes and was smoking as he watched. When she had finished, he said: 'Another boyfriend?'

'Just a friend who happens to be a boy.'

Micky stubbed out the cigarette and slipped his hand under the towel. He tried to pull her down. 'Once more,' he said. 'You like it.'

She slapped his hand away. 'I told you. I have to go to work.'

'But I was good. You said so yourself. You enjoyed it.'

She looked at his handsome face, like a schoolboy, sulking on the corner of the bed.

She started to get dressed, in a hurry now.

'I *was* good.'

She felt the savage indignation. His arrogance. His presumption, waiting like some performing dog for a reassuring pat on the head. 'No, Micky. You were only average. Five out of ten.'

She met Paul on the terrace of the Monaco Bar at the back of Grafton Street at seven o'clock after they'd finished filming for the day. It wasn't really warm enough to be sitting on the terrace but it seemed like the chic thing to do. They drank kir and watched the crowds shopping along the Powerscourt complex or drifting into the restaurants for an early meal.

The evening was coming down and the light was beginning to fade. There were a few other couples on the terrace and inside, the hubbub from the bar, waiters in long white aprons rushing around with trays, the tinkle of glasses, brittle laughter. The street-lights were coming on at the top of Chatham Street, up near the Green. If it hadn't been for the slight chill in the air it might even have been romantic.

'Why did you want to see me?' she asked.

'You know I always want to see you.'

She looked into his eyes. He was wearing a soft blue suit, pale shirt, blue tie and pocket handkerchief. His hair was neatly trimmed. It seemed that every time she met him he had just been to the hairdresser. She could smell his aftershave.

'Did you have a busy day?' he asked.

'Frantic. You know that. One damned take after another. Make-up on, make-up off. Costume on, costume off. The director doesn't know what the hell he wants. Keeps changing his mind. He only knows what he wants when he sees it in another magazine.'

She took a sip from her kir and lit a cigarette. She felt tired. She'd been running around too much of late. Maybe she'd have an early night.

'I'm worried about you,' he said.

She laughed.

'I'm not the only one. I hear things. You should slow down.'

'What the hell?' she said indignantly. 'I'm not a child.'

'You should take a break. When's the last time you had a holiday?'

It was like he was reading her mind.

'It's not that easy. I can't just get up and walk away. I'm booked solid for the next six weeks. You should see my schedule.'

'Forget your schedule. What's more important? Your health? Your looks? You go on like this, you're going to have a breakdown.'

She laughed again, nervously this time.

'You look tired right now. You should take a break.'

'But my agent would go apeshit. He's signed contracts.'

'Look,' he said and took her hand and she saw the blue of his eyes. 'Don't fool yourself about this business. Your looks are your main asset. You know that old nursery rhyme? "My face is my fortune.'' When your looks go, they won't want to know you. I read in the papers the other day. Some Brazilian kid at the Milan Show. Thirteen years of age. Thirteen fucking years of age. That's what you're up against.'

She looked away from the terrace, down towards Grafton Street. There was a busker in a doorway with a crowd around him, playing the uileann pipes. She could hear the sweet sound carried along the busy street on the breeze. There was a sadness in the music, a plaintive quality.

'I care about you,' he said. 'That's why I tell you these things. If your bloody agent was doing his job, he'd tell you too.'

She stubbed out her cigarette. He's right, she thought. I'm getting on. The competition is getting hotter. Maybe it's time to pack it in. Get out while I'm still ahead. Settle down. Raise a child. She lifted her kir and swirled the sticky liquid in her glass.

'What's bothering you?' he said softly. 'There's something on your mind.'

She shrugged. She could hear his voice, low and probing. It reminded her of the confessional, the shadow of the priest's face in the darkened box: *How many times? When? Where?*

A tall Italian-looking waiter came and brought them fresh drinks.

'You know that Harpo Higgins is dead?' she said.

'Yes. I heard.'

'Who might have done it?'

Paul laughed. 'How the hell would I know? Probably some of that druggie crowd he was mixing with. They're not nice people.'

'I can't help thinking. It's like a chapter was closing. The end of an era. I remember the first time I met him. It was at a gig in the Olympia. I was about seventeen. We were all so young and innocent then. We thought we could do whatever we liked.'

'He's better off,' Paul said. 'Poor fucker was going to die anyway. Overdose or something.'

She turned a shocked face. 'How can you say that?'

'Because it's true.'

'But to be murdered?'

'Try to look at it rationally. It was probably all over in a couple of seconds.'

There was a certain sense in what he said, even if it sounded cold, detached, void of feeling.

'Sometimes when I think about it, it makes me sad.'

She felt him take her hand. 'Then don't think about it,' he said.

'I keep wondering who might have done it.'

He leaned closer to her and she could smell his aftershave again. 'Put it out of your mind. Think of something else.' He paused. 'Are you hungry? What did you eat today?'

'I had a sandwich.'

'That's not enough. I'll tell you what. Why don't I take you to dinner? We'll go to Cooke's.'

'I don't know. I should get some sleep.'

'I'll make sure you get home early. C'mon. It'll lift you out of it.'

His voice sounded reassuring. Paul had this quality of always sounding right.

She thought for a moment and then said: 'Give me a couple of minutes.'

She got up and walked off the terrace and through the bar. It was getting crowded, people coming in for a drink on their way home from work.

She pushed open the door of the Ladies and saw the sparkling titles, the gleaming taps, the clean towels. There was a smell of air-freshener.

She opened a cubicle door and went inside, sat down and lifted her handbag. She took out her face mirror and found the little bag of powder. She tapped out a line and pressed her thumb against one nostril, bent down and sniffed.

She felt a buzz of pleasure, a rush of energy. She sat for a moment and let the feeling invade her. The tiredness fell away.

After a while, she got up and put the mirror and the powder back into her bag. She left the cubicle and washed her hands, went to the mirror and began to adjust her face, eye-liner, mascara, pancake.

She was feeling wide-eyed now, as if she'd just wakened

from a long sleep. She started back through the bar. There was music playing somewhere, a traditional band, a jig or a reel, notes swelling, guitars throbbing. She felt the rhythm bouncing about in her head.

Paul was sitting where she'd left him on the terrace. It was dark now, the place ablaze with a hundred lights, like so many stars in the sky. She ran her finger along the back of his neck and he looked up and smiled.

'You fox, you,' he said.

'Try me,' she said.

14

For the next two days Megarry was confined to bed, nursing his cold. He was a bad patient. He complained and argued with Kathleen who insisted that he take vitamin tablets and stay warm. She confiscated his cigarettes and fussed around the darkened room till she got on Megarry's nerves.

'I don't need this,' he said. 'I'm not dying, you know. All I've got is a simple cold.'

'You want to get better, don't you?'

'I've had colds before. All I need is a few hot whiskies. These things take care of themselves.'

She frowned. 'Don't argue. Just do as I say.'

Megarry snuggled deeper into the bedclothes. She hadn't forgiven him for the damage to the car and the theft of the radio. The bill had come to £175. What annoyed Kathleen more than the cost of the repairs was the fact that he had been caught out deceiving her.

They'd had a heated argument in the bathroom, all the more ridiculous because it was conducted in subdued tones so that no one else in the house could hear. Megarry's nose was streaming and he could feel the sweat gathering on his forehead and the back of his neck. He was in no mood for fighting. In the end he had retreated as gracefully as he could to the sanctuary of his bed.

He read the papers and listened to the radio and dozed. He hadn't realised how tired he was. At one o'clock and six o'clock each day his sister-in-law came into the bedroom with a tray of food and each evening, when he got home from work, Andrew would come and sit with him. He would tell him about the little trials of his day. But the visits had their positive side.

Andrew would bring with him cigarettes and the two men would sit in the room, smoking and drinking Guinness out of teacups for fear that the women would find out. Megarry concluded that Andrew wasn't such a bad guy after all.

On the third day he decided to get up. It was a glorious morning, the sun streaming into the house through the branches of the trees outside, casting strange shadows on the furniture of the room. Megarry sat down at the breakfast table and the two women observed him closely.

'I'm fully recovered,' he said, then added tactfully, 'Thanks to you pair and your nursing skills. You were right all along. What I needed was a good rest.'

'You don't look recovered,' Kathleen said doubtfully.

'But I am.'

He stretched his arms to show how fit he was and his shirt tightened like paper across his chest.

'You should be careful,' Nancy said sympathetically. 'You know how easy it is to have a relapse.'

Megarry smiled and poured a cup of tea. 'Don't worry about me. I'm going out for a breath of air. Bit of exercise will do me the world of good.'

'The car stays where it is,' Kathleen said firmly.

'Of course. Of course.'

'And lunch is at one o'clock.'

He walked down through the village to the harbour. There were a couple of fishermen drinking at a table outside the Pier House Inn. Megarry went past them and along the pier to the abandoned lighthouse and stood staring out across the sea to Ireland's Eye.

The little island was bathed in light. He could see the way the colours contrasted, the sand along the shore, the heather, the dark green of the cliffs. There was a martello tower at the end of the island where it merged into the sea. He remembered someone telling him once that it had been put up in Napoleonic times as a defence against a French invasion that never came. Near the shore he could make out the decaying shell of an oratory, ivy clinging to the walls, a place of fasting and prayer built by the monks in the seventh century.

This place is soaked in history, he thought. Not just here, the whole country. There is hardly a hill or a field that could not tell a tale. He started back towards the village and when he got half-way along the pier, he felt tired and sat down to rest.

He took out his cigarettes and watched the boats tossing at their moorings in the breeze. He found himself thinking once more about his interview with the superintendent in the fine office he had in the station in Barrack Street. He had been curt and dismissive and Megarry had seen that he didn't like him. His manner had offended him, the brusque way he had ordered him off the case without even one word of thanks for the work he had already put in.

He realised now how sick he had been, how meekly he had accepted his dismissal without argument. He had driven home with his spirits bruised, defeated, feeling the superintendent's ingratitude like a lash across his back. And then he remembered, with a start, that no one had called to sympathise with him, neither Mulqueen nor Kelly. There had been no phone call to thank him, no offer of support, no whispered words of comfort. He felt a wave of regret like a sense of loss. He stubbed out his cigarette with his shoe and started walking again, back towards the village.

The bar of the Royal Hotel was crowded when he arrived. A business lunch was planned for one o'clock. He fought his way through the ranks of middle-aged men in striped shirts and women with padded shoulders, and ordered a pint of beer. He found an empty stool at the end of the counter and sat down to read his paper. He looked up when a young waiter approached and set down his glass.

'How much?' Megarry asked, reaching into his pocket for change.

'It's already paid for,' the youth said.

'What?'

The waiter pointed to a table near the window. 'That gentleman paid for it, sir.'

Megarry peered across the room. A familiar face was smiling at him. Harry Dempsey raised a hand and beckoned for him to join him.

Reluctantly, Megarry folded away his paper and went across. Dempsey had a table to himself and a half-eaten sandwich beside a pot of coffee. He reached out his hand and Megarry took it.

'I just spotted you, there,' he said. 'How are you?'

'I'm fine.'

'And the c-case? How's it going?'

'The case is going well,' Megarry said. 'We're making progress.'

'G-good. There's too much crime in this city. I remember when I was growing up. We were a tough b-bunch. We weren't averse to a little bit of thieving now and then, but we'd never dream of attacking old ladies and stealing their handbags. Not like these little gurriers today.'

Megarry examined the man beside him, the fine features, the tan, the healthy skin that came from good care. 'Things have changed,' he said.

'For the worse.'

'Yes. Unfortunately.'

'But you think you'll c-catch this guy? The man who killed poor Higgins?'

'Yes,' Megarry said. 'We'll catch him in the end.'

Dempsey lifted the coffee cup to his lips and looked at the policeman over the rim. 'Why aren't you at work?' he said.

'I had to see some people.'

'And your walks? Are you still getting out for a walk now and then? The c-case isn't taking up all your time?'

'As a matter of fact I went for a nice walk this morning. Down to the end of the pier. There's a beautiful view out to Ireland's Eye.'

'You know you can get a b-boat across? You can spend the whole day over there. It's worth exploring.'

'I didn't know that.'

'Oh yes,' Dempsey said with enthusiasm. 'In fact, there was a famous m-murder committed over there. About a hundred years ago. Man took his wife over and she was found drowned. He was hanged for it. That should interest you.'

Megarry finished his drink and made to leave but Dempsey put out a hand to restrain him. 'What are you doing this evening?' he asked suddenly.

'I don't know. I haven't decided. Why do you ask?'

'Just something that struck me. We're having a little p-party, Claire and I. Just some neighbours and friends. Why don't you and your wife come along? Give you a chance to meet some local people.'

'I'm not sure.'

'Relax,' Dempsey said. 'You're working too hard. Look.'

He took out a silver pen and drew a map on the back of a beer mat.

'The house is called Elsinore. B-big white house. Up at the Bailey. You couldn't miss it. Any time after seven. Why don't you come?'

He snapped the pen with a flick of his thumb and put it back inside his pocket.

'I'll see,' Megarry said.

'Try to make it. Claire would love to m-meet you.'

He walked up the hill, past the church and the fine houses lining the front of the road. As he climbed, the village fell away behind him, till at last he was able to stand and look down over the housetops and the harbour. There was a sleepiness about the place that he remembered from when he was young, old linen towns in Antrim and Down where he would go with his father to bowling tournaments. Afterwards they would visit some ancient village pub and drink pints of Guinness while the cool summer evening came down all around them.

He remembered other nights, his father in the front room of their little house, going through his insurance accounts, computing the sums in a dog-eared exercise book, totting and adding and sucking the end of his pencil till he was satisfied that everything was in order. He had been a scrupulous man, honest and decent. He had never got promotion. Megarry was convinced it was because he had been too easy with his customers, allowing them to build up arrears, lacking the ruthlessness that would have brought him to the attention of his superiors.

He missed his father, missed his steadiness and common sense, his humour and kindness and compassion. His death had scarred him, shaped his life, set him off on a vendetta that had almost destroyed him. But it was over now, the old ghosts laid to rest at last, even if the sadness remained.

When he arrived back at the house, he found that he was out of breath from the exertion. He could smell the rich aroma of cooking chicken and when he went into the kitchen he saw that Kathleen had bought a bottle of wine and uncorked it.

'It's a little celebration,' she said as she bent her face to be kissed. 'A thanksgiving for your recovery.'

Nancy smiled silently from the cooker where she was stirring gravy in a pot.

'Well that's nice,' Megarry said. He poured a glass of wine and stood at the window looking out over the garden. The light was shimmering through the trees.

He raised the glass to his lips and sighed. 'Good health,' he said.

15

Elsinore was a big white house, just as Dempsey had described, and they found it without much trouble. It was set in about half an acre of lawns and trees and had a commanding view out over the bay. As they approached, Megarry could see that the roadway was blocked with cars and he had to drive on till he found a place to park.

The light was beginning to fade and the night air was suddenly filled with the scent of gorse and lilac, and from the cliffs nearby, borne occasionally on the breeze, the strong salt smell of the sea.

Kathleen was in a cheerful mood. He had half expected her to reject the invitation, to make some excuse. He was in two minds himself, was even looking forward to a night with Andrew in the Anchor Bar, but Kathleen had surprised him by agreeing at once.

'I like meeting new people,' she had said. 'And I want to find out how they live down here, the cost of everything. All this grand life-style. Do they pay any taxes? How do they do it?'

'This man isn't typical,' Megarry had said. 'He owns a factory, remember.'

'Yes, but you said he had started with nothing.'

'That's true.'

As they got closer to the house they could hear the sound of music, the chatter of voices coming from the lawn at the back. The front door was open and a small cockerspaniel watched them warily from underneath a chair, his sad eyes alert for strangers.

Megarry reached for the bell and the dog began to growl. 'Good boy,' he said and bent to pat its head.

They listened to the bell ringing somewhere inside the house, but there was no response, so Megarry pressed once more. The voices sounded louder now and they could hear laughter from further down the garden as someone told a joke.

'Maybe we should go round the back,' Megarry said, turning to Kathleen. 'I don't think they can hear us.'

But Kathleen had a horrified look on her face. 'For God's sake,' she said. 'We can't do that. We can't just go barging into someone's house. Try again.'

She held tight to the bottle she had specially wrapped, while Megarry stood on the doorstep looking foolish.

He reached out once more and a door inside the house suddenly opened and they could see someone approaching. A small middle-aged woman appeared in the lighted hallway. She looked fit and athletic. Her hair shone in the light.

'Hello,' she said in a pleasant voice. 'I'm Claire Dempsey. You must be the Megarrys. Come in. We've been expecting you.'

She ushered them inside and began to make a fuss. 'Let me take your coats. Can I get you a drink?'

Megarry stood uncertain.

'Who's doing the driving?' Mrs Dempsey asked.

'I am,' Kathleen said.

'I'll have a Bushmills and water,' Megarry said quickly and glanced at Kathleen, who smiled.

'And I'll have a glass of white wine please,' she said.

Mrs Dempsey led them into a drawing-room, which gave on to a kitchen and left them while she went off to get the drinks. The music sounded louder now. Outside they could see a patio and lights and little groups of people standing around talking.

The room they were in was large and comfortably furnished. There was a stone fireplace with a copper canopy and sofas and settees and heavy drapes shading the windows. On a sideboard beside the door there was a collection of photographs and mementoes. Megarry bent to look. One of them showed a young couple on their wedding day and he immediately recognised Harry Dempsey, a thinner, more earnest version in a suit and tie. Beside it was a picture of a teenage girl holding a tennis racquet in a garden. He could see the marks left by the mower.

He looked up and Mrs Dempsey was back with a tray of drinks.

'Now,' she said. 'If you're ready, I'll take you out and introduce you. Harry'll be delighted you could come.'

She took them through the kitchen and out to the patio. Even though it was not yet dark, the garden was hung with lights. The smell of the sea was stronger now and down at the bottom of the lawn, beyond the shadow of the trees, Megarry could see the dying sun reflecting off the water.

As they came out, the talking stopped and several people turned to look. In the middle of the group, in blazer and slacks, was Harry's tall figure. He came forward at once to meet them.

'Ahhh,' he said. 'You were able to c-come.'

He bent to kiss Kathleen's cheek and took Megarry's hand.

'Did Claire g-get you a drink? Did she get you B-bushmills? Cecil is a B-bushmills drinker.'

'Of course, I did, Harry. What do you think I am?'

Megarry thought there was a little tension in her voice, but she concealed it skilfully and shook her head at Kathleen.

'C-come and meet the folks,' Harry said. 'The folks that live on the hill.'

He brought them forward and began making introductions. A portly man in a white tennis shirt shook hands politely.

'Pleased to meet you.'

'You too,' Megarry muttered.

There was another face that he recognised, pale, with blue eyes and hair like straw.

'You've met P-paul before, I believe,' Dempsey said and Byrne came forward and shook the policeman's hand. Megarry remembered him from the interview at the factory. He had the same air of deferential confidence, as if he knew his place but also his own ability.

'P-paul's my private secretary,' Dempsey said and ruffled the young man's hair. 'He does my dirty work for me. Don't you P-paul?'

Byrne blushed. 'How is your case going?' he asked Megarry.

'So-so.'

'Did you find Marie O'Gorman?'

'No,' Megarry said. 'She wasn't living there any more, but I spoke to her father.'

'So you think you might be able to trace her?'

'I hope so.'

'I wish you luck,' Byrne said and Dempsey turned to the rest of the group.

'The Megarrys are visitors. They're staying with friends in Howth. Cecil is a p-policeman.'

'That's interesting,' Megarry heard someone say. 'Where did you meet Harry? Was it the yacht club?'

'No, I . . .'

'Harry's mad about boats. If it's not boats it's golf.'

'Or making money,' someone else said and everyone laughed.

'Where do you find the time, Harry?' an earnest young man in a maroon jacket said. 'You seem to have a finger in every pie.'

Dempsey beamed. 'I make t-time. It's all to do with organisation. You decide what's important and you prioritise.'

'He never has time for the garden,' Claire said. 'That's left to me and the gardener.'

Dempsey smiled. Megarry took a sip at his whiskey. He could see that Harry was enjoying himself. He was relaxed, the centre of attention, surrounded by admiring friends and neighbours.

'I've only g-got so much energy,' Dempsey said. 'It's called the opportunity c-cost in economics. It wouldn't pay me to do the gardening. My time's more valuable.'

'Listen to him,' Claire said. 'He'll be quoting Aristotle next.'

The group laughed.

'Why not?' Dempsey said. 'He talked a lot of sense. He had a lot of interesting things to say.'

A thin woman with glasses moved closer to Kathleen and Megarry heard her say: 'How long are you staying in Howth?'

'Just for a few weeks.'

'Have you been in to Dublin yet?'

They bent their heads together and began to talk. Megarry was about to join them, but at that moment Dempsey detached himself from the group and came and stood beside him.

'It's a beautiful evening,' he said. 'This is the b-best time of the day to be in the garden. You can smell things. Take a deep breath.'

He watched as Megarry did as he was asked.

'Did you c-catch the scents?'

Megarry nodded.

'You see. Evening is the b-best time.'

He began to lead Megarry away from the group, further down the lawn where a small garden table and chairs had been placed. The sky was dark blue over the bay and they could see the lights begin to come on along the southern shore.

Dempsey lowered himself into a chair and motioned for Megarry to join him. 'I really love this view,' he said. 'You should see it in the daytime. This house is worth five hundred thousand p-pounds for the view alone.'

Megarry stared. 'That much?'

Dempsey shrugged and waved his hand. 'I don't know for certain. But that's what I'd p-pay. It's got the best view in Dublin. Listen, c-can you hear the sea?'

Above the noise of the music and the chatter, Megarry could hear the soft lapping of water as the waves sucked against the shore. It was a soothing sound. He thought how peaceful this garden must be when there was no one here, no noise or distraction, when the only sound would be the gulls and the sea and the wind sighing in the trees.

'It's a magnificent house,' Megarry said in admiration. 'You're a lucky man.'

Dempsey smiled. 'But money brings p-problems, you know. Responsibilities.'

'How do you mean?'

'Well security for one thing. Crime, kidnapping. It's every-where now. You being a p-policeman know that. I must talk to you some time. Get your advice.'

'Why did you choose to live in Howth?'

'I'll t-tell you,' Dempsey said and bent forward. 'When I was a little boy, my father used to take us out here on Sundays. Here or over to the other side, Dalkey or Dun Laoghaire. I fell in love with this place. I used to envy the p-people who lived in these b-big houses. I wanted to be like them. My father inspired me. He was a wonderful man. I owe everything to him.'

'And to your own efforts, surely?'

'Yes, that too. But I loved my father. I thought he was the greatest man who ever lived. You know the b-bond between father and son is a wonderful thing. Do you have any children?'

'I have a daughter,' Megarry said.

'Me too. But it's not the same. I would love a son. We could do things together. I could t-teach him the business. My daughter isn't interested. She has her own life.'

He fell silent for a while and the two men sat in the gathering darkness watching as one by one the stars came out in the empty sky.

'I did have a b-boy,' Megarry heard him say. 'Colum.' There was a sadness in his voice.

'What happened?'

'He was drowned. He was only ten. We were on holiday. He went out in a canoe. Claire has never g-got over it.'

'I'm sorry,' Megarry said gently.

He felt the breeze from the sea, cool upon his face. He was lost for words. He heard an owl hooting somewhere in the darkness, its call like the sound of a muffled pipe. 'Maybe you could have more children,' he said.

'No,' Dempsey said. 'It's too late. Claire c-can't have any more.' He lifted his drink and drained it. 'You remember I told you about control being the secret. Well some things you can't control. Some things only G-god can control.'

Megarry heard him sigh. He thought: Why is he telling me

these things? Why has he invited me here in the first place? We've only just met. We're still comparative strangers.

Just then there was a burst of laughter from the group on the patio and Megarry turned his head to look. He saw that Kathleen had been joined now by some more women.

At that moment Claire came out from the house and he saw her clap her hands. The chatter stopped. The music had been turned down and was now barely audible.

'Food's up,' Claire said. 'It's in the dining-room. Help yourselves.'

Dempsey put his glass on the little table and stood up. 'Are you hungry?' he asked and started to walk up the garden towards the house. 'There's salmon and stuff. Claire g-got it all fresh. She always does a g-good spread.'

They left shortly after one o'clock. The party was beginning to break up, the guests making their farewells, shaking hands, confirming engagements, all but the plump man in the white tennis shirt whom Megarry had been introduced to first. He had graduated to whiskey and sat alone on the patio in the moonlight, as if planning to settle in for the night.

Dempsey walked with them to the gate. 'I hope you had a g-good time,' he said and kissed Kathleen once more on the cheek.

He seemed to have regained his humour. The melancholy mood he had displayed in the garden was gone.

'We had a very good time,' Kathleen said. 'I learnt a lot.'

'Knowledge is money,' Dempsey said and smiled. 'Don't forget that.'

Megarry stretched out his hand. 'I enjoyed talking to you,' he said. 'Thank you for the invitation.'

Dempsey waved his hand. 'It was my p-pleasure. We must keep in touch. Have you a phone number?'

'It's in the book,' Megarry said. 'Under Andrew Agnew.'

'Right then,' Dempsey said and turned to go. 'Take care.'

They drove to the Summit and then down the hill. The roads were silent and empty of traffic. There was a stillness in the night.

'Did you really enjoy it?' Megarry asked.

Kathleen turned to look at him. 'Of course. They were nice people. No airs or graces. Just honest-to-God friendly folk.'

'Did you get a chance to talk to Harry?'

'Only a bit. Mostly it was Claire and the women.'

'They had a child who died,' Megarry said softly. 'A little boy of ten.'

'My God,' Kathleen said. 'That's dreadful. The death of a child. That tears my heart.'

As they went past the church, Megarry spoke again: 'I wonder why he invited us?'

'Because he wanted our company. Maybe he just likes entertaining new people. Maybe he just wanted to be friendly.'

'I wonder,' he said.

Kathleen punched his shoulder. 'Give over,' she said. 'Why do you always have to analyse things? Stop being a cop. You're on holiday.'

After a few days he felt his strength return. He fell back into his old routine. He would get up about nine o'clock and have a leisurely breakfast and then go for a stroll along the cliffs. He made a point of dropping in to one of the local pubs for a drink.

One day he called into the Cock Tavern. There was a music session in full swing. He was about to leave but something in the subtle rhythm of the music held him. There was a piper and a man playing a banjo and another man with a flute. Megarry went to the bar and bought a pint and sat in a corner listening to the ebb and flow, the songs, the jigs and polkas. It was like a whole new world had been discovered to him. It was past three o'clock when he started up the hill for home, the plaintive lilt of the music still ringing in his ears.

Another time, he called Nelson in his office in Belfast. 'How's it going?' he asked.

'Quiet.'

'Well that makes a change.'

'Yeah. But this peace dividend isn't all it's cracked up to be. They've started to cut police overtime. A lot of the guys are complaining.'

'Jeeesus,' Megarry exploded. 'Some people are never satisfied. At least you can go to work in the morning without having to check if there's a bomb under your car.'

'I still check,' Nelson said.

'How's Harvey?'

'He's fine. He's got a new assistant.'

'Well that should keep him happy.'

'No,' Nelson said. 'You know Harvey. He's never happy.'

Megarry put the phone back and immediately he thought to himself: Why did I call? Do I miss them? Do I miss the work, the camaraderie of the office? Is that the reason?

Increasingly he found himself thinking back to Higgins's murder. He was still irked that no one had called him, even to let him know how the case was continuing. He read the papers every day, listened to the radio and television, hoping to hear some news of a breakthrough, that someone had been arrested or charged with Higgins's death. But he heard nothing.

He thought that maybe the case had been quietly abandoned, Kelly taken off and reassigned to other duties. It happened all the time. As the superintendent had told him at the interview, all the divisions were understaffed. The crime load was heavy. If a case had no prospect of a solution there was no point in wasting people's time. There were too many other tasks awaiting their attention.

He remembered the powerful sense of disappointment and ingratitude that had overwhelmed him when he had been ordered off. He had felt crushed, useless, as if the time and effort he had put in had counted for nothing. He realised now that he had been too presumptuous, butting in like that on someone else's patch. There was a protocol in these matters. He should have observed it.

Why had he involved himself in the first place? Was it really to help Mulqueen, or was it something else? Something he wanted to prove to himself? Was it simply the challenge, a diversion to fill the long days as he convalesced from the heart attack?

He had enjoyed the work. There was a satisfaction in interviewing suspects, using the skills that he had built up over the years, putting together the tiny bits of the jigsaw that went into building a case. There was an excitement. He missed it now. It was like the days when he was drinking heavily, separated from Kathleen, living in the grotty flat on the Lisburn Road. The mornings when he would wake up with a hangover and the first thing he would think of was another drink.

He realised what he was suffering from. It was withdrawal.

One afternoon, when her sister was out of the house, Kathleen took him aside. 'We'd better think soon of making tracks. We've been here two weeks.'

'That's fine by me,' Megarry said.

'Nancy has been very good, but we don't want to overstay our welcome. I'll talk to her this evening. You don't mind?'

'No,' Megarry said solemnly.

'Anyway, Jennifer will be getting worried. How long is it since she saw us?'

'Almost a month.'

'It's long enough. We should really go back. And you look rested. The break has done you good. You're sure you don't mind?'

'Jesus Christ,' Megarry said. 'I just told you.'

Kathleen's face clouded.

'I'm sorry,' Megarry said. 'I didn't mean that. If you want to go, we'll go.'

That evening he took Andrew down to the Anchor for a drink. There was only a handful of people in the bar and they had the dartboard to themselves. Andrew took off his jacket and rolled up his shirt-sleeves, eager to get started.

'There's a lot of skill in this game. Most people don't know that. They think it's just a matter of throwing darts at the board. But it's not like that at all.'

He sighted along the shaft and pulled his skinny arm back and scored a forty. He turned to Megarry with a smile of satisfaction. 'There you are,' he said.

Megarry sipped his whiskey and put down the glass. 'You're too good for me, Andrew. I don't think I'm any competition.'

'No, not at all,' his brother-in-law hastened to say. 'You're getting better all the time. Why, since you've been here, you've improved in leaps and bounds.'

Megarry took the dart and prepared to throw. He felt his heavy stomach wobble over his pants.

'Just take your time. Sight your dart. Think of it like shooting a gun. You've shot a gun plenty of times, haven't you?'

'Yes,' Megarry said. He hurled the dart and watched in horror as it struck the wire and bounced off the board. The barman looked up from the counter at the dart skidding along the floor towards the door.

There was a silence. Megarry's face burned.

'Don't worry,' Andrew said. 'That happens to everybody. It's just like falling off a horse. You've got to get back up and start again.'

They returned to the house around ten o'clock. The whole way back Andrew talked about work, the pressure he was under, the carelessness of the younger people who were coming into the firm.

'It's not like when you and I were young,' he said. 'Nobody cares any more. There's no professionalism. Nobody takes a pride in their work.'

'I understand,' Megarry said.

'Young people today have things too easy. You and I had to fight for anything we got. It makes you sharper, more appreciative. Don't you think so?'

'Yes,' Megarry said and gritted his teeth, wondering how Andrew could know anything about young people since he and Nancy had no children.

By the time they reached the house, Megarry's head was swimming. He wanted Andrew to go to bed so that he could pour himself a nightcap and sit with Kathleen watching late-night television.

The phone was ringing in the hall. Andrew rushed past the door and stretched out his bony arm to lift the receiver, while Megarry took off his coat. He heard his brother-in-law mumble into the phone for a moment. Then he turned and said: 'It's for you.' He sounded disappointed.

132

'For me?'

Megarry took the instrument and pressed it close to his ear.

'Cecil,' a voice said.

'Yes?'

'It's Kelly.'

'Ahhh.'

'Something's happened. I thought I'd better tell you.'

Megarry caught the tension in his voice. 'Yes?' he said again.

'There's been another murder.'

'What?'

'Butcher. Eddie Butcher's been shot.'

16

George Buchanan hurried past the imposing façade of the Shelbourne Hotel with its newsboys and commissionaires and taxis. It was all bustle, people coming and going. In the big bay windows, he could see couples already seated for dinner, lit candles, shining glass, elegant women and men, waiters fussing with menus or pouring wine.

He envied people like that, people with money who would think nothing of tipping a waiter £20. He had been in there once or twice. He remembered the rich carpets, the mirrors, the chandeliers, the buzz in the Horseshoe Bar, journalists and celebrities greeting one another, ordering rounds of bullshots. That was the sort of life George aspired to.

He crossed the road towards the gates of St Stephen's Green and at the traffic junction he stopped and looked back. The day was fading fast and the sky to the west over the spires of the city showed a cold blue light, empty of cloud. Down along Grafton Street the neon signs were coming on, twinkling like pin-points in the gathering gloom. In the other direction, along Baggot Street, he could see crowds of drinkers jostling for space outside the pubs. He could hear the chatter, the laughter, smell the rich aroma of cooking meat from the kebab house.

He started walking by the railings of the Green, wet now after the recent rain. He had given up on Dee Dee out in Dalkey, watching from a table near the window of a pub as the camera crew had done one take after another, the director and the producer and the production assistants running around like headless chickens posing her this way and that, trying to make up their minds what was the best angle, what was the best shot.

George had watched them with growing boredom, the costume manager and the make-up artists and the lighting crew and a fat man in a tweed suit whom George took to be her agent, all fighting and arguing while Dee Dee sat patiently waiting for them to come to a decision. Glamorous it might be, George had concluded. But boring. Definitely boring.

In the end he had given up and got the train back into town. He went for a quiet drink in Doyle's off College Street. He would pick up Dee Dee later at Jangles night-club. She went there every night.

He had sat in the little snug and chatted to Peggy, the barmaid. He liked Peggy. She listened to him. He turned things over in his mind. He would have to make a report soon, go and see the Quare Fella, get a top-up of expenses. And then he remembered once more what he had seen in Brannigan's the night Harpo Higgins was killed and he felt a tightness in his chest.

George wished he hadn't seen it. He had tried to forget it, to put it out of his mind, but it kept coming back. Should he mention it to the Quare Fella? Was it something he would want to know? It was tricky. George wasn't sure what he should do. But one thing he knew for certain, knew instinctively. The information was dangerous.

As he walked, he listened to the sound his shoes made as they crunched on the loose gravel of the path. It was much quieter here, the street practically deserted, only the occasional chug-chug of a car on its way towards the Concert Hall, a dying bird-call from the darkening recesses of the park.

At the corner of Leeson Street George turned and looked back again, just in case, but there was no one there. It was a feature of his business always to be on his guard, suspicious, distrusting. But since he had started to keep watch on Dee Dee, following her around and monitoring her activities, his distrust had swelled to an obsession. He imagined that people might be listening to his phone calls, intercepting his mail. In bars, he automatically lowered his voice and looked about before he would speak. It was as if the conspiratorial world that he had entered had now enveloped him completely. He didn't trust anyone any more. It was like a virus, something he had caught, something over which he had no control.

He looked at his watch. It was too early for the clubs. They wouldn't really get into swing until after the pubs had closed. But it suited George. He would be able to get a good vantage point, somewhere in a quiet corner where he could watch what went on. And there was a bonus. If he went early, he wouldn't have to pay the admission charge. He felt in his pocket for the tightening roll of money. He was getting low.

On his way past Dwyer's pub he stopped for a moment to examine himself in the mirrors of the window. He found a comb in his breast pocket and flicked back his hair. He straightened his tie, pulled down the corners of his jacket, brushed some imagined specks of dandruff from his shoulder. He took out a paper napkin and rubbed his shoes till they shone.

A big green bus went panting along in a whoosh of exhaust fumes. It stopped half-way down the street and a group of young women got off in a flurry of handbags and flashing jewellery and laughter. George felt the excitement start to rise like sap in his breast.

As he went past the various clubs along the Strip, he could hear dance music echoing up the steps. Just warming up. The clubs would be empty now. He passed a restaurant with a fancy menu in a little glass case, the food spelled out in French in neat copperplate writing. There was a smell of garlic issuing from a grill. When he came to Jangles he stopped once more and straightened his tie. Jangles was the premier club, the place to go and be seen. It had a strict admissions policy. Only glitterati and people with proven spending power. But George was all right. They all knew George. He bounced down the steps with a jaunty tread.

The entrance to the club was a heavy black metal door with a blue light burning in a little bowl. It was guarded by two rough-looking men with cropped hair and scuffed dinner-jackets. They watched George approach and, as he got to the bottom of the steps, one of them raised a beefy hand to detain him.

'You a member here?'

George laughed, as if this was just a little private joke. 'You know me, Anto. George Buchanan.'

He took off his sun-glasses so that the doorman could recognise him.

'Doesn't matter. You have to be a member, George. Them's the rules.'

'Of course I'm a member.'

'Got your card?'

George fussed in his pockets but already he knew the answer. 'Not with me.'

'Sorry, George. No Card. No admission.'

George tried to laugh again, but he only managed a smile and it died on his lips. 'For God's sake, lads. I've been here dozens of times. I've left my card at home.'

'Too bad.'

'C'mon,' George said, realising now that this was serious. 'Don't be acting the bollix. Let me in.'

'What did he say?' the first man asked. He drew back his shoulders and George heard the dinner-jacket crack.

'He made a derogatory remark.'

'Did he now?'

The first man smashed his closed fist into the palm of his hand and took a deep breath. 'That's one sure way of waking up in hospital and getting your dinner through a tube.'

'Lads, lads. Let's be reasonable.'

'Why don't you move on?' the second man said. 'You're causing an obstruction.'

George sighed. 'How much?'

'Five.'

'*Five* bleedin' quid? Just to get into the gaff?'

'Three, George. Seeing as we know you.'

The man held out his hand and George fumbled in his pockets for the change.

'We're doing you a favour,' the man said, grasping the coins.

'Thanks,' George said. 'For nothing.'

'Enjoy yourself,' the man said, and he heard them laugh as he pushed past and into the gloomy interior of the club.

There was a blast of disco music and flashing lights and a smell of scented disinfectant. George stood for a moment and surveyed the scene. There was only a handful of people in the club. No one was dancing. The barman stood behind his little counter and was already looking bored.

George searched for a familiar face. In a corner near the stage he spotted Pinky Somerdale's rotund figure. He was sitting by himself, a bottle of champagne sweating in its bucket. He made his way across.

'George,' Pinky said. 'You're early.'

'Wellll,' George said and wiped the seat with a handkerchief before sitting down. He was still feeling the effects of the encounter at the door. 'I thought I'd pop in just for a while. Catch the scene. Know the way it is?'

'Have a glass of champagne,' Pinky said and reached for the bottle.

George already had a glass extended.

'You look tired, George.'

'I *am* bleedin' tired.'

'You should slow down,' Pinky said and lowered his glass. 'What are you doing anyway that has you so tired?'

'Just bits and pieces. A little consultancy work.'

'Oh,' Pinky said and looked impressed. 'Who are you working for?'

George glanced around and lowered his voice even though there was no one close. 'I'm not at liberty to tell you that.'

Pinky looked offended.

'It's a surveillance job,' George said quickly. 'Fella's playing the field. Wife's suspicious. She wants to get evidence.' He closed one eye slowly and looked away.

'I see,' Pinky said. 'And does he come in here?'

'Sometimes.'

'They're all doing it,' Pinky said. 'I don't know why these guys get married in the first place.' He took out the champagne

138

bottle and topped up George's glass. 'If you ask me, women aren't worth the bleedin' trouble. Take my brother for instance.'

Pinky began to relate a tale of marital discord. George looked away. A few more people had drifted in. Near the door, beneath the strobe lights, two tables had filled up with women and men, already drunk from somewhere else and singing in time with the music. It looked like an office party.

Jesus, George thought, they're letting anyone in here now, and he thought again of the altercation at the door.

'Hit him over the head with the baby's bleedin' bottle, she did. Split him open. What about that?'

Pinky was continuing to relate the story of his brother's marriage woes. George began to think of escaping. Trouble was, Pinky was buying champagne. At three quid for a glass of poxy red wine at the bar, it was not a decision to be taken lightly.

'Have some more,' Pinky said and poured again.

'You're in here a lot,' George said.

'I'm enjoying myself. What's the point of working yourself into the grave? What's the point of that?'

'Not much.'

'Anyway it's a sort of a celebration. I came into a few bob.'

'Yes,' George said eagerly and bent his ear forward to hear, but Pinky was not about to inform him.

'Did a little deal.'

'I see.'

'Made a few shillin's.'

'That's nice,' George said.

'Well I've been working on it for a couple of months. It only came together last week.'

Pinky yawned and put his hand up to cover his mouth. He's putting me to sleep, George thought, and looked around again. A couple of the newcomers had got up to dance, the women in T-shirts and short skirts, gyrating wildly to the music. Rednecks, George thought. Bleedin' civil servants up from the sticks.

He thought of Dee Dee and her smart set, seriously stylish. Faces pale, the men like something out of an advert for Calvin

Klein, the women thin and undernourished with eyes that glinted with practised indifference. They had money and nice clothes. They said all the right things, knew all the right people.

When they got up to dance from time to time, the crowd separated to let them through. The disc jockey shouted encouraging remarks above the din, the people stood aside and applauded when it was over and the music stopped. They didn't even acknowledge the applause, just accepted it as their due.

Pinky had started off again on some other tale. He's drunk, George thought. That's what it is. He's bleedin' pissed. He's boring me to death. No amount of free champagne is worth putting up with this.

He finished his glass and put it down on the table. 'Excuse me,' he said. 'I have to go to the Gents.'

'See ya,' Pinky said.

'Game ball,' George said and made his way to the bar. 'Glass of your poxy wine.'

'Red or white?'

'Red. The white tends to keep me awake.'

The barman ignored the remark and splashed some wine into a glass. He slid it across the counter. 'If it's so poxy, why are you drinking it?'

'Because I've no bleedin' choice,' George said and slapped down the money.

He turned to go, searching for a quiet spot, an alcove well away from Pinky Somerdale where he could observe the action without being seen. As he did so he caught sight of something that made his heart leap.

He stared again to make sure, but there was no mistake. Through the smoke and the haze and the flashing lights he could see Dee Dee making straight for the bar. And beside her, escorting her by the arm, was Paul Byrne. George froze.

He looked around quickly for somewhere to hide. Once they spotted him the game would be up. His cover would be blown. He started to retreat but it was too late. They were almost upon him. And they were on their own too, none of the usual gang of hangers-on that accompanied Dee Dee.

140

George felt the colour drain from his face. Dee Dee and Paul Byrne. He didn't even know they were acquainted. And here they were together, like lovers, bearing down on him.

Paul Byrne stopped when he got to the bar. 'If it isn't George Buchanan,' he said.

George tried to smile, to cover his confusion. He noticed Byrne's nice new suit, the haircut, the fancy tie, his eyes, blue and cold like the sea.

'Hello Paul,' George said without enthusiasm.

Dee Dee was already at the bar, leaning across examining the bottles stacked in a neat row along the back. She turned to face Paul Byrne and George noticed the light in her eyes. She seemed to be all energy. She's on something, he thought. As sure as hell she's doped up to the eyeballs.

'I think I'll have a campari,' Dee Dee said and Paul Byrne took a twenty-pound note out of his pocket. He looked in George's glass.

'What's that you're drinking?'

'Red wine.'

Byrne wrinkled his nose in disgust. 'Here, put it away.' He reached out and took the glass from George and put it on a table. 'Have a decent drink.'

'I'll have a whiskey,' George said.

Byrne gave the order to the barman and came back with fresh drinks. 'You know Dee Dee Clarke?' he said.

Beside them, Dee Dee had started moving to the music. She saw someone she knew across the room and gave a little wave of her hand. So far she had barely acknowledged George, as if he didn't exist.

'I've seen you before somewhere,' she now said.

'I get around.'

She raised the campari to her lips and took a sip. 'You were in here last night. Didn't I see you here last night?'

'No,' George lied. 'Not me.'

He glanced nervously between the two of them and gulped at his whiskey.

'I could have sworn you were here.'

'Somebody who looks like me.'

'What are you doing here now?' Byrne said.

'Just passing through. I drop in from time to time.'

'Give me a cigarette,' Dee Dee said and Byrne reached into his pocket. He held out a lighter and she inhaled deeply. George watched the movement, the way he attended her. A terrible thought came hurtling into his head.

'I'm feeling great,' she said. 'Jangles always cheers me up. What time is it anyway?' She looked at her watch. 'Where's the gang? Where's Louise? Where's David?'

Byrne smiled. 'Aren't you supposed to get your beauty sleep?'

'Hump that,' she said. 'I'm starting to enjoy myself. If you knew the kind of day I had, hanging around that freezing railway station while that bunch of idiots tried to make up their minds.'

She looked at George and he saw once more how beautiful she was, her dark hair falling down around her face, the lights casting shadows on her skin.

'What do you do for a living?' she said. 'You're in PR or something. Maybe that's where I saw you.'

'Yes,' George said. 'I am in a way.'

'He's a friend of the Quare Fella,' Paul Byrne said.

'Oh,' Dee Dee said and looked at George with renewed interest.

'Not really a friend,' George said quickly. 'More a business associate.'

'He does little jobs for him from time to time. Don't you George?'

George shifted uneasily. The conversation was taking a dangerous turn. 'I'm a consultant.'

'What does that mean?'

'It means he consults people,' Byrne said and laughed. He ruffled George's hair. 'You're getting low,' he said and pointed to George's glass. 'Dee Dee, what about you?'

'I'm all right.'

New people were getting up to dance, willowy blondes with long legs, dark Latin-looking women with bright lipstick. More like the usual crowd. The rednecks had retreated to their corner table and were getting morosely drunk.

'How long have you known the Quare Fella?' Dee Dee said.

'Years.'

'He's a bastard,' she said and George felt a little wave of shock.

'I wouldn't say that.'

'I would. He's ruthless. He's not a man to tangle with. Don't cross him.'

Suddenly it seemed to George that the place had got very warm. He felt a trickle of perspiration along his brow. The music had got louder. I'll have to get out of here, he thought. I don't like the way things are turning out.

Byrne came back from the bar and pressed a tumbler of whiskey into George's hand.

'I saw him break a man's arm once,' Dee Dee said. She had suddenly got serious.

'What's that?' Byrne said and bent his head.

'I'm telling George about the Quare Fella. I saw him break a man's arm. One chop with his fist and the man's arm was hanging off like a piece of cardboard. He didn't even blink. The man was in agony and the Quare Fella didn't even blink.'

Byrne stared at her and then at George. His face had grown dark. 'You're talking rubbish,' he said. He took her hand. 'Let's dance. C'mon. You said you wanted to dance.'

George watched them make their way out on to the floor. His head was feeling fuzzy. I need some air, he thought. I need to get out of here. He put the new glass of whiskey down and started for the door.

The bouncers stood aside to let him pass.

'You're leaving early, George,' one of them said.

He heard them laugh as he made his way up the steps and into the cold night, his head teeming with outrageous possibilities.

17

Megarry had arranged to meet Kelly the following morning at a hotel near the police station. On the train he kept thinking about Butcher. It was hard to imagine him dead. He remembered the day he had called on him in his house in Daffodil Grove, the swagger and bravado, the smart suit he had worn, his smooth chin jutting out in defiance.

He had almost come to like him in the end. He recalled the simple way he had reacted to praise about the gaudy house, the obvious pride he took in showing it off, pulling open the drinks cabinet and displaying the rows of bottles like he was the chairman of some important company. He was a criminal with a violent record, but there was also something childlike about him. Now he was dead and his murder had changed every-thing that Megarry had thought about the case so far.

He chose a seat in the lounge shaded by a palm tree, where he could observe who came and went at the door. He ordered coffee and waited. There was a convention at the hotel and lots of people milling around the foyer and the reception area. He had told Kelly ten o'clock. He checked his watch and saw that it was now ten to ten.

He thought of last night, the aftermath of the phone call. He had waited till Andrew and Nancy had gone to bed, till only he and Kathleen were left watching television in the parlour.

'Did you talk to Nancy?' he said softly.

'Yes.'

'And what did she say?'

'She doesn't want us to leave.'

'Maybe she's just being polite.'

Kathleen shook her head. 'No. I think she means it. She's a kind soul. She enjoys our company.'

They sat in silence for a while and Megarry sipped his nightcap. At last he said: 'Why don't we stay? Just for a few more days?'

'Why have you changed your mind?'

'I haven't. I was only agreeing with you.'

'Something's come up,' she said. 'I can tell.'

Megarry finished his drink. 'Yes,' he said at last. 'Something *has* come up. Some business I have to finish. Do me a favour. Stay till the end of the week.'

Kelly came bustling into the foyer at two minutes past ten. He was wearing a smart blazer and slacks and carried a briefcase under his arm. Megarry stood up and waved. 'Here,' he said. 'Over here.'

The young policeman came across quickly.

'Sit down,' Megarry said. 'Have some coffee.' He poured a cup and waited till Kelly had composed himself. 'Now tell me what happened.'

'We found him last night. In his car. Back of Smithfield market.'

'Gunshot wounds?'

'Yes. I have a copy of the preliminary forensic report. Heavy-calibre revolver.'

'.375 Magnum?'

Kelly nodded. 'The same as Higgins.'

He took a thin folder from his briefcase and gave it to Megarry. 'I copied that this morning. It's for you.'

Megarry opened the report and started to read. It was almost a repeat of Higgins's murder. Gunshot wound to the back of the head. He had been found by a man out walking his dog at ten past six the previous evening, slumped over the wheel of the

145

car in a side-street near the market. There were all the usual details of the analyses that had already been carried out by the Technical Bureau: fibres, blood, fingerprints, carbon traces from the weapon.

He finished reading the report and put it down carefully on the table beside him. Kelly was finishing his coffee.

'Someone has informed his widow?'

'Yes.'

'Has she been interviewed?'

'Not yet. The poor woman was devastated. We just brought her in to make a formal identification.'

Megarry felt in his pocket for his cigarettes. 'You know I talked to Butcher again after we released him from the station?'

'No. I didn't.'

'I went to his house. He told me that someone had been threatening Higgins over a drug debt. A man called Joey Morton. I had to extract the information. He seemed very edgy.'

'Afraid?'

'More than afraid. Terrified, I'd say.'

'Did you check out this Morton guy?'

'I tried but I drew a blank.' He lit a cigarette and looked at the other man. 'Who's handling this?' he asked.

'I am.'

'As well as the Higgins case? I take it it's still active.'

'Of course. I've got support. The superintendent has drafted in a couple more detectives. The Higgins case is going nowhere. But now with another murder, and the same weapon and everything, they're running around like headless chickens.'

'What about Mulqueen?'

'He's in a panic. He seems to have gone to pieces. I don't think he can take the strain. I think he'd just like the whole business forgotten about. Files closed. Case buried. He has the look of a very worried man.'

Megarry said nothing. He sat for a while.

'Why did you come to me?'

'Because I want you to help me.'

'But you know what happened? You know I was ordered off the case by the superintendent?'

146

'He doesn't have to know.'

'For God's sake, Peter. He gets to hear. People tell him things.'

'Nevertheless I'd like you to help.'

Megarry studied the young man. 'You know the risk you're running? You know the danger? Nothing can happen to me. But you have a lot to lose.'

'I don't care.'

'Don't say that.' Megarry crushed out his cigarette and stood up. 'Did you come by car?'

'Yes. It's outside.'

'Okay,' he said wearily. 'Let's go and talk to Mrs Butcher.'

They parked beside the house. As they were getting out of the car, Megarry tapped Kelly's shoulder and pointed to the radio. 'Take it out and put it under the seat. I had a bad experience here.'

The Butcher household was in turmoil. It seemed to be filled with neighbours and friends of the dead man. The widow sat in the flashy kitchen surrounded by a couple of tough-looking youths, whom Megarry took to be Butcher's sons. She had a tumbler of brandy in her hand.

When she saw the policemen she began to weep, her heavy bosom shaking beneath her white blouse. Megarry squeezed her hand and the youths stood aside so that he could sit down.

'I'm terribly sorry, Mrs Butcher.'

She wiped her eyes and sniffed but didn't speak.

He said: 'Poor Eddie. He was a good man.'

The mention of her dead husband brought on another flood of tears. Beside him, Megarry could sense the youths watching him warily. It was obvious that their experience with policemen had not been good. He sat for a while and gently patted the woman's hand.

'We'd like to get the people who did this,' he said.

'Bleedin' right,' one of the youths said.

'Maybe you could help?' Megarry said.

Mrs Butcher raised the tumbler to her lips and took a drink, then wiped her chin with a plump hand.

'Did Eddie have any enemies, anybody with a grudge against him?'

The woman looked at him with large, innocent eyes. 'Eddie didn't have an enemy in the world. Everybody loved him. Isn't that right, Christy?'

One of the youths muttered. Megarry exchanged glances with Kelly who had also sat down at the kitchen table.

'So why do you think he got killed?'

'Some bastard was jealous of him, that's why,' the second youth said.

'Did he have a row with anyone recently? Anyone threaten him? Anything like that?'

'No way,' Mrs Butcher said. 'Sure Eddie only minded his own business. He just lived for his family. Me and the kids.'

'Did he owe money to anybody?'

The woman looked at the policeman as if he had just insulted her. 'Eddie never owed money to nobody in his life.'

She was weeping again. Behind him Megarry could hear the two youths shifting uneasily.

'Do you know a man called Joey Morton?'

'Who?'

'Joey Morton.'

'Never heard of him.'

'He mentioned a man called Joey Morton to me the last time I talked to him. I thought you might know who he is.'

'Eddie knew loads of people in his business. He knew hundreds of people. He was always meeting people all the time. Eddie was very gergarious.' She turned once more to the eldest youth. 'You ever hear of him, Christy?'

'No, Ma.'

She drained her glass and one of the youths uncorked a bottle and silently filled it up again. She looked at Megarry.

'I'm not the better of this,' she said by way of explanation. 'The shock. To see a man in the whole of his health one minute and the next minute he's dead.'

'It must be hard for you.'

'You've no idea,' she said and shook her head and took another gulp from the glass.

148

'Tell me exactly what happened. What was he doing at Smithfield? Did he go there to meet someone?'

'Well,' Mrs Butcher said and wiped her chin once more. 'We were sitting here watching the video. Just right here. Where you are now.' Her eyes filled up with tears again. 'And I heard Eddie's mobile ring. So he got up and says: "Just a mo, Margie." And he went off into the hall and I could hear him talking to somebody for a few minutes, and then he came back in and put his coat on. "I'm going out, Margie," he said. "I won't be long." So I thought nothing about it. Eddie's always meeting people, like I told you, for his business.

'So off he went and when he didn't come back for his tea, I just assumed he'd called in to the boozer on his way home. I didn't think nothing about it. And then, Mother of God, about eight o'clock, the police came from the station to say he was murdered. I'm telling you no lie, I'm not the better of it yet.'

'You'll never get over it Ma,' the oldest youth said and squeezed her shoulder and Mrs Butcher dabbed her eyes.

'Tell me something else,' Megarry said. 'After the phone call, how did he look?'

'What do you mean?'

'Was he frightened? Did he look scared?'

'Not at all,' Mrs Butcher said. 'Eddie didn't look scared. Why should he? Didn't I tell you that Eddie didn't have an enemy in the world.'

'Did he say who it was? This person he was meeting?'

'No. Eddie never discussed his business with me. He always kept that to himself. "You've no head for business, Margie," he used to say. "You wouldn't understand it." '

'But you think the person he went to meet was someone he knew?'

'I assume so. Who else would it be? I assumed it was something to do with his business, just like I said.'

At that moment there was a bustle at the doorway and more people came into the kitchen to pay their respects. Mrs Butcher composed herself for further tribute. She had finished with Megarry now. He had wanted to ask her about Higgins but he realised that the interview was at an end.

'Thank you for giving us your time,' he said and stood up. 'I'm sorry this has happened.'

Mrs Butcher ignored him. The oldest youth accompanied them to the front door. Megarry took his hand, a cold, calloused hand with blackened nails.

'If you think of anything that might help, give us a ring.'

Kelly had taken a card from his pocket and gave it to the youth.

'Sure thing,' the youth said and closed the door.

Ballymoss was bathed in sunlight when they arrived. From the tower blocks long shadows spread like a blanket across the grey forecourt and out as far as the waste ground where some kids were kicking a ball.

As he stepped from the car Megarry thought of the last time he had been here, the pools of water after the rain, the dogs running in wild packs across the field, the smell of cooked chicken coming from the butcher's shop.

As he began to walk with Kelly towards the flats he was conscious of people watching them, groups of sullen youths in doorways, a woman leaning from a balcony to hang out clothes. We are conspicuous, he thought. They know us as strangers.

The entrance to the tower block was cold and damp. He could smell the stale odour of decay, of human detritus. He started to climb the stairs, his breathing laboured from the exertion. An old man in a long overcoat passed them by, but turned his face away when Megarry tried to exchange a greeting. When they came to the door of the flat he stopped to catch his breath.

He pressed the bell and waited. He could hear noise inside, the same sounds he had heard the first time, a video machine turned up too loud, children shouting. After a while, the door was opened slightly and a child's face peeped out.

'Is your mother in?' Megarry asked.

The child regarded them for a moment, then closed the door without speaking and went back inside the flat. He heard the video being turned down, then the door opened again and Mrs

Nolan was standing in the hall. He saw her examine their faces, searching for recognition.

'Remember me?' he said softly.

'Yes.'

'I'm sorry to trouble you again. I have to ask you some questions. Can we come in?'

Mrs Nolan stood aside and they followed her into the tiny flat. He saw the faces of the children watching from the sitting-room. She led them into the kitchen and closed the door.

There was a table and four chairs and scraps of a left-over meal scattered on some plates in the sink. Kelly sat down and Megarry walked to the window and looked out over the roofs of the houses stretching away towards Santry.

'Would you like a cup of tea?' The woman held out a kettle, its bottom burnt black from constant use.

'That would be nice,' Megarry said. There was a soft plopping sound as the cooker ignited.

'It's Annie, isn't it?' he said.

'Yes.'

'Where's your husband, Annie?'

'He's scarpered.'

'Gone?'

'Yes, these four years.'

'Where is he?'

'God knows. England, I suppose.'

'And how many children have you got?'

'Three.'

The woman sat on the edge of her chair with her hands clasped before her and tried to avoid his eyes. She's afraid of us, he thought. Policemen always bring trouble.

He cleared his throat and began again. 'Tell me more about Harpo,' he said. 'What kind of guy was he?'

He heard her response, soft and quiet as a mouse. 'He was a good brother.'

'But the drugs?'

'The drugs destroyed him. If he hadn't been murdered, he would have died anyway. In a way, I was glad, because it put him out of his misery.'

There was something shocking about the remark, even though it was kindly meant.

'How bad was he?'

'You saw him in the morgue. In the end he was only skin and bones. He used to be a lovely boy. When we were growing up, he was the best-looking boy on the street, the girls went mad for him. But the drugs done him in.'

She paused.

'When he was staying here with me, he used to wake up in the morning before it was light and he'd be strung out. I used to hear him crying with the pain. It was awful. He'd have the shakes, the withdrawals.'

She looked up and he caught her eye. She had the same defeated look that he had seen the first time he had been here, the same resignation. She wore it like a uniform.

'If he had any drugs left, he'd shoot up and he'd be all right for a while. He used to always try to keep some for the mornings. The mornings were the hardest time. But if he had no drugs he'd be in bits, pacing up and down, throwing up in the toilet. He'd go off as soon as it was bright to look for a fix.'

He saw Kelly look up as the kettle began to boil. Mrs Nolan rose quickly and poured water into the teapot.

'What was he doing here in the first place?' Kelly said. 'He had his own house didn't he, in St Martin's Gardens?'

'Some people were after him.'

'What people?'

She shrugged.

'And what were they after him for?'

'I don't know. He never told me. I supposed it was to do with drugs.'

'And the last time he came here, before he was killed, was that the same thing?'

'Yes. He just arrived here one morning in a taxi and said he'd have to stay for a few days. I was used to him coming and going. I didn't mind.'

She poured the tea and came back to the table with three cups.

Megarry leaned forward. 'He left home to stay with you

152

because some people were chasing him. Is that what you're saying?'

'Yes.'

'And how often did this happen?'

'A few times. Two or three.'

'And where was his partner, Marie O'Gorman? Did she come with him?'

Mrs Nolan shook her head. 'He came on his own.'

'And where did she go? Did she stay in the house?'

'I don't think so. I think she stayed with friends.'

'So they all cleared out. Harpo and Marie O'Gorman. What about the boy, Henry?'

'She took him.'

'How old is he now?'

'About eight or nine.'

'But he's not Marie O'Gorman's child, isn't that right?'

'No. He's Harpo's. He kept the boy when he split with his wife.'

Megarry sat back and sipped at his tea.

'Where is his wife?' Kelly said.

Mrs Nolan turned in her seat at the sound of the new voice.

'Around town somewhere. Her and Harpo didn't get on. I think she took up with somebody else.'

'Do you know her address? Where we could contact her? Somebody should tell her that Harpo's dead.'

Mrs Nolan shook her head. 'She doesn't care. She's got a new life.'

'And how did Harpo get custody of the boy? He was hardly in any position to look after him.'

'She didn't want him. She couldn't be bothered.'

'Couldn't be bothered?'

'She just wanted out. She left Harpo. Just got up one morning and took herself off. Later she changed her tune and tried to get custody of the boy. Threatened to take Harpo to court. There was a big row over it. But Harpo wouldn't let go. He really loved that child. In the end she backed off and left him alone.' She fell silent.

Megarry watched her, her thin hand trembling as she raised the teacup to her lips. 'Was Harpo a violent man?' he asked.

Mrs Nolan looked startled. 'No,' she said. 'Harpo wouldn't have hurt a fly.'

'You're sure? I've been told by people that he was violent.'

'No,' she said firmly. 'Whoever told you that was telling you lies.'

Megarry considered for a moment. 'Tell me about Eddie Butcher. Did you know him?'

She nodded. 'He was a friend of Harpo's. Well not exactly a friend. Harpo didn't have any real friends. He was more a sort of . . .'

'Acquaintance?'

'Yes,' she said. 'That's right. He used to come round here from time to time to see Harpo.'

'He was a drug dealer?'

'Yes.'

'And Harpo and him used to do business together. Is that it?'

'Yes.'

'Harpo was a dealer too?'

'Only in a small way,' the woman said. 'Only to support his own habit. He wasn't a bad man.' She shook her head and he could see the tears forming in her eyes. 'He was a good brother, a good father. If it hadn't been for the drugs.'

I'll have to go gently, Megarry thought. God help her. She's had enough troubles without me adding to them. 'Do you know a man called Joey Morton? Did Harpo ever mention him?'

'No,' she said. 'I don't know everything.'

On impulse, he reached out and touched her cheek. She hung her head and he heard a low sob like the sound of the wind rustling in the trees.

'I'm sorry, Annie. I don't mean to interrogate you. There's just one more piece of information. Marie O'Gorman? Where would I find her?'

Mrs Nolan sniffed and wiped her eyes. 'At the funeral. She's bound to be there.'

'Harpo's funeral? You mean he hasn't been buried yet?'

154

'No,' she said. 'They only released the body yesterday. They were doing tests.'

'And when is it?'

'This evening. Church of the Redeemer. Five o'clock.'

18

The Church of the Redeemer was a modern building with a spire and an enormous cross on a green copper dome. It dominated the drab, grey landscape, amid the rows of box-like houses. As they approached the entrance, the policemen saw a small group of men, poorly dressed in jeans and jackets. They hung about outside the porch, puffing at cigarettes, shuffling uneasily in the pale evening light. They stood aside as the two men drew near and Megarry and Kelly entered the church.

There was a smell of polish and candle-wax and a gloom that settled over the place like a shroud. There were only a few people inside and Megarry thought at first that they had come to the wrong place or had misheard the time. And then, up near the altar, he saw the thin yellow coffin, resting on its lonely trestle and the small knot of mourners huddled together in the first few rows.

He could make out Mrs Nolan, a black scarf tied loosely round her head. She sat with her children and some other women in the first pew. They looked small and frightened as if the business of the funeral intimidated them. Megarry thought of other funerals he had attended, the church packed, people standing at the back and along the aisles, politicians and dignitaries jostling for recognition. This was the poorest funeral he had ever seen.

His first instinct was to find a seat near the door so as not to draw attention. And then some impulse drove him forward, some barely recognised sympathy for the miserable group of mourners, clinging together for support at the front of the church. There was an empty pew about half-way down the aisle. He pushed Kelly before him and together they slipped into the seat, just as a bell began to toll. A plump little priest in billowing vestments appeared quickly beside the altar and the service began.

The priest approached the coffin and stood for a moment looking out over the tiny congregation. The church fell silent. The mourners waited. Megarry watched as the priest took out a little spoon and sprinkled holy water on the yellow casket. Then he began the prayers for the dead and a mumble of responses rose like a muted wave from the first few pews. The priest began to talk about Harpo.

He called him James. He spoke of the life he had lived, the suffering, the misery inflicted by his drug addiction. He called it a scourge that was wrecking the lives of whole communities. It was mainly the poor who were suffering, the young, the dispossessed. He spoke in a compassionate voice. He said that Harpo's life was just as important in the eyes of God as the life of the greatest statesman or the richest potentate. In God's eyes they were equal and no one had the right to take that life away.

Megarry heard a woman begin to sob, the cries echoing round the empty church. The priest finished and walked to the rows of mourners and began to speak to them, gently commiserating, pressing his hand on their shoulders as he dealt out reassurance. Then he turned and went back to the altar to begin the Mass.

Megarry watched Kelly, awkwardly following his responses, the crossings and blessings and genuflections. He had never been at a Catholic Mass before. He remembered the fear and suspicion he had picked up as a child on the streets of Belfast, the hostility to all things Popish.

When the service was over, there were more prayers and then some men got up from the congregation and Megarry watched as the coffin was taken from its trestle and raised on

157

their shoulders to begin its slow progress down the church. Mrs Nolan and her children came next, walking together in a pitiful group, then some more women and a handful of men. He waited till they had passed, then he and Kelly followed them down the aisle and out into the failing light.

There was a shiny hearse waiting at the door, a few pathetic wreaths and two men in black undertakers' overcoats. The policemen stood in the porch and waited as people began to press in on Mrs Nolan, shaking hands, whispering condolences. When at last the little band had thinned out, Megarry and Kelly approached. She seemed surprised to see them.

'I didn't think you would come.'

'Why not?' Megarry asked.

'You're too busy. Harpo wasn't important.'

He let the remark slip past.

'I'm sorry Harpo's dead. Even though I didn't know him. He was too young to die.'

She looked at him and he could see that her eyes were red and swollen from weeping. 'Maybe it was for the best.'

He stood for a moment and gently pressed her hand.

'Marie O'Gorman. You said she would be here.'

'She is,' Mrs Nolan said. 'I saw her earlier.'

She scanned the small group of mourners. 'There,' she said.

Megarry's eyes followed the pointed finger. A thin woman with fair hair stood near the church gates. She was poorly dressed, just like all the others. She had a little boy, holding him tight by the hand.

Mrs Nolan was speaking again. 'Will you be coming to the cemetery?'

'I don't think so,' the policeman said. 'But I might call on you again. I might need to talk to you.'

The woman nodded. 'We'll be having a few drinks later in the Blackthorn. After the cemetery. It's a sort of a wake for Harpo. You'd be welcome to come.'

'Maybe,' Megarry said.

Someone else came to speak to her and the two men turned away. They waited now for Marie O'Gorman. She too was surrounded by people who were shaking her hand, expressing regrets. He wondered if Dee Dee Clarke was here, the woman he had seen that day when he visited Harpo's house. He recalled the anguished reaction when he had told her that Harpo was dead, the tears. But as he searched the remaining knots of mourners, dispersing now into the evening, he could find her nowhere.

At last the people who had been talking to Marie O'Gorman drifted away. She stood alone by the gates of the church. The two men walked quickly across.

'Could we have a word with you?' Megarry asked.

She was smaller than he had thought, her features pale and pinched, her hair a mousy blonde. She looked at them with alarm, her eyes examining them, trying to decide who they might be.

'What about?'

'Harpo. We're police officers. We'd like to ask you some questions.'

She gripped the child's hand tighter and he could see the fear in her face. 'I know nothing about it.'

'Nothing about what?'

'His murder. I wasn't even living with him when it happened.'

Something in her manner struck him as odd, the fear, the defensiveness.

He lowered his voice and tried to speak gently, to reassure her. 'You have nothing to be afraid of. We'll protect you. You might know something. Even something small and insignificant. Something you might not think is important.'

She looked from one man to the other. 'Are you going to the cemetery?' she asked.

Megarry shook his head.

'Have you got a car?'

'Yes.'

'Then take me to St Martin's Gardens. I have to pick up some things.'

They walked together in silence till they came to Kelly's car. Megarry studied her as they went. She was in her late twenties and had once been pretty but care and trouble were beginning to wear her down. There were thin lines in the corners of her face that the make-up couldn't hide and shadows, like dark smudge marks, beneath her eyes. She had put on a black blouse and coat for the occasion and dark stockings on her thin legs.

'Who's this guy?' Kelly said as he unlocked the car. With his free hand he ruffled the boy's hair.

'He's my son.'

Megarry heard the lie but decided to ignore it.

'What's his name?'

'Henry.'

The woman continued to hold the boy tight by the hand as if she feared that someone would come along and take him away.

'I've a boy his age,' Kelly said. 'How old is he?'

'Eight.'

'That's what I guessed.'

The boy stared back at Kelly with big, suspicious eyes, as if life had already taught him to be wary. He had the look of a child who had been hurt, who had witnessed the terrible things that adults could do to one another.

Kelly put his hand on his head once more. The child pulled away from the touch.

'What do you like to do, Henry? Play football?'

The boy hung his head and didn't reply. Marie O'Gorman shook him by the arm.

'Tell the man what you like.'

'Football.'

'Any favourite team? Who do you support?'

'I don't support anybody.'

'Where do you go to school?'

'St Patrick's.'

'Do you like it?'

'No.'

Kelly opened the car door and Megarry got in beside him, while Marie O'Gorman and the boy got in the back.

They drove away from Ballymoss and into the city. It shone before them in the dying light, spires and roof-tops and steeples. In the distance they could see the mountains, and as they got closer to the river, the polish of light on the dark water. They crossed at the toll bridge. There was a ship ploughing up the channel, gulls screeching in its wake. In the mirror, Megarry saw the boy press his face to the window to watch.

He heard Marie O'Gorman speak.

'Is it all right if I have a fag?'

'Of course.'

'I'll open the window,' she said. 'Some people don't like you smoking in their car.'

'I don't mind,' Kelly said. 'It's up to you.'

'No,' she said. 'I'll open it,' and began winding down the window.

There was a rush of cold air. Megarry saw her rummage in her handbag till she found her cigarettes. She held out the packet but he waved it away.

He had decided not to question her till they got to the house. It would be easier for the boy. He wondered how much the child knew, how much he understood. He glanced once more in the mirror and saw him sitting with his cold, silent eyes watching as the streets slipped by.

Kelly parked the car outside the house and waited while they all struggled out on to the pavement. Marie O'Gorman had a key. She put it in the lock and pushed hard and the front door opened with a shudder.

Immediately, Megarry smelt the odour of must and decay that he remembered from the last time, the smell of trapped air, of putrefaction.

She saw his reaction and said: 'Look at this place. Jesus Christ, it's a kip.'

She stood in the doorway and waved her hands around the stark, empty hall. 'This used to be a cosy little house. Oh, I could tell you a tale. Look at it now.'

She turned to the boy who was standing passively beside her. 'You go out and play in the garden. Me and the men have to talk.'

Together they trooped down the hall and into the kitchen. The smell was stronger.

'I should open some windows,' Marie O'Gorman said. 'Let in some air.'

She walked to the sink and threw the windows open wide, then turned back to address the policemen. 'I don't suppose there's any point in offering you tea, even if I could find something to make it with?'

'It's all right,' Megarry said and sat down at the table. He took out a packet and fumbled with a box of matches. 'This shouldn't take long.'

She sat down across the table from the two men and took one of Megarry's cigarettes.

'When's the last time you were here?' he said.

'Two or three weeks ago.'

'What happened?'

He saw her avoid his glance.

'Harpo and I had a row. I couldn't take any more. I decided to get out.'

'Where did you go?'

'To stay with friends. Then I found a flat.'

'What was the row about?'

She sighed and kept her head down. 'Those fucking drugs.' For the first time he detected a flash of anger. 'They destroyed him. When I first met Harpo he was such a lovely guy, carefree, generous, full of life. He was such fun to be with. But that damned heroin did him in. You've no idea.' She gestured around the room. 'He sold everything in here that wasn't nailed down. He robbed. I couldn't even leave my handbag lying around or he'd take anything I had. In the end it was getting impossible. All he thought of was drugs. Where the next fix was coming from. That's all he cared for. It was hell. That's what it was. A living hell.

'The only one who escaped was Henry. He never stole anything belonging to him. In fact to give him his due, even when he was desperate for a fix he would be bringing home little presents for him, toys, things like that.'

Megarry kept his voice low. 'You used drugs yourself.'

'What?' She looked up sharply. 'That's not true. I never took drugs. I saw what they did to Harpo. There's no way I was going to get involved in that shit.'

'You're lying.'

'How dare you?' He saw the colour rise in her cheeks. 'Who told you that?'

'You were hospitalised with an overdose.'

'What?'

'Isn't it true?'

'No, it's not bloody true. Why don't you check? Jeeesus,' she said. 'The lies that people tell.'

Megarry decided to let the matter rest.

'What sort of guy was Harpo?'

'He was a lovely guy. Decent, full of life. Generous. He loved the kid. It was the drugs that ruined him.'

'Was he violent?'

'No he wasn't.' She was dismissive. 'Harpo was as easygoing a guy as you could meet. Where did you hear that?'

'I heard it.'

'Someone's been filling your head full of shit,' she said.

'Do you know Eddie Butcher?'

'Yes. He was a friend of Harpo's.'

'Did you know that he was dead?'

For a moment, her face froze.

'He was murdered,' Kelly said. 'Just like Harpo. Same weapon.'

She looked from one man to the other. 'Jesus,' she said.

'We found him last night.' He leaned forward to peer into her face. 'Who is it? Why is it happening?'

'I don't know,' she said and shook her head and Megarry could see that the fear had returned. 'He was a friend of Harpo's. He got his drugs from him sometimes.'

'Did they ever argue?'

'No. They were good friends.'

'Did they ever fall out over drugs?'

'I don't think so. Jesus. Harpo and now Eddie.' She gripped Megarry's arm.

'Why did Harpo leave here?' he said. 'He left in a hurry. Just

163

packed a bag and fled. He didn't even take time to finish his meal.'

He pointed to the table, the plates, food congealing and mouldering green and blue.

'I don't know.'

'You do know. Someone was after him. The Quare Fella. Who is that?'

'It's just an expression.'

'Joey Morton?'

'Who?'

'C'mon,' Megarry said. He spoke harshly as if he was trying to shock her. 'You know who Joey is. Don't lie to me. You've lied to me enough.'

'What do you mean?'

'Henry. He's not your son. Why do you try to pretend that he is?'

'I've raised him,' she said. 'As far as I'm concerned he is my son.'

'Where is his mother. His real mother?'

'I don't know.'

'For God's sake,' Megarry said. 'Who are you covering for? I know Harpo beat you up. I know you were taking drugs. Why do you persist?'

'Who told you that?'

'Your father.'

She threw her head back and for a moment the tiny room was filled with laughter. 'I might have guessed. My father.'

'Guessed what?'

'My father is a complete bastard. He threw me out of my own home. Told me not to come back. He doesn't give a damn about me.'

'He knew that Harpo was a bad influence on you. He didn't like him.'

'Didn't like him? Jesus, that's an understatement. He fucking hated him. They never got on from the moment they set eyes on each other.'

'Because he cared for you?'

'My arse. He didn't care about me. He was jealous. He

164

wouldn't let me out of his sight. I couldn't have a boyfriend. I was the only girl in the neighbourhood who didn't have a boy. My father couldn't bear the thought of another man having me.'

For a second, Megarry thought he had misheard, and then the awful truth came rushing in. He took her hand and held it softly in his own. 'I'm sorry,' he said. 'I should have realised. Forgive me.'

She turned her head away. Across the table, Kelly was watching them.

'He was abusing you?'

She hung her head, and didn't answer. When she looked up, he saw the shame in her face. 'That's why I fell for Harpo. He gave me a chance to get out of there.'

'Why didn't you tell someone?'

'Who would have believed me? My own father?'

'Forgive me,' Megarry said again.

From the back garden, in the gathering gloom, they could hear the sound of a ball being kicked against a fence. Henry had found some distraction.

'Do you know why Harpo was murdered? Have you any idea?'

She shook her head.

'Someone was after him. Who was it?'

She looked away, avoiding his eyes.

'Please,' Megarry said. 'Help me. Tell me what you know.'

She stared but didn't speak.

The policeman crushed out his cigarette and stood up. 'You wanted to get some things,' he said.

'Yes.'

'You're not going to stay here?'

'No. Too many memories.'

Megarry nodded. 'We'll wait for you. We'll take you back.'

She bit her lip. 'Poor Harpo,' she said. 'He was a good man. You'll never know.'

'What will you do now?' Kelly asked.

'I'll try to go on. I've got a little job. It doesn't pay much. Henry and I will be okay.'

'Why do you do it?' the young policeman said.

'For Harpo. He loved that boy.'

Megarry thought of the picture he had taken from the house, Harpo and the boy at the fairground, happy, carefree. Maybe he had been wrong about Higgins. Maybe he had misread the situation.

'Are you finished now?' Marie O'Gorman asked. 'No more questions?'

'Just one more. Who is Dee Dee Clarke and why does she have a key to this house?'

He saw her face grow dark. 'That cow,' she said. 'Why do you want to know about her?'

'I met her here. In this house. She said she was a friend of Harpo's. Why does she have a key?'

'How would I know? I didn't know she had a key.'

'But this was your place. Who would have given it to her?'

She shrugged. 'Harpo.'

'Why?'

Marie O'Gorman almost spat out the words. 'Because she's his bleedin' wife. That's why.'

19

Marie O'Gorman had a flat on the North Circular Road in a large terrace house tenanted by nurses from the nearby hospital. They dropped her there with the boy, then drove back into town. Megarry was hungry. They parked the car by the river and went to Bewley's coffee shop in Westmoreland Street.

It was crowded with shoppers and kids on a school outing, rushing around the café, making a lot of noise. He took a tray and queued for beef casserole. He was about to order chips when Dr Henry's injunction flashed into his head. Nothing greasy, nothing fried. Potatoes are all right but no butter, no dressing. He chose a salad instead and a small bottle of red wine, then searched for a table in the Smoking section.

'What are you going to tell them about this, back at the office?' he asked Kelly as he put down the tray.

'I'll tell them what I did. Where I went, who I talked to. The usual stuff. I have to make out a daily report for Mulqueen and a copy for the superintendent.'

'You know to keep me out of it?'

'Of course.'

They ate in silence for a while and then Kelly said: 'Why *were* you removed? No one ever said.'

'You don't know?'

'No. You were never mentioned again. It was as if you hadn't existed. One day you were there, next day you were gone. Mulqueen never said a word. I got the impression he was embarrassed.'

'I was a casualty of protocol,' Megarry said and forced a smile. 'I belong to a different police force, in a different jurisdiction. The superintendent said there could be problems. He was very civil about it. But adamant. He wanted me off the case.'

'How did he find out?'

Megarry sighed. 'Somebody must have told him.'

Outside, it began to grow dark, street-lights coming on, rush-hour traffic clogging the road. Megarry finished his meal and pushed away the plate. He looked towards the coffee counter, changed his mind, searched in his pocket instead for his cigarettes.

'Tell me something,' he said, rattling a matchbox. 'How did you get involved in this racket? Was your father a cop?'

'No,' Kelly said. 'He was a builder's labourer. A Wicklow man, up from the country. But he was responsible nevertheless.'

'How come?'

'It was like this. He used to work in all weathers, rain and snow. And when the weather was so bad that he couldn't work, he didn't get paid. He was determined that I would do better. There was a breed of men in those days who worshipped the idea of a steady job with a pension. When I left school, he suggested the police. He said I'd never look back.

'I'll always remember the day when the letter came from HQ. He was as pleased as punch. He put on his best coat, an old tweed thing that he kept for Mass on Sunday mornings. Nothing would do him but we'd go down to the Cat and Cage to celebrate. That's where he used to drink and he knew that all his old cronies would be there. He wanted to show off, you see.

'He marched up to the bar. I'll never forget it. He ordered drinks for everybody in his loudest voice. And then he made a little speech about how this was the last drink he would ever buy me, because from now on I'd be buying *him* the drinks. I was mortified, all those old men, pressing their skinny hands, clapping me on the back, telling me I was a credit to my parents. And when I turned to look back, there he was at the counter with his glass of whiskey tight in his hand and the tears were rolling down his cheeks.'

'He was proud of you,' Megarry said. 'You made good.'

'Yes. I suppose he was.'

'Where is he now?'

'In a nursing home. Over in Blackrock. My mother died a few years ago. He was on his own.'

'Does he like it there?'

'He misses home. I should visit him more.'

'We underestimate our fathers when we are young,' Megarry said. 'We think they are foolish. We only realise when it's too late.'

He toyed with his cigarette and got ready to go.

'Are you making any sense of this?' Kelly asked suddenly. 'Higgins and now Butcher. The same weapon. Do you still think it's related to drugs?'

'It's the most obvious link. We know Butcher was a dealer. We know that Higgins was an addict and a dealer and that he got drugs from Butcher. One thing intrigues me, though. Higgins fled his home in St Martin's Gardens. He was terrified. Just like Butcher was terrified. Somebody was really putting the frighteners on them. If we could find out who that was we might begin to understand it.'

'Joey Morton?'

'Possibly,' Megarry said. 'You could run another check on him.' He drummed his fingers gently on the edge of the table. 'But don't be surprised if you come up with a blank.'

'Why do you say that?'

'Because I had no luck. I'm beginning to wonder if he exists at all. I think it's just a name that Butcher made up. Something that came into his head. He wanted to get rid of me, so he produced this name and sent me off on a wild-goose chase. He wanted to protect the real person who was threatening Higgins, and who presumably killed them both.'

'You think he was lying?'

'Don't be so surprised. I think most of the people we've

169

talked to have been lying. Or at least not telling us the whole truth.'

'Marie O'Gorman?'

'Particularly Marie O'Gorman. I don't think she's told us half of what she knows. In fact the only person who has been totally honest with us is Mrs Nolan.'

Kelly looked across the café. It was beginning to thin out, people drifting off into the cold night. 'What about Marie O'Gorman's father?' he said. 'Of all the people we've interviewed, he has the strongest motive. He hated Higgins and he didn't sound like he had much time for Butcher either.'

'You're right,' Megarry said and looked at his watch. 'I suppose we'd better go and talk to him again.'

It was Mrs O'Gorman who came to the door this time. She was a small, mousy-looking woman who peered out at the two policemen and immediately retreated as soon as Megarry had declared their business.

'Charlie. It's for you. Two coppers here.'

O'Gorman's broad figure appeared in the hallway. He was in his vest. It seemed to Megarry that the same stubble was still on his chin. He advanced to the door and stood with his arms folded.

'You again?'

'Afraid so,' Megarry said.

'What do you want now?'

'There's some more questions we need to ask.'

'Jeeesus,' O'Gorman swore. 'I thought I told you everything you wanted to know the last time.'

'Not quite.'

They followed him into the lounge. The television was on. There was a soccer game in progress. A can of beer stood on the carpet beside the armchair.

'What is it?' O'Gorman said wearily and lifted the can from the floor.

'We found Marie.'

O'Gorman looked up. 'Oh. How is she?'

'She's fine. She's not living at St Martin's Gardens any more. She's moved out.'

'I'm not surprised. It was a dump. Why doesn't she come here, to her own home? There's always a place for her here.'

'Maybe you could answer that,' Kelly said.

O'Gorman looked up quickly. 'What do you mean? Has she been talking? Has she been saying things about me?'

Megarry coughed into his fist. 'Did you know that Eddie Butcher had been killed?'

O'Gorman swung his focus back. 'The Fat Man? Dead?'

'Yes,' Megarry said. 'The same weapon that was used to kill Higgins.' He kept his eyes on O'Gorman's face, watching for his reaction.

'They've crossed someone. That's what it is. You mark my words. This is all to do with drugs. They were a right pair. Dublin's a better place without them.'

He pulled up his vest and scratched his chest.

'You feel no emotion?'

'Are you kidding? Emotion? After what Higgins put me through?'

'Do you know a man called Joey Morton?'

'Never heard of him. Who is he? Another bleedin' druggie?'

'Do you have a weapon?' Megarry said. 'A gun? Smith and Wesson pistol?'

O'Gorman laughed.

'We could get a warrant to search the house.'

'Get all the warrants you like.'

He laughed again and took a swig out of the can.

'Why were you threatening Higgins?'

O'Gorman stared. 'What are you talking about?'

'You threatened him, didn't you? You forced him to leave home.'

'No, I bleedin' didn't.'

'You're lying.'

'What?'

'Just like you lied to us the last time we were here. You told us that Marie was using drugs. You told us that Higgins was beating her up. Lies, all lies.'

O'Gorman's mouth opened and quickly closed again.

'You were abusing her, weren't you?' Kelly said. He sat closer so that he was staring into O'Gorman's face. 'That's the real reason she left home. The real reason she took up with Harpo Higgins. It was because of you. Isn't that right?'

'No,' O'Gorman said. His face had gone pale. 'Keep your voice down. That's a terrible accusation. I don't want the missus hearing that.'

'Why not? It's true isn't it?'

'No. It's not. Did she tell you that?' He looked from one face to the other. 'Is that why you're here?'

'Partly,' Megarry said. 'We're here to find out the truth.'

O'Gorman was scared now, most of the jauntiness gone out of him. 'I told you the truth the last time.'

'No, you didn't.'

'Well maybe not about Marie. But everything I said about Higgins was the truth.'

'No,' Megarry said and shook his head. 'You told us lies. Why would you do that? Only a man who has something to hide tells lies.'

'Jesus,' O'Gorman said. 'What is this? Tell me what you want and I'll try to answer you.'

'Were you threatening Higgins?'

'Not really.'

'Not really? What does that mean?'

'I told you the last time. I told him if he ever showed his face around here again I'd break his neck. I warned him to stay away. But I never threatened him to leave his house.'

His mouth fell open. Suddenly the realisation rushed in on him. 'You think it was me, don't you? You think that I killed Higgins?'

'You had a reason. You had more reason than anyone else we've talked to.'

'No,' O'Gorman said. 'I'd nothing to do with it. Honest.'

'But maybe you know who did?'

'No,' O'Gorman pleaded. His hand was shaking now and he could scarcely hold the can. 'I'll tell you the truth. I'd no love for the guy. I'm glad he's dead. But you've got to believe me. I never killed him.'

20

Kelly left Megarry at Tara Street DART station. It was turning cold, a wind whipping up off the river. As Megarry got out of the car, the young man held his arm. 'What about tomorrow?'

'Ring me.'

'Okay.'

Megarry waited at the station entrance till the car disappeared into the traffic moving quickly along the quays. Then he pulled his jacket close against his chest and turned to the row of taxis waiting patiently at the rank. He pulled open the door of a cab and got into the back seat. 'Lancaster Gardens.'

The driver put down the paper he had been reading and started the engine. 'Where is it?'

'Ranelagh,' Megarry said.

It turned out to be a pleasant tree-lined street of Victorian houses. Number twenty-nine was half-way along. Megarry paid the fare and stepped out. It was dark and deserted, the street-lamps casting a pale glow on to the cold pavement. He pushed open the gate and walked quickly along the gravel path. He took out the little card he had been given and pressed the button for Flat Three. A woman's voice came buzzing over the intercom. It sounded distorted and he wasn't sure if it was her. He spoke his name into the mouthpiece.

'Who?'

'Cecil Megarry. I'm a policeman. We met at St Martin's Gardens. Remember?'

'What do you want?' she said. 'I'm busy right now.'

'I need to talk to you. It won't take long.'

'Can't you come back some other time? This doesn't suit.'

'No,' Megarry said firmly. 'It has to be now.'

There was a pause and then she said: 'You'd better come up. It's the top floor.'

He heard a click and the front door opened. He entered a wide hall with a staircase. There was a smell of paint. He started to climb, pausing for breath when he came to each landing.

Dee Dee met him at the door. She was wearing a silk dressing gown with a dragon motif. He thought she looked tired.

'What is it?' she snapped. 'I was just about to have a bath.'

'I've some more questions for you.'

She led him into the flat. It was a large place, tastefully decorated in pale pinks and yellows. The furniture looked new and expensive.

'I told you everything I know the last time we spoke.'

'Not everything.'

'No?'

She turned to face him. There was anger in her eyes. She is used to getting her own way, Megarry thought. She doesn't like this.

'You didn't tell me you were married to him.'

For a moment she stared and then her face broke into a smile. 'You didn't ask.' She ran her hand along a row of bottles in a cabinet. 'Can I get you a drink? If you've come to interrogate me, we might as well enjoy it.'

'I'll have a whiskey. Bushmills, if you've got it.'

'Of course. I've got everything here.'

Her attitude had changed. She fussed with an ice bucket.

'I didn't see you at the funeral,' Megarry said.

'I couldn't go. I was busy. I had a shoot.'

'A shoot?'

'Photographs. I was working. Modelling.'

'Of course,' Megarry said. He looked once more around the flat, the sumptuous drapes, the carpets. There were one or two little paintings that he recognised.

'You own this place?'

'Yes.'

'Modelling must pay well.'

'It pays very well. But it's very demanding. And a lot of the time it can be boring. Just hanging around waiting for people to make up their bloody minds. I'm thinking of getting out.'

She gave him his drink and sat down opposite. She pulled the dressing gown closer around her. She's beautiful, he thought. She's one of the most beautiful women I've ever seen.

'Were many there? At Harpo's funeral?' She took out a packet of cigarettes. Megarry remembered the scene in the little house in St Martin's Gardens when he had told her that Harpo was dead. The tears, the dramatics. Yet she couldn't even turn up when he was getting buried.

'No. Not many.' He leaned across and held out a match and she bent her face into the flame. 'His sister, Mrs Nolan. Some neighbours.'

'Mrs Nolan,' she said and puffed out smoke. 'Poor woman. She must have taken it hard. Harpo and her were very close.'

'Marie O'Gorman.'

She looked up quickly, then ran her hands along the dressing gown, straightening the folds.

'Why didn't you tell me you were married to him?'

'I didn't think it was important.'

'In fact you lied to me. When I asked you if he was married, you told me No.'

'Technically that was correct. Anyway, it didn't last long.'

'Long enough for you to have a child.'

She paused and studied him through the threads of smoke from her cigarette. 'You seem to know an awful lot about me.'

'It's my job. Finding out things.'

'You've been talking to Marie O'Gorman?'

'Yes.'

'I should have known,' she said. 'That's the real reason I didn't go the funeral. I didn't want to meet her.'

Megarry lifted his glass and took a sip of whiskey. 'She just told me her side of the story.'

176

'With a good spin against me, no doubt.' She sighed. 'It doesn't matter, I'm used to it by now.'

'Why don't you tell me about it,' Megarry said.

'There's not much to tell. It was all a mistake. A stupid mistake. I was only eighteen. Everyone makes mistakes when they are young.'

'But some mistakes last longer than others. Some mistakes last all your life.'

'Yes. That's true.'

She took Megarry's glass and recharged it and poured herself another drink.

'I met Harpo and fell in love. He was older than me and very good-looking. I was only a kid. Harpo was very exciting. I thought he was the most exciting guy in the whole world. Everybody was against it. Everybody told me I was mad. My friends, my parents. My father was furious. He wouldn't come to the wedding.'

'He was right.'

'Yes, he was right. But I didn't know that at the time. It was only later when things began to go wrong that I realised what I'd got myself into.'

'Where did you meet Harpo?'

'At a gig. He was a roadie with a band. He was in charge of the equipment. We used to travel all over the country. It was a great time, playing till the early hours, partying, sleeping till the afternoon.'

'Was that when he started using drugs?'

'Yes. Everybody was doing it. It was the scene at the time. But it was only small stuff. Blow mainly and sometimes a bit of skag. He was only skin-popping. I've told you all this before. Nobody dreamed he'd get addicted. We were so innocent.'

'And then the baby was born?'

'Yes. That's when the shit really hit the fan. My father went ballistic. He wanted me to leave Harpo and take the baby. I wanted Harpo to settle down and get a steady job. We were living in flats around the town, moving from place to place. It was no life. That's when the arguments began in earnest.

'Harpo got a job with a PR company promoting bands. It wasn't

177

bad for a while. We got the place in St Martin's Gardens and everything seemed to be going well. But then he started on the drugs again. He'd be going in to work doped up to the eyeballs, some days he wouldn't go in at all. In the end he lost the job.'

'He got other jobs.'

'Yes, for a while. He drifted in and out of jobs, but he lost them all because of drugs and in the end I had to go out to work. In a strange way he did me a favour. That's how I got into modelling.'

'He was working recently. For a company called Dempsey Engineering.'

She stubbed out her cigarette. 'Was he? I didn't know that.'

'When did you finally decide to leave him?'

'Nineteen ninety-one. He was getting impossible. You've no idea what it's like living with an addict. They only think about themselves and their drugs. Their whole life revolves around getting drugs, getting the money for drugs. It wasn't that Harpo was a bad guy. He wasn't. He was a very loving guy, very kind and gentle. But the drugs were taking control of him.

'I couldn't see myself being stuck in that house for the rest of my days with Harpo the way he was. He wouldn't work. He was living on the dole. He'd be gone half the night with his junkie friends, and when he was home he'd be going around stoned out of his head. Then he got busted. That was the final straw. I made up my mind to get the hell out of there and start a new life without him.' She was rattling on now, the words pouring out.

Megarry put up a hand to restrain her. 'Something you said. Harpo got busted?'

'Yes. He got done for possession.'

'Was he sentenced?'

'Sure. He got six months in Mountjoy.'

He leaned forward. 'How many times did he get done?'

'Several times.'

'When was the first time?'

She screwed up her face. 'About 1991. It was the summer. I remember that because he got busted at an open-air rock festival. Anyway that made my mind up for me. When he was released I told him I'd had enough.'

'And you left the child with him? What's his name?'

'Henry.'

'You left him with Harpo?'

'Yes. That was another mistake.'

'Why did you do that? Why didn't you take him?'

'I wanted to make a clean break.'

'Wasn't that a strange decision? To leave a child with a man who was abusing drugs? Didn't you care about the boy?'

'Of course I did. But I was confused and angry. We'd just had a big row about me going. I wasn't thinking straight. I just wanted to get away from him. I couldn't take any more hassle. I just wanted out.'

'But later you changed your mind and wanted the child back?'

'Yes. When I realised what I'd done. I still want him back.'

'And he wouldn't part with him. Why was that?'

'Who knows? Spite. He wanted to spite me for leaving him.'

'Maybe it was love. Maybe he loved the boy?'

She lowered her eyes. 'Yes. Maybe it was.'

Megarry took a deep breath. He looked at the beautiful woman sitting opposite him and thought about the turmoil in her life. There was a table lamp beside her and it cast a shadow on her face. He was suddenly reminded of a photograph he had seen, a young girl in a garden.

'You maintained your relationship with Harpo after the marriage broke up?'

'Yes. We were sort of friends. There was nothing sexual. Nothing like that.'

'Even after all the trouble over the child?'

'Yes,' she said. 'You can't hold grudges for ever.'

'How often did you see him?'

'Now and again.'

'The day I saw you at his house, what were you doing there?'

'I told you at the time. I was paying him a social call.'

'You told me he was a dealer.'

'So he was.'

'Did you go to his house looking for drugs?'

He saw the anger flare once more.

'Did Marie O'Gorman tell you that?'

'She didn't tell me,' Megarry said. 'I figured it out. That's the reason you backed off when you went to Harpo looking for custody of the child. He threatened to expose you. Isn't that right? He threatened to say that you were as bad as he was. You realised that it could ruin your career and you backed off.' He lowered his voice. 'How long have you been using drugs?'

'Since I was living with Harpo. But it was only toot. A little line now and again.'

'Toot?'

'Cocaine. I used it to relax. It can give you a buzz. Some people use alcohol. Other people use drugs. But I was never as bad as Harpo. I was never an addict.'

'And you're still using?'

'No,' she said and shook her head. 'Not any more.'

Megarry finished the whiskey in his glass. 'Who do you think did it? Who murdered Harpo?'

'I don't know. That's your job.'

'But you have a suspicion?'

'What use is suspicion? It's proof you need.'

Megarry stood up. 'What's your relationship now with your parents? Are they supporting you in this?'

'Of course.'

'Your father? Are you reconciled with him?'

'No,' she said. 'My father and I don't get on. It's not just the business with Harpo. It's . . . well . . . other things.'

She turned her face away and got up indicating clearly that the interview was at an end. She followed him to the hall. On the landing, she gripped his arm. 'Now that Harpo's dead, I'm Henry's only surviving parent. I want him back. I'm very determined. I'm going to commence legal proceedings.'

Megarry stopped.

'I expect you to be neutral in this. I don't want any of that shit about me not being a fit mother.'

'Where would you keep him?'

'Here with me. He'd want for nothing. He'd have a better life than Marie O'Gorman could ever give him.'

'It's not my business,' Megarry said. 'In the end it will be a matter for the courts. And the social workers. They'll decide.'

'I won't give up,' she said. 'Now that Harpo's dead, I won't give up.'

Outside, there was a big orange moon in an empty sky. He hurried along the street towards the bright lights on the main road and stood for a while waiting for a bus. He gave up and hailed a taxi and rode into the city centre. He got off at the bridge and walked through streets crowded with late-night revellers till he came to the station. He took the lift up to O'Toole's office. He knocked on the door and heard a voice telling him to come in.

The chief of the Drugs Squad had his long legs stretched on his desk. He was wearing the same leather jacket that Megarry remembered from the last time he'd been here. O'Toole was leaning back in a chair and scrolling through a computer screen. He seemed surprised to see Megarry.

'Sit down,' he said. 'Coffee?' He gestured towards the percolator on a little tray in a corner of the room.

'No thanks,' Megarry said coolly.

O'Toole slowly withdrew his legs from the desk and sat up straight. 'How's your cold?' he said.

'My cold?'

'Yes. The last time you were here you were sneezing all over the place. You were coming down with something.'

'That's gone now,' Megarry said. 'I'm fine.'

'It's this damned Irish weather,' O'Toole said. 'You never know what to expect. Warm one day, cold the next. Rain, wind. You never know what clothes to wear.'

Megarry studied the other man. He had been right the first time. There was an arrogance about him. Arrogance and now deceit.

'How is the case going?' O'Toole said. He stretched a hand and switched off the computer screen. 'Getting anywhere?'

'I'm not working on the case any more,' Megarry said. 'I was taken off it. Didn't you hear?'

O'Toole looked surprised. 'No. I didn't.'

'Well that's what happened.'

'So what are you doing here?'

'I came to ask you something.'

O'Toole seemed to catch the coldness in Megarry's voice. He sat back slowly in his seat. 'What is that?'

'Why did you withhold information about Higgins?'

Megarry saw the other man's face grow dark.

'What are you talking about?'

'Higgins had a record for drug possession. He served several prison terms. Why did you withhold that information?'

He saw O'Toole begin to smile. His chest shook and he was laughing. 'You're a cheeky Northern bollix,' he said. 'Coming here to my office and throwing around accusations. Who do you think you are?'

'Why didn't you tell us about Higgins's record when we asked?'

O'Toole stopped laughing. He leaned forward so that he was staring into Megarry's face. 'Have you spoken to Mulqueen about this?'

'Yes. He told me you were unable to come up with anything.'

'Did he now? Well there must have been a breakdown in communication. Yes sir. A breakdown in communication. I already gave Higgins's file to Mulqueen.'

Megarry's voice sounded small and subdued. 'When was that?'

'Last week. The day after you called here.'

O'Toole had started laughing again, a deep, sarcastic guffaw.

Mulqueen's office was in darkness. He rapped on the glass but there was no reply. He grasped the door handle and to his surprise it opened. He pushed the door and slipped inside.

He wondered if he should put on the light, but it might draw attention. He could feel his heart thumping now inside his shirt. He moved first to the big desk near the window. There was a thin light from the corridor outside. He rummaged in the debris on Mulqueen's desk. There were statements, progress reports, forensic files, but not what he was looking for.

One by one he tried the drawers but they were locked. He felt perspiration begin to break on his forehead. In a corner of the room, beside the door, stood a heavy metal filing cabinet. He pulled on the first drawer and it rolled out with a gentle clicking sound.

He paused and waited for approaching footsteps but no one came. He began to examine the contents of the drawer in the dim light. There was a bundle of green folders. They seemed to be in alphabetical order. He riffled through them till he came to H and started again, slowly this time.

It was stuck in the middle as if someone had carelessly jammed it in among the other files, a slim folder with an official stamp on it. He took it out and glanced at the cover. STRICTLY CONFIDENTIAL. PROPERTY OF THE DRUGS SQUAD.

He opened it and started to read. JAMES ANTHONY (HARPO) HIGGINS it said. CRIMINAL RECORD.

Book Three

21

Megarry slept badly. He dreamt of plane crashes and disasters, buildings collapsing, rivers bursting their banks. Once or twice he woke in the night to find Kathleen dozing gently beside him. He crept closer to her, put his arms round her and heard her mutter in her sleep. He thought of the previous day's events. He felt a sadness at the certain knowledge of betrayal. He fell asleep and dreamt that Mulqueen was lying on the cold slab in the morgue. Harpo Higgins was leaning over him. He turned to Megarry and his eyes seemed like empty sockets. He could smell his breath. It reeked of decay. 'He's dead,' Harpo said and pointed to Mulqueen. 'As sure as anything he's a goner.' The phone woke him. It was ringing downstairs in the hall. The room was flooded with sunlight. He looked at his watch and saw that it was half past eight.

There was a smell of breakfast cooking in the kitchen. He got out of bed and padded along the landing to the bathroom. He heard Nancy shouting to him from the hall. 'It's for you,' she said.

He imagined that it would be Kelly. He had promised to ring. He lifted the phone and heard a man's voice speak his name.

'Cecil?'

'Yes,' Megarry said.

'It's Harry Dempsey here. Did I get you out of b-bed?'

The unexpected voice confused him.

'Yes,' he said. 'I mean, no. I was up already.'

'I wanted to get you early. Before you went off for the d-day. I was going to ring you last night, but I didn't know what t-time you got home.'

'What is it?' Megarry said irritably.

'I was wondering if you could drop up to see me?'

'This morning?'

'Yes. Is that c-convenient?'

'I don't know,' Megarry said. He thought of his work with Kelly, the things he had to do.

'It won't take long,' Dempsey said. 'Just something I wanted to t-talk to you about.'

'Can you tell me what it is?'

'Not on the phone.'

'All right,' Megarry said reluctantly. 'I'll get up there as soon as I can.'

He had a shower and got dressed. When he went down to the kitchen, Kathleen and Nancy had already started breakfast.

'That was Harry Dempsey,' he said and smiled. 'He wants me to call up to see him.'

'Whatever for?' Kathleen asked.

Megarry shrugged. 'I haven't a clue. Maybe he's going to offer me a job.'

Nancy laughed but Kathleen kept her face straight and he realised that his sortie had misfired.

'This business you're working on,' she said. 'Is it any closer to completion?'

Nancy looked puzzled. 'Business?' she said and glanced from one to the other.

'Cecil is doing a little bit of work for someone. But he expects to have it finished by the end of the week. Don't you, dear?'

'Yes,' Megarry said meekly.

'Then we'll be able to get out of your hair, Nancy. You and Andrew will be able to get on with things without us getting in the way.'

'But you know we don't mind,' Nancy said quickly. 'We enjoy you here. You don't have to leave on our account.'

'We've been away from home too long. Cecil has to consider his options. He has to decide whether he's going to take early retirement. Cecil's not a young man any more. He wants to enjoy his life. And anyway, they don't appreciate him. I'm sick of telling him that.'

'I understand,' Nancy said and poured more tea into Megarry's cup. 'Sometimes wives can see things that their husbands can't.'

Megarry lowered his head and ate his meal in silence.

Claire Dempsey met him at the door and took him through the house and to the patio where Harry was waiting. There was someone else with him. As Megarry drew closer he saw that it was Paul Byrne. The young man got up and shook Megarry's hand.

'Beautiful morning,' he said.

'Yes.'

There was the sound of bird-song from a tree nearby.

'Sort of morning makes you glad to be alive,' Byrne said. 'Sort of morning makes you want to go for a swim or a good hard jog. Something physical.'

'Not for me,' Megarry said. 'A walk is about as much as I can manage.'

Byrne smiled. 'How is your case going?' he said and folded away a pen inside his coat pocket.

Megarry realised that every time they met he asked about the case. It was the only topic of conversation that they had between them. And he remembered how Byrne had helped him, had pointed him in the direction of Marie O'Gorman. 'I'm not working on it any more,' Megarry said.

'Really?' Byrne said with interest. 'Have you solved it? Have you got the murderer?'

'Not yet. But I think we will.'

'I hope you do,' Byrne said. 'There's too much crime in this city. Human life has become cheap.' He had a briefcase with him and some papers. He gathered them up quickly.

'Is there anything else?' he said to Dempsey.

'No,' Dempsey said and waved his hand. 'I think you have it

all there. Tell Stella I'll be delayed and I'll t-talk to her when I get in. Tell her just to monitor any phone calls.'

Byrne walked away across the lawn and they heard the sound of a car starting up at the front of the house.

'I'd be lost without him,' Dempsey said. 'My g-good right arm. Paul is the most loyal employee I have. He p-puts the interests of Dempsey Engineering first, last and always.'

Megarry remembered the previous conversation he had had in this garden, Harry lamenting the loss of his boy, drowned in a canoeing accident. I could have taught him the business, he had said, showed him all the little tricks. Was that what Byrne was to Dempsey? A surrogate son?

'Sit down,' Dempsey said and pulled out a chair. There was a newspaper folded on a little table beside him, the remains of a breakfast, orange peel, eggshells, bread crusts. Harry pointed to a delft pot and some cups. 'Have some c-coffee.' He lifted the pot and poured. 'Milk? Sugar?'

'Just milk, please,' Megarry said. 'I have to watch my weight.'

He saw Dempsey smile.

'A b-bit of exercise is all you need. You're not in b-bad nick. Now look at me.' He patted his stomach. He had a little paunch but otherwise he seemed fit.

Megarry could see that he was seeking to be complimented. 'You're in excellent shape,' the policeman said. 'It's your good life-style.'

Dempsey beamed. 'I try to take care of myself.' He turned his tanned face to Megarry. 'What age do you think I am?'

'I don't know. Fifty-five?'

'I'll be sixty next b-birthday.'

'You don't look that old.'

'Sometimes I feel it.' He sighed. 'Sometimes I feel very old.'

Megarry looked down along the lawn. There was a mist on the sea far out towards Dun Laoghaire. At the bottom of the garden, through the trees, he could see the gulls swooping and diving into the waves. There was a stillness in the air. When he listened, he could hear the sea lapping at the shore at the bottom of the cliffs.

'You know,' Dempsey said, 'there are d-days when I don't feel like going in to work. There are days when I just feel like sitting here and letting the world go by.'

'Why don't you?' Megarry said. 'Why don't you take it easy?'

'Because I have a b-business to run.'

'But you have other people don't you? You have a board, senior managers?'

'I have no b-board. I own the company lock, stock and b-barrel. Just me and Claire.' He waved his arm. 'I don't believe in b-boards. Too many busybodies poking their noses in. Too many p-people trying to tell you what to do. I believe in control. Total control. I told you that before.'

Megarry lifted his coffee cup and waited for Harry to come to the point of the visit, the reason he had brought him here.

'You know my company is worth a lot of money. I built it up from nothing, just a van and a shed. The b-bigger companies tried to put me out of b-business. They ganged up on me, tried to fix the prices, tried to squeeze me out. But I saw them off.' He lowered his voice. 'Sometimes I had to employ a b-bit of muscle.'

'Muscle?'

'Yes. Sometimes things happened. By accident of course. B-buildings went on fire. Lorries were destroyed. It was all right. They were insured. But they g-got the message.'

He smiled and Megarry recognised the pride in his voice, a poor boy from the Liberties taking on the might of the establishment and winning. It was clear to him that Harry would be a ruthless opponent.

He remembered the conversation this morning over the breakfast table, the refrain that Kathleen had been singing for months past.

'Maybe you should retire,' he said. 'Have you ever thought of that?'

Dempsey snorted. 'But what would I do? And who would run the b-business? I've no one to hand over to.'

'What about your daughter?' Megarry said quickly. 'What about her?'

'No.' Dempsey shook his head vigorously. 'She's not interested. She's got her own career. I tried to get her involved in the b-business when she was younger but she didn't c-care.'

He turned and looked at the policeman. 'Now if I'd had a son,' he said sadly. 'If Colum had lived, things would have been different. He could have d-done it.'

There was a pause. Megarry stared out over the sea. 'Tell me about your daughter.'

Dempsey shifted in his chair. 'We rarely see her. She visits us sometimes. She t-talks to Claire on the phone. She's closer to Claire than to me.'

'Why is that?'

Dempsey shrugged. 'Who knows? It's the way with g-girls and their mothers. Maybe she thought I was too strict when she was younger.'

Megarry thought fleetingly of his own daughter, Jennifer, the way he had neglected her when she was growing up, always working, never at home. He had punished himself for that.

'What does she do? For a living, I mean.'

'She's an actress.'

'That's an interesting career.'

'There's no m-money in it,' Harry said dismissively.

They sat for a moment in silence, then Dempsey said: 'So you see. To answer your question. I c-can't retire. There's no one to take it on.'

He laughed and pointed once more to the coffee pot. 'Some more?'

'No,' Megarry said. He had taken out his cigarettes. 'Do you mind if I smoke?'

'Not at all,' Harry said and pushed a little ashtray across the table. He cleared his throat. 'You're wondering why I asked you to c-come here. Well let me tell you. I have something I want to talk about. It's c-confidential, you understand that? Just between you and me?'

'Of course,' Megarry said.

'How much do you earn?'

The question surprised the policeman. He smiled. 'What on earth do you want to know that for?'

'D-don't be offended,' Dempsey said. 'I know already. I've made inquiries. You're a superintendent, isn't that right?'

Megarry felt his face flush.

'I know what you earn. It's not a lot. Not when you consider the work you put in, the stress, the responsibility, the long hours. P-policemen never stop working, even when they're away from the job. Not good policemen anyway. They're like good b-businessmen, except they don't get paid as well.'

Megarry said nothing.

'I have a proposition to put to you,' Dempsey said. He stretched his legs. 'I've been thinking.' He suddenly sat forward and pointed to the house. 'Look at this p-place. What do you see?'

'How do you mean?'

'It's wide open. I'm a sitting d-duck. Any little fucker who wanted to kidnap me could just walk in and do it.'

'Kidnap you? What put that idea in your head?'

Harry looked offended. 'Why not? They kidnapped a d-doctor only last month. Don't you think I'm worth more than a bleedin' d-doctor? Me and Claire. They could just come and get us any time they wanted.'

'But you have security gates and an alarm system. It wouldn't be that easy. Maybe you're exaggerating.'

'No,' Dempsey said. 'It worries me. I lie awake some nights thinking about it. There's p-people out there would like to steal my money. The money I've worked hard to earn.'

Megarry tapped ash from the end of his cigarette.

'Anyway,' Dempsey said. 'It's not just the house. It's the factory. Do you know how much thieving is going on in our p-place?'

Megarry shook his head.

'Thousands of pounds a year. Thousands of p-pounds. You should see the insurance bill. It would scare you. P-petty thieving, pilfering. F-fellas sticking things in their pockets when they're going home at night. They think nothing of it. They think it's a p-perk of the fucking job. It's costing us a fortune.'

'But don't you have security staff?'

'Of course. I hire a firm to guard the premises. But it's a waste of t-time. I'm thinking of setting up my own security system.' He looked at Megarry. 'How would you like to run it for me?'

Megarry gasped. 'Me?'

'Why not?' Harry said quickly. 'You're an experienced c-cop. You've seen it all. Terrorists, paramilitaries. You've been through the whole damned shooting gallery. This would be a piece of p-pie for you.'

Megarry smiled. 'I'm flattered. But I think you've got the wrong man. My wife wants me to get out altogether. Retire. Take it easy for the few years that are left to us.'

'B-but what would you do?' Dempsey said. 'You're like me. You love your work. And you're only a young man. Fifty-three . . .'

'How did you know that?' Megarry said.

'I told you. I made inquiries.'

Megarry frowned.

'Don't be upset,' Dempsey said. 'I only did what any sensible p-person would do. I want to hire someone for a job like this, I check them out.'

'What would be involved?' Megarry said.

'Setting up the system. Recruiting the staff. Making sure it runs smoothly. I'd p-pay you well. Make it worth your while.'

'Like what?'

'D-double your current salary. Company car. G-good expenses. I'd leave you alone. It would be your show. As long as you did your job, I wouldn't interfere.'

Megarry closed his eyes. He could hear Harry talking on, in his halting voice, the inducements pouring from his lips like a practised salesman. No wonder he had been successful.

'You could take early retirement, g-get your pension. Life here in Dublin can be very pleasant. I'd introduce you to p-people. You could join the yacht club, golf. I'd look after you.'

Harry suddenly leaned forward and put his arm around Megarry and pulled him close. 'What are you worried about? You could do it in your sleep.'

The policeman struggled free. 'It's just so sudden. I need time to think.'

194

'I'll give you a written c-contract. Five years. A legal c-contract. If it doesn't work out you can walk away. What have you g-got to lose?'

Harry sat back in his chair and Megarry heard him sigh.

'I'm giving you an opportunity. If I was you I'd grab it with b-both hands. It might never come again.'

Megarry stayed silent.

'You know sometimes in life things happen to you and you've g-got to go with them. It's the same in b-business. Sometimes you meet a challenge and you must face it. If you turn away, you spend the rest of your days regretting it.'

22

Kelly had suggested that they meet at a car-park at the bottom of Townsend Street. Megarry found it after getting lost a couple of times. He pulled open the front door of the car and got into the passenger seat.

The young detective was excited. 'Guess what? They've organised a press conference for tomorrow morning. Ten o'clock.'

'Who has?' Megarry was irritable. His wanderings through unfamiliar streets had not improved his temper. Now he found the perspiration beginning to form like a damp poultice on the back of his neck.

'Mulqueen, the superintendent. I even think they've roped in O'Toole. They've decided to bare their breasts. Make a public appeal for information. What do you think of that?'

'Whose idea is this?'

'The superintendent's.'

'They must be worried.'

'Sure they are. Two murders and the media on their backs asking difficult questions. Here, look at that.'

He gave Megarry an evening paper. A large black headline screamed: CRIME IN DUBLIN OUT OF CONTROL.

Megarry started to read: 'Detectives have admitted that they are no closer to solving the murders of two men in Dublin in the

196

last two weeks, Mr James Higgins and Mr Edward Butcher. Police sources have admitted privately that they believe the murders are linked and that they centre on a dispute over the control of drugs in the Inner City. However no early arrests are planned.'

He gave back the paper.

'The media always like easy answers. Something the public can understand. Something that can be packaged in a couple of simple sentences. Here you've got murder, drugs, gang warfare, inner-city poverty. All that's missing is sex and no doubt they'll get round to that eventually.'

He took out his cigarettes and wound down the window.

'What's happening at the office?'

'They're in a tizz, chasing their tails. The superintendent has drafted in more detectives from the Serious Crimes Squad. They've been told to drop everything and concentrate on the murders. Right now they're combing the files on every murder committed in the city right back to 1985. The trouble is these new guys aren't familiar with the cases and they're tripping over one another.'

'But it gives the impression of activity,' Megarry said. 'And in situations like this, that is very important.' He struck a match. 'How is Mulqueen?'

Kelly shook his head. 'Not good. Technically he's in overall control, but he's going to pieces. He looks like a man who's about to have a nervous breakdown. He can't take the strain. The superintendent is busy laying all the blame on to him.'

'There's nothing new under the sun,' Megarry said.

'You must be feeling some satisfaction,' Kelly said. 'They ordered you off the inquiry and now it's falling apart on them. I'll bet they're sorry now.'

'I get no satisfaction from seeing criminals go free.' Megarry blew out a plume of smoke. 'C'mon. We'd better get going.'

'Where to?' Kelly started the engine.

'North Circular Road. I want to talk to Marie O'Gorman again.'

Marie O'Gorman looked surprised when she found them once

more on her doorstep. There was a rattle of bolts and chains sliding from locks and the door was pulled wide. Earlier Megarry had spotted the little spyhole and knew they were being observed.

'Who were you expecting?' he said staring around the tiny flat. He noticed that she had even got bars put on the windows. He stood for a moment and let his eye travel along the dingy hall. 'You've enough security here to guard Fort Knox.'

Marie O'Gorman tossed her mousy hair. 'I feel safer this way. This is a tough neighbourhood. I don't like to take any chances. A woman like me, living on my own, with only a kid . . .' She let the sentence trail away.

He looked at her, the bags gathering beneath her eyes, the wrinkles, the occasional thread of grey along the temples. She would be no older than Dee Dee Clarke and yet the difference was enormous. In a few years' time she would be an old woman.

'What do you want?' she asked with an attempt at defiance. 'I thought you'd finished talking to me.'

'Not quite,' Megarry said. 'There are a few loose ends. Have you got a moment?' He smiled.

Marie O'Gorman sighed. 'I was about to go out,' she said.

'We could wait.'

'No. Let's get it over with.'

She turned away reluctantly and led them into a bare sitting-room. It was sparsely furnished, a settee and a table and a few chairs. There was a television in the corner of the room and a little pot with a spider plant. There were no pictures or ornaments, nothing that would give the place a homely effect, apart from the plant. There was a smell of cooking, minced meat, spaghetti, something like that.

'Where's Henry?' Megarry asked.

'At school. That's where I was going. I pick him up every day and bring him home for lunch.'

'Can't he stay at school? Don't they provide school meals?'

'They do. But I prefer to bring him home. I like to feed him myself. God knows what sort of gunge he'd get at school.'

198

Megarry nodded, not convinced. 'How much do you pay for this place?'

'Two hundred a month.'

'That's a lot of money,' Kelly joined in. 'For someone in your situation. Why don't you just go back to St Martin's Gardens?'

'I told you before. Too many bad memories.'

'But think of the money you'd save.'

Marie O'Gorman shrugged. 'It's complicated. Harpo owned the house jointly with his wife. Technically she owns it now, although God knows, she doesn't need it. Anyway, I can manage. I'm not complaining. I like it here.'

'Do you mind if we sit down?' Megarry said. 'Or if you like, we could drive you to the school. Talk on the way. When does school get out?'

'Half-twelve.'

'We've got time,' he said, checking his watch. 'This shouldn't take long.'

She sat down at the little table and waited patiently for the questions. Megarry had taken out a notebook and was flicking the pages. He smiled again to put her at ease.

'The last time we talked you said you left St Martin's Gardens because of a row with Harpo. That wasn't really true, was it?'

'It was true.'

'No,' Megarry said and shook his head. 'You left together. The table in the kitchen was set for three. You, Harpo and Henry.'

'How do I know what the table was set for? I was gone. I'd had enough. I told you that the first time.'

She looked from one policeman to the other.

Kelly sat back and folded his arms and let Megarry conduct the interview.

'You left together. Harpo was seen with a suitcase getting into a taxi. But you were already in the taxi, you and Henry. Isn't that right?'

'I don't know what you're talking about.'

'You do, Marie. You left together. You'd barely time to pack. You just gathered a few things and got to hell out. You went to

199

stay with friends till you got this place and Harpo went to his sister. Now why did you do that?'

She didn't reply.

'You fled that house as if your lives depended on it. You got a phone call, a letter, something like that. Some kind of warning. Someone was putting pressure on you and Harpo. Enough pressure to make you run. Isn't that what really happened?'

She lowered her eyes.

'Why don't you tell me?' he said softly. 'I'll get the truth in the end.'

'I can't.'

There was a tremor in her voice. She reached for her handbag and took out a packet of cigarettes. Megarry struck a match and held it for her.

'What are you afraid of?'

'Afraid? Who's afraid?' Her hand was shaking as she held the cigarette.

'For God's sake,' Megarry said. 'You won't go back to St Martin's Gardens. You've got this place barricaded like it was a prison. You don't even trust the kid to stay in school over lunchtime.'

He put a finger under her chin and raised her face.

'If you want us to get the people who murdered Harpo, you have to help us. Someone was threatening him. The pressure got too much and you both decided to flee. I thought at first it was some drug debt but I don't believe that now. I'll tell you what I believe.'

He took a deep breath. He could see Kelly watching him intently.

'It was to do with Henry.'

She gave a little cry.

'Dee Dee Clarke wanted him back. She's wanted him back ever since she split with Harpo. But Harpo loved the boy. He wouldn't let go. Then the rough stuff began, the threats, the bribes. You were worried that the boy was going to be kidnapped.'

He paused.

'Who is the Quare Fella, Marie?'

200

'I don't know. Honest to God.'

He took a letter from his pocket and spread it on the table. ' "Need to see you urgently. Tried ringing but no one in. The Quare Fella is very annoyed with you. Get in touch. Soon." That letter was found in Harpo's pocket when he was killed. If we knew who the Quare Fella was, we might be getting somewhere.'

They heard a church bell chime the half-hour.

She began to stand up. 'I'm late,' she said. 'I have to go.'

Megarry leaned out and held her wrist. 'You're trying to cover for someone. Why don't you trust me? Who was threatening Harpo? Was it Dee Dee Clarke? Was it someone acting on her behalf?'

'I don't know. Honest.'

She shook her head and struggled to get up.

'You've got to help me. I can't do this on my own. Who was threatening Harpo? Who made the phone call that caused you to abandon the house?'

She hung her head.

'Who was it?'

'I don't know.'

'You're not leaving here till you tell me.'

He saw the desperation in her face. 'The Fat Man,' she said. 'It was Eddie Butcher.'

'Eddie Butcher? You told me he and Harpo were good friends.'

'They were good friends. But then he started leaning on Harpo. He kept telling him he'd have to give Henry back, but Harpo refused. At first it was kind of friendly advice. You know, one good pal to another. Then it got heavier, threats of violence. He tried to stab Harpo once. In the end, Harpo was terrified of him.

'That letter you just read. He got that about a week before he was killed. Harpo went to meet him and Eddie Butcher said that if Henry wasn't given back, then matters would be taken out of his hands.'

'What did that mean?'

'Harpo took it to mean he was going to get killed.'

'And the morning you left St Martin's Gardens? What happened then?'

'Harpo got a phone call. I'll never forget it. He'd had a bad night. He'd no drugs and he was strung out. You know, the shakes, stomach cramps. He was in a bad way. The phone rang and this man asked to speak to Harpo. He took the call and when he came back it was as if he had seen a ghost. He said they were coming to get him.'

'Who?'

'I don't know, but Harpo was terrified. He said we'd have to get out, for me to take Henry and he'd get in touch. We just packed a couple of bags and rang a taxi. It was like you said.'

'This Quare Fella that's mentioned in the letter. You've no idea who that might be?'

She shook her head. 'No.'

'And was that the last time you saw Harpo?'

'No, he came to visit us a few times, brought things for Henry, little toys, things like that. He loved the boy. It was breaking his heart to be separated from him.'

She stubbed out her cigarette. 'I'll have to go,' she said. 'I don't like leaving him there on his own.'

'We'll take you,' Megarry said.

He motioned to Kelly and they both stood up.

He put his arm around her and whispered in her ear, 'Don't worry. We'll protect you. We'll find those responsible.'

They drove to the school and waited while Marie O'Gorman picked up the boy, then took her back again to the flat. She fussed over the child, holding him tight by the hand and cuddling him. As they left her, Megarry said: 'We'll arrange a guard for you. Someone to keep an eye out.'

She started to protest but he silenced her.

'It'll be low-key. You won't even notice. It's better. Just till we get this business sorted out. You'll feel safer.'

He turned to walk back to the car and suddenly she put her arms around him and kissed him. He could see that her eyes were filled with tears.

'Thank you,' she said. 'You're a good man.'

202

'It's okay. You should have come to us sooner.'

He was about to say that it might have saved Harpo's life, but he decided not to. Who was to tell? They weren't omnipotent. They couldn't cover all eventualities.

He got into the car and waved goodbye. The last time he was to see her, she was standing at the door of the flat, holding the boy close to her side, the sun casting long shadows across the grey pavement.

They drove back into town. As they got closer to the river, he spoke to Kelly. 'Where is the registry of births, deaths and marriages?'

'Pearse Street, I think.'

'Take me there.'

It was a drab building of black stone. It felt warm, as if the central heating was turned up too far. There was a smell of polish and papers long kept in filing cabinets. A busy little man in an official uniform showed them up to the second floor.

There was a long hall like the reading room of a library. A few people sat at tables, poring over documents. All was silent.

Behind a desk was a middle-aged woman with spectacles and a cardigan. She smiled as the two men approached. 'Can I help you?' she asked in a subdued voice.

'I want to check some information about a marriage,' Megarry said.

'What name?'

'Higgins. James Anthony Higgins.'

'And the date?'

'I'm afraid I don't know that.'

'Do you know where the ceremony was performed?' The woman was brisk and efficient.

'No,' Megarry said.

'Was it Dublin or some other part of the state?'

'Dublin, I think.'

'Take a seat,' the woman said and pointed to an empty desk.

The two men sat down and waited. Megarry thought of the last time he had been in a place like this. The Central Library in Belfast. He had been seeking information about Barbarossa. A Barbary Pirate, a Holy Roman Emperor, the code name for a

203

military operation against the Soviet Union. It had helped to unmask a murderer.

He looked up quickly when he saw the woman return. She had some papers in her hand. She sat down across the desk from them and straightened them out.

'Do you want to write this down?'

Megarry searched for his notebook and pen.

'James Anthony Higgins, bachelor, of Seagrove Terrace, Ballymoss, Dublin, was married on 20 May 1987 at St Margaret's RC church, Howth, County Dublin.'

'And the bride's name?'

'I was coming to that,' the woman said. She consulted the papers once more. 'The bride was Deirdre Dempsey of Elsinore, Bailey, Howth.'

23

George Buchanan watched Megarry and Kelly leave Marie O'Gorman's flat on the North Circular Road. He turned away as their car approached and pretended to look into the window of a chemist's shop, waiting till they had passed.

He had followed them from the car-park in town, just as he had earlier followed Megarry from Howth, sitting further along the carriage with his head buried in a newspaper, as the train rattled past Kilbarrack and Killester and into Tara Street. He'd been following Megarry all day.

He had first picked him up the previous night when he had visited Dee Dee out in Ranelagh. George had been watching her house, noting everyone who approached. Most of the people had been innocent enough. But there was something about Megarry's plump figure which struck him as different. He had stood under the trees across the street from her flat and watched the policeman enter. Megarry had stayed in the house for over an hour and when he finally left, George had trailed him back to Barrack Street station. That's when George had decided he must be a cop.

The knowledge filled George's head with all kinds of possibilities. What was Dee Dee doing with a cop in her flat? Maybe he was from the Drugs Squad? Maybe she'd been busted. His first instinct was to ring the Quare Fella, but then he realised that it was too late. He'd be gone home for the night and he never liked being bothered at home.

Some cunning, some caution, caused George to pause, to find out more. He waited till Megarry left the police station and he followed him out to Howth, all the way up the hill from the train station, keeping in the shadows, out of the light, watching as he entered the house and closed the big front door firmly behind him.

George had gone home to bed. He had lain awake for a long time trying to figure out what was going on. He didn't like getting involved in anything to do with the police. And then he thought of that other thing he had seen and he felt fear creep over him. Maybe it was time to see the Quare Fella and tell him he was getting out.

He watched now as the car with the two policemen disappeared up the street and he started to walk quickly away. There was a cold breeze, a spring breeze coming in from the sea, and George pulled his jacket up closer around his chest to keep warm. He saw the sign for Hourican's pub and he nipped smartly inside.

It was cosy, a fire blazing in the grate, a television set showing the racing on a little shelf on the wall. George took off his dark glasses and looked quickly round the bar. There was only a handful of drinkers at this time of the day, pensioners, mostly, by the look of them. George felt in his pocket for his last remaining twenty-pound note.

He ordered a pint and turned to look for the phone. It was at the end of the room. While the barman was pouring, George made up his mind. He lifted the instrument and heard the coins drop into the box.

'I want to speak to Harry Dempsey,' he said.

There was a pause and he heard the switchboard put him through.

It was Harry's secretary. 'Mr Dempsey is busy,' she said.

'Not too busy for this,' George said in a rush of disregard. 'Tell him it's George Buchanan. Tell him it's urgent.'

There was another pause. George wished now that he'd had a drink before he had done this, a small one to bolster his spirits.

The seconds seemed to tick away and then he heard Harry's stammering accent on the line.

He looked around to make sure there was no one within earshot and lowered his voice. 'It's me. George.'

'What do you want?'

'I've got something for you, Harry. About Dee Dee.'

'What about her?'

'I've been keeping an eye on her, like you said. I've got news for you.'

'Jeeesus,' Harry said. 'I'm a b-busy man. What is it? Get to the point.'

George glanced nervously over his shoulder and cupped a hand closer around the phone. 'I don't trust this bleedin' thing, Harry. I'd rather talk to you face to face.'

'You're wasting my t-time.'

'No. Listen. The cops have been to see her.'

'The c-cops?'

'Yes, Harry. The bleedin' cops.'

He heard a sharp intake of breath.

'Where are you?'

'North Circular Road.'

'Hop in a c-cab. I'll see you here in twenty minutes. Tell the security man to let you through.'

'Game ball,' George said and put down the phone.

Harry met him in his office, the big office at the top of the building with the view out over the bay and the Dublin mountains. He seemed to be in good form. He pulled out a chair and sat George down.

'Cigar?' he said and pulled a wooden box from a drawer in his desk and pushed it towards him.

'No, thanks,' George said. 'I don't smoke.'

'Drink?' Harry got up and walked to the drinks cabinet. 'What would you like?'

'I'll have a whiskey, Harry, if that's all right.'

'Sure, it's all right. You're my g-guest. I always treat my g-guests well.' He poured the drink and brought it back and gave it to George. 'You ever been up here before?'

George shook his head.

'Look at that view,' Harry said and waved his hand.

George followed with his gaze.

'You ever see a view like that?'

George might as well have been looking at a field of potatoes. 'No.'

Harry nodded. 'You're a D-dublin man, George, aren't you? You were b-born in Dublin?'

'Yes,' George said and sipped his whiskey. 'Inchicore.'

'You should be p-proud of your city. Do you know what's wrong with this p-place? Too many begrudgers. Too many p-people always trying to drag things down. There's not enough p-positive thinking. That's what the country needs instead of all this wheedling and c-carping.'

He sat down again at his desk. Harry had his shirt-sleeves rolled up to the elbows and George noticed the firm muscles along his forearms, the little freckles from too much sun. He remembered what he had heard Dee Dee say that night in Jangles about how Harry had smashed a man's arm with a blow of his hand.

'I'm sorry if I sounded a b-bit sharp on the phone earlier,' Harry said. 'I didn't realise it was you. I'm up to my t-tonsils with work right now.'

'That's all right, Harry. I know you're a busy man.'

'You've no idea.'

George sipped his whiskey and waited.

'Anyway. What were you saying about Dee Dee?'

'I've been following her, like you asked. I thought I'd touch base and bring you up to date. I don't think there's much more I can do. It's cost me a pile of money,' George said quickly. 'She goes to Jangles a lot. Five bleedin' quid to get in and then it's £30 for a bottle of champagne. Not to mention taxis and all the rest of it.'

Harry nodded. 'Has she been keeping clean? No drugs?'

'I couldn't swear to it. I've seen her a few times and she looked to me like she was tanked up.' George tried to pick his words carefully. He didn't want to offend Harry. 'Anyway, I thought I'd just tell you. Collect my expenses, like, and call it a day.'

'You said something about the c-cops?'

'The cops were at her place last night. Well one cop. Plump guy. Lives out in Howth near you, Harry.'

Harry thought for a moment. 'It could be nothing,' he said dismissively. 'It could have been a p-parking ticket.'

'I don't think so. I followed this guy again this morning. Him and another younger cop. This time they went to Marie O'Gorman's flat on the North Circular Road.'

'And?'

'You know who she is, Harry. She's Harpo Higgins's mot.'

He saw Harry's face darken.

'Where does she live?'

'Near Dorset Street. I wrote it down.'

George pulled a piece of paper from his pocket and gave it to Harry.

'You're g-getting low,' Harry said and got up once more and filled up George's glass. 'Tell me about this c-cop. The one who lives in Howth.'

'He's a middle-aged guy. About fifty, I'd say. Five feet ten or eleven. Plump. Going bald.'

'Did you speak to him?'

'No way. Are you kidding?'

'Did he see you?'

George shook his head and took another sip at his whiskey. 'I made quite sure of that.'

Harry sat for a while and stroked his chin. 'It could be nothing,' he said again. 'You could be reading too much into this.'

'But what about Harpo Higgins?' George said.

'What about him?'

'He was murdered.'

'I know that.'

'But Dee Dee and him were married weren't they? And then Marie O'Gorman. Maybe the cops are on to something.'

'No,' Harry said. 'It's nothing. Just your imagination.'

'My imagination?'

'You're putting two and two together and coming up with six.'

'There's something else,' George said in desperation. He gulped his whiskey. He wasn't sure how to say this. 'I saw Paul Byrne and Dee Dee together the other night. In Jangles. She was on something, Harry. She was flying. It struck me . . .'

'Yes?'

'Maybe he's the one's supplying her.'

Harry shook his head. 'Not at all. They're friends. He was probably looking after her, keeping her out of trouble.'

'I saw him one other night. The night Harpo was murdered. In Brannigan's Bar. He was with Harpo. They left together.' The words came tumbling out and George felt a terrible release, mixed with a feeling of fear.

'You saw *what*?'

'I saw Harpo with Paul Byrne. They were up at the bar drinking and then they left together.'

For a moment, Harry said nothing. There was a stillness in the room. Then his face spread in a smile. 'I know all about that. I sent P-paul to talk to him.'

'You did?'

'Harpo used to work here. P-poor devil lost his job because of these bloody drugs. He didn't show up for a medical. I asked P-paul to go and talk to him, see if we couldn't take him back. I felt sorry for him.'

'Ah,' George said and felt relief wash over him like a wave. 'So that's what it was all about.'

'Sure,' Harry said. 'What did you think?' He was smiling again. 'You know you should have been a detective, George. You've got the nose for it. And you've g-got a suspicious mind.'

He opened a drawer in his desk and took out a cheque-book. 'These expenses you were t-talking about. What do I owe you?'

George did a quick calculation. 'There's Jangles, there's taxis, there's meals, there's bottles of champagne. I've no receipts, Harry. They don't give you receipts in Jangles.'

'That's all right.'

'Five hundred?' George said quickly.

Harry had a pen out and was starting to write. 'Five hundred for your expenses and say I give you f-five hundred more for your work. A thousand p-pounds. A nice round figure. Are you happy with that?'

'Sure,' George said, trying not to appear too enthusiastic.

Harry wrote out the cheque and gave it to George. He stood up and stretched out his hand and George grasped it. 'You've done g-good work watching Dee Dee. I worry about her. She's so headstrong. I suppose she g-gets it from me. You've no idea the worry that daughters bring. I don't want her to g-get into trouble, mix with the wrong types.'

'I know,' George said. He finished his drink and put the empty glass on Harry's desk. 'You should see the crowd they're lettin' into Jangles now.'

'How are you g-getting back?'

George thought of the few pounds that he had left. He would have to get to a bank at once, cash Harry's cheque. 'I'll get a bus.'

'No you won't. You'll g-get a taxi.' He lifted the phone and started to ring. Then he put it down again. 'I've a b-better idea. Wait here.'

He got up and left the room.

George stretched out his legs. He was feeling good. The whiskey, the cheque, the knowledge that Paul Byrne's meeting with Harpo that night had been innocent after all. It was like a weight had been lifted from his shoulders. Harry was right. He did have a suspicious mind.

He heard footsteps approaching and voices in the corridor outside. The door opened and Harry was back. Paul Byrne was with him. He had car keys in his hand and he rattled them on the end of their chain.

'Now, George,' Harry said. 'Where do you have to g-go?'

'Town.'

'Paul will drive you. Won't you P-paul?'

'Pleasure,' Byrne said.

They had left Kelly's car on double yellow lines in a side-street near the Registry building. It was the only place they could find.

As they hurried back along the street, Megarry said to the young detective, 'Have you got your personal weapon?'

Kelly pulled back the flap of his coat to show the revolver in its leather shoulder holster.

'Fine,' Megarry said and waited while Kelly fumbled with the car keys. He settled into the front seat and pulled on his safety-belt.

'Where to now?'

Megarry checked his watch. It was almost two o'clock. 'Dempsey Engineering. It's out by Clontarf. I'll give you directions.'

They went along Pearse Street and Tara Street and over the bridge. There was a brittle sun in the sky and it felt cold, as if rain was threatened. The Custom House shone white in the pale afternoon light.

Megarry sat silent as they passed the river and out by Fairview. There was a schoolboy soccer game in progress in the park and he saw Kelly turn his head to watch. He remembered what he had told him about his boy. 'How is Jamie?'

'He's grand.'

'Still playing football?'

'Yes. He has a game today. Seeing those kids back there reminded me.'

The reply told him all he needed to know. 'Spend time with him,' Megarry said gravely. 'Remember my advice.'

'When?'

'Just make time.'

He closed his eyes and for a moment it appeared as if he had gone to sleep. He thought of the way events had spun out. He had come here to recuperate, intending to relax, and instead he had become embroiled in this. Had he sought it out, or did it seek him?

He thought of those lazy mornings, walking Howth Head in the sun, the afternoons fishing from the rocks, the dart games with Andrew in the Anchor Bar, the relaxing pints in the Royal Hotel where he had first met Harry Dempsey.

It had all gone so fast, and now it was coming to an end. Tomorrow or the day after, he would have to return to Belfast.

What would he do then? Go and talk to Chief Superintendent Drysdale and tell him what? That he was leaving? That he was bowing to Kathleen's wishes and taking early retirement?

It was a decision that he had been putting off, hoping in some strange way that it would solve itself, that the answer would come by some magical process that would require no effort of will from him. He knew in his heart that things didn't happen like that. Very soon he would have to make his choice.

He opened his eyes again as they were going past the yacht club. He could see the boats, their tall masts jangling in the breeze. He tapped Kelly lightly on the shoulder. 'Next turning on the left.'

They went along a street of fine houses, large, neat gardens. A few cherry trees were in blossom, their petals like a pink carpet on the grass.

He saw the engineering complex rising before them, the flat roofs of the factory, the shining glass of the administration building. There was a security boom in place, a man in uniform checking cars as they went in and out.

They slowed down as they approached, and at that moment, the boom was raised and a car came out, a new BMW with two men in the front seats. One of them was wearing sun-glasses, the other man, the driver, looked like a businessman, nice new suit, white shirt, neatly trimmed fair hair.

Megarry craned his neck to look but the car was picking up speed now, accelerating away.

The security man kept the boom raised, waiting for them to approach.

'Pull in,' Megarry said urgently. 'Turn the car.'

Paul Byrne took the car along Verdon Avenue and out on to the main road. He had the radio on. It was playing dance music and Byrne tapped his hand to the rhythm. He turned to speak to George. 'Why do you wear those glasses?'

'Because the light hurts my eyes.'

'They're stupid. Did anyone ever tell you that, George? They're old-fashioned. They draw attention to you.'

'Do they?' George said. He'd never considered that before.

'Sure they do. You go into a pub with those things on and everybody turns to look. The work you do, you need to be unobtrusive, melt into the background. Those sun-glasses make you stick out like a sore thumb.'

'Right,' George said and took off the glasses and put them in the breast pocket of his suit.

'That's better,' Byrne said. 'Now you look normal.'

George thought of the cheque he had in his pocket. A thousand lids. Harry had been very generous. He could have been sticky, asking for receipts and details of expenditure. He supposed Harry would write it off against his income tax.

His admiration for Harry swelled. A self-made man, a real Dub, who never forgot where he came from. That little speech about being proud of the city. He was dead right. There were too many knockers, too many whingers, complaining all the time, expecting the Government to do everything for them. What the country needed was a few more people like Harry. People who got things done.

He thought what he would do with the money. He owed a few bob rent on the flat. He'd pay that off and maybe he'd get some new clothes. He might even take a little break somewhere. He'd been working hard. He deserved a break.

Everything had turned out fine in the end. He looked at the man beside him and saw Byrne smile.

'Music bothering you, George?'

'No, it's game ball.'

He thought of the way he had doubted Byrne, the suspicions he'd harboured and in the end it had all been so simple. A job for Harpo. That was typical of Harry, looking after the underdog. And after all the hassle that Harpo had given him over the marriage to Dee Dee and everything.

The traffic was heavy on the road, trucks heading into the docks.

'What are you going to do now?' Byrne said. 'Anything lined up?'

'Not at the moment. I might take a break.'

'You should talk to Harry,' Byrne said. 'He could find

something for you. Something permanent. He's thinking of setting up his own security system.'

'Oh,' George said.

'Yeah. You wouldn't believe the thieving that's going on in that place. Petty pilfering. It's costing the company thousands. You should see the insurance bill.'

'Do you think he could use me?'

'Sure he could. A bright guy like you. And you've already got the inside track. He thinks very highly of you, George. He told me so.'

'Right,' George said. 'Maybe I'll do that.'

'Tell him you talked to me.'

'Game ball,' George said.

They'd got stuck behind a delivery truck, the traffic almost down to a crawl.

'Tsk, tsk. We'll never get into town at this rate,' Byrne said and swung the car into a side-street at the next junction. 'We'll take a short cut.' He put his foot down on the accelerator and the car surged forward.

George looked at the houses flashing by in a blur of colours. 'I could always get out and take a bus,' he said.

'Not at all. I'll drive you.'

George sat back and thought of what Byrne had just said. A job with Harry. A permanent job. A steady income. No more rushing around from pillar to post, huddling in corners of pubs, listening to people's conversations. And he'd be good at it. Security. Didn't Harry just say that he'd make a good detective?

Byrne was pushing the car hard, taking corners in a screech of brakes and burning rubber. They came out at another road and then another.

George struggled to get his bearings. 'You're sure you know where you're going?'

Byrne smiled. 'Of course.' They passed a church and a cinema.

George turned his head as they went by. He recognised the church. He spoke to Byrne. 'You're going the wrong way. You're heading back out of town.'

'Relax.'

215

George felt panic grip him. Something was wrong. He glanced at Byrne and saw that his face had grown hard and intent. Byrne turned up the radio and the music flooded the car.

'What the hell?' George said, but Byrne didn't reply.

They had turned off the road again and were entering an industrial estate. It seemed to have been abandoned, buildings boarded up, windows broken, glass and debris littering the ground.

Byrne pulled the car in and stopped. There was no one in sight. George saw the overgrown grass, the weeds sprouting from the footpaths, a burnt-out car like a beached whale in the middle of the road. He felt his heart hammering in his breast. He reached for the door and struggled to get out, but Byrne detained him.

He had taken a heavy pistol from his pocket.

'Jesus,' George said and put his hands up to his face. He felt his body shake with fear.

'I'm sorry about this,' Byrne said. 'I genuinely am. Trouble is, George, you know too much.'

'Please. I don't know nothing.'

'You know enough to put me and Harry away.'

He pointed the gun at George's head and pushed open the door. 'Get out of the car, George, and kneel on the ground.'

He unhooked the safety-belt and shoved George on to the road. George fell in a heap. He struggled to get up but Byrne's hand was on his neck.

'You should have done as you were told, George. Just kept an eye on Dee Dee. That's all Harry wanted you to do. But you had to go and get involved with me and Harpo Higgins.'

'I couldn't help it. I just saw you. I can forget all about it.'

'You'll forget it all right.'

George heard a sharp click as the revolver was cocked. He saw the sun glinting off the burnt-out car. My God, he thought, is this to be my last sight on earth? 'Let me say my prayers.'

'You've got thirty seconds.'

The words came trembling out. 'Hail Mary, Mother of God . . .'

There was another sound, the screeching of car brakes, a door

216

being slammed. George felt the gun being removed from his neck. He turned to see.

The fat cop was running along the road and another man beside him. He had a pistol held in both hands and he was roaring.

24

Claire Dempsey met him at the door. She had an apron on and there was a smell of cooking coming from the kitchen.

She looked surprised to see him. 'I'm just preparing dinner,' she said. 'If you like, I could . . .' And then she saw Kelly, standing behind Megarry. She looked from one policeman to the other, the grim set of Megarry's jaw. 'It's Harry you want. Isn't it?'

'Yes, Mrs Dempsey.'

She led them through the house and out to the patio without saying a word. Dempsey was sitting at the little table. He had a glass of wine beside him and books and papers spread out. The evening was coming down, the light fading over the bay.

He stood up when he saw them come through the kitchen. 'Cecil, why didn't you ring?'

'I didn't have time,' Megarry said.

He turned to Kelly and introduced the two men.

'Sit down,' Dempsey said. 'Can I offer you a d-drink? Claire . . . ?'

'It's all right,' Megarry said quickly. 'Don't bother her. We won't be drinking.'

He lowered himself into a chair beside Harry. The dog appeared and sniffed at Megarry's trousers, then disappeared down the lawn.

'You know why we've come?' Megarry said.

Harry smiled. 'You've come to accept my offer. The job we t-talked about.'

Megarry sighed. 'On another occasion, perhaps, that might have been attractive.'

'It's still available.'

'No.'

In the chair beside him, Kelly shifted.

'We arrested Paul Byrne this afternoon,' Megarry began. 'He's been charged with two counts of murder. James Higgins and Edward Butcher. And a further charge of attempted murder on George Buchanan.'

Dempsey lifted his glass and sipped his wine. 'What's that got to do with me?'

'He has signed a statement implicating you.'

'What?' Dempsey said and put the glass down so firmly that some wine spilled on to the table.

'He claims that he was acting on your instructions.'

'The b-bastard.' Dempsey's face had gone red. 'There's loyalty for you,' he said. 'I've given that g-guy everything. I've treated him like he was my own son. G-good job, g-good salary, nice car.'

'Nevertheless,' Megarry said quietly, 'we have his statement.'

'I'll c-contest it. It's only his word against mine.'

'We may have other witnesses.'

'Who?'

'I'm not at liberty to say right now.'

Dempsey turned away and Megarry heard him curse under his breath. 'Jesus Christ,' he said. 'Is this what you've c-come here to tell me? A heap of bloody lies made up by an ungrateful bloody b-bastard?'

'Ungrateful?' Megarry said. 'Hardly that. He murdered to protect you.'

'He's a psychopath. He enjoys violence. He has a criminal record.'

'I know that. But you found him useful. You encouraged him. What was it you once said to me? "Paul does my dirty work for me." You needed someone like Byrne around you. Someone who wasn't afraid to use violence, who was prepared to murder if necessary. You paid him well, looked after him. You're very good at manipulating people. It's all part of this philosophy of control that you are so proud of.'

'He's a liar,' Dempsey said. 'A criminal. I took pity on him. And this is the thanks I get.'

Megarry waited for the anger to abate.

'Why do they call you the Quare Fella?' He spoke softly.

Dempsey laughed. 'It's just a name. A D-dublin expression. You Northerners wouldn't understand it.'

'What does it mean?'

'Quare, queer. It's an expression of respect. I g-got it first when I was building up my b-business. People looked up to me. They admired me for the way I d-did things.'

'The way you used muscle? The way you burnt your competitors' vehicles, flooded their premises, intimidated drivers?'

Dempsey waved his hand. 'It was them or me. They were trying to force me out. I fought b-back. There's nothing wrong with that. Let me tell you something I've learnt. There's no morality in b-business.'

'But there is in life.'

'Look,' Dempsey said. 'I came from nowhere. I had no silver spoon in my mouth. I was up against all these v-vested interests. Guys with good educations, all the right connections. They looked down their noses at me. They tried to squash me, the way you would squash a worm or a b-beetle. What was I supposed to do?'

It seemed to Megarry that Dempsey was proud of what he had done. He showed no shame. He had used the only tools available to him. Cunning, ambition, determination, the tricks he had picked up struggling for survival in the back streets around the Liberties. There was no doubting that he had been successful.

He looked down along the lawn to the trees. He could hear the sound of the sea washing along the shore. He remembered it from the first time he had come here, the night of the party.

220

'Do you mind if I smoke?' Megarry said. 'The boy. Henry. He's named after you, isn't he?'

'What?'

'You opposed your daughter Dee Dee marrying Higgins. You felt he was too wayward, too disorganised. You didn't like his attitude to life, the way he drifted along without ambition. You felt that he might be marrying her to get at your money. So you broke with her over it.'

'I was right, wasn't I?'

'Given that the marriage didn't last and Higgins turned increasingly to drugs, I suppose you *were* right. But there was also something decent about Higgins. He loved that boy. And as he sunk deeper into addiction and his marriage broke up, he tried to care for him, to hold on to him. He bought him little presents, toys.

'You were happy to see the marriage break up, but you were devastated when Dee Dee left the boy with Higgins. You wanted a son. Desperately wanted a replacement for your real son, Colum, who was drowned. But there was nothing you could do. Higgins was his natural father after all.

'After a while, you persuaded Dee Dee to go to Higgins and try to get Henry back. But he saw her off, threatened to reveal the fact that she was also a drug user. If it came to court it would be one unfit parent versus another. And she had walked out on the child. Plus there would be all the dirty linen washed in public.'

It was growing dark and the lights were coming on along the southern shore. Dempsey sat quietly in the gloom, his hands pressed in his lap.

'You decided that if you held on, Higgins would eventually end up in prison and you would get custody. And in fact he did go to prison. Several times. But by then, Marie O'Gorman had come on the scene, and she was providing some kind of stability for the boy. So in the end you decided to apply some of the tactics that had made you successful in business. Threats, bribes, intimidation.

'You gave Higgins a job in your factory, hoping to win him over. He didn't even have to go for an interview. That's why when I checked with your personnel department they couldn't find any application from him. But it didn't last. His addiction was too far gone and there was no prospect of him holding down a steady job. So then you began to lean on him. You used an old contact from the days when you were starting up in business. One of your muscles. The Fat Man. Eddie Butcher.'

He drew softly on the cigarette. Kelly sat beside him, listening carefully. Dempsey stared out over the sea.

'Butcher had known Higgins for a long time. He was a drugs dealer. Higgins owed him money. Butcher began to threaten him, to suggest it would be better for him to give up the boy. He offered him drugs, he suggested that he would forgo the debts. He threatened him with a knife. But still Higgins resisted. So in the end you resorted to murder.'

The word seemed to shatter the silence of the garden. For a moment no one spoke and then Dempsey stirred in his chair and lifted the glass of wine.

'This is all supposition. Eddie B-butcher is dead.'

'I'm coming to that,' Megarry said. He tapped ash from his cigarette. 'Paul Byrne murdered Higgins after luring him to Brannigan's Bar. He took him to the quays and shot him. He has signed a statement admitting it.'

'That's his b-business,' Dempsey said.

'You thought that would be the end of the matter. But you couldn't be sure. So you got Byrne to keep an eye on Butcher. He saw us bringing him into the station for questioning and you began to get worried. And then when I went out to his house to question him again, you panicked. You thought that Butcher was going to spill the beans, so you had Byrne murder him too. Isn't that right?'

'No,' Dempsey said.

'Byrne says it is.'

'He's a liar. It's his word against mine. Who is a jury likely to believe? A confessed murderer or a respectable b-business-man?'

He smiled and Megarry saw the confidence in his eyes.

'I'm not finished,' he said. 'The loose cannon in all of this was George Buchanan. You had been using him to keep an eye on

222

your daughter. You were worried about her cocaine habit. Why is she called Clarke by the way?'

Dempsey sniffed. 'It's her professional name. For modelling. They all use fancy names.'

Megarry nodded. 'George is a fool. The trouble is, he had seen something in Brannigan's Bar. He'd seen Paul Byrne with Harpo Higgins the night Higgins was murdered. He added things together and unfortunately for him, he came up with the truth.

'His big mistake was telling you. It almost cost him his life. The trouble is once you embark on murder it's hard to stop. It gets easier. And if I hadn't seen Byrne driving out of your premises with George and decided to follow them, George would certainly he dead now and there would be no one left to tell the tale.

'I've had doubts about Byrne for some while. He tipped me off about Marie O'Gorman. At the time I thought he was just being helpful. Later I realised that he'd sent me there because he knew of the bad blood between Higgins and Marie O'Gorman's father. He was simply trying to throw me off the scent. It was a crude attempt to draw suspicion on to O'Gorman.'

'Is that it?' Dempsey said and finished his wine.

'Almost. You also interfered with the police investigation, didn't you?'

Megarry saw Kelly glance up sharply.

'Did I?'

'You tried to bribe me. The security job you offered.'

Dempsey laughed. 'I was doing you a f-favour. I thought you could do with the money.'

'I think you succeeded in bribing another officer. I think you know what I'm talking about.'

They sat for a while and no one spoke. Then Dempsey slowly stood up.

Megarry motioned to Kelly who got up too and put a hand on Dempsey's shoulder.

'I'm arresting you in connection with the murders of James Higgins and Edward Butcher and with the attempted murder of George Buchanan. I think we can bring a charge of aiding and abetting the commission of these murders.'

He spoke the words in a steady voice, a bit more formally than he would normally speak. Megarry suspected it was the first time he had used them. It was probably something they had taught him at police college.

Dempsey looked from one man to the other and shrugged.

They walked through to the kitchen. Claire Dempsey had turned off the cooker and was watching television. She got up quickly and Megarry could see from the look on her face that she knew something was wrong.

'I have to go with these p-police officers,' Dempsey said. 'Ring Cahill at once and tell him to come immediately to . . .' He turned to Megarry. 'Where are we going?'

'Barrack Street.'

'B-barrack Street station. Tell him to b-bring money for bail. Tell him this is urgent.'

They walked through the house and out to the hall. It had grown dark outside.

Dempsey took an overcoat from a rack and put it on. He smiled at Megarry as he buttoned it up. 'I find it gets quite c-cool in the evenings,' he said.

25

The following morning Megarry woke early. He lay in bed listening to Andrew rustling about as he prepared to go to work. Then, after he had heard the big front door close and the car drive away from the house, he got up and went downstairs and rang Mulqueen from the phone in the hall.

He got put through to his office. He heard Mulligan answer, 'He's not here right now.'

'This is Cecil Megarry speaking.'

'Oh,' Mulligan said. 'Tell you the truth, he won't be in at all today. He's called in sick.'

'Right,' Megarry said.

'You could try him at home. Have you got his number?'

'Yes, I've got it.'

Megarry put down the phone and searched in his contact book. Outside, the sky was overcast and it looked like rain. He rang Mulqueen's number and got his wife.

'He's in bed,' she said. 'He's not well.'

'I need to talk to him. It's important.'

He waited while she plodded away and then he heard Mulqueen come on the line.

'Dan. It's Cecil here. You're not feeling good?'

'I'm dying. I've twisted my back or something. I've had to get the doctor.'

'You heard what's been happening? Kelly has arrested two men in connection with the murders.'

'I heard.'

'I need to talk to you, Dan.'

He listened as Mulqueen started to complain. 'Jesus, Cecil. I'm dying. I'm running a temperature and it looks like it's going to piss rain any minute.'

'I have to see you,' Megarry said. 'We have to talk.'

Something in his voice alerted the other man.

'What is it?'

'Something that's come up. Something important.'

'How long will it take?'

'It shouldn't take long.'

'Where do you want to meet me? I can't be seen walking the streets and me that's supposed to be sick.'

'Name somewhere.'

'I'll see you in the White Hind. It's a pub along the quays. Do you know it?'

'I'll find it.'

'I'll see you there in an hour.'

Megarry went back upstairs and got washed and dressed. When he came down again, Kathleen and her sister were sitting at the breakfast table.

'You're going home?' Nancy said. There was genuine regret in her voice.

'Yes,' Megarry said and buttered some toast. 'All good things must come to an end.'

'But we've hardly seen you at all. You've been running around on this business of yours. You know you can stay here as long as you want. Andrew was just saying last night how he'll miss you at the darts.'

'He'll have to find another partner,' Megarry said and topped up his tea.

'He has plenty of partners. It's you he'll miss.'

Megarry smiled.

'We *have* to go, Nancy,' Kathleen said. 'We haven't seen Jennifer for ages. And Cecil has to report back to work. He's got some serious decisions to make.' She leaned across and squeezed Megarry's hand. 'Haven't you, dear?'

'Yes,' Megarry said.

He walked down to the station. It was a dull morning, one of those brooding, dark mornings that sometimes appear in late spring, with menacing clouds louring across the sky. The sea beyond the harbour was in turmoil. He could see the waves lashing against the rocks of the lighthouse.

He took the train, listening to the clatter of the wheels as it rattled past Sutton and Bayside and into the city. He thought of what he would say to Mulqueen and how he would talk to him.

He felt a tired sadness take hold of him as if his mood was matched by the weather, the rain that was now beginning to beat against the windows of the train. He was glad he had brought his coat and hat. It was a wise precaution.

He got off at Tara Street and walked out along the river. The rain was blanketing the city now, a dull grey mist falling relentlessly from a leaden sky. He found the pub and chose a seat near the door where he could watch for Mulqueen. He ordered a large Bushmills and waited.

He thought how long he had known him. Seven years. That conference on cross-border police co-operation in the quiet County Louth hotel all that time ago. A bright young detective asking all the right questions, clearly destined for promotion. The fact that he was there at all showed that he had already come to the attention of his superiors.

And yet, he thought, what do I really know about him? All we have done is exchange cards at Christmas, talk on the phone. At the end of the day, I know nothing about him at all.

Mulqueen came in out of the rain, hulking into his overcoat, shaking himself like a dog, cursing and swearing. 'Christ Almighty,' he said. 'This better be important.'

'Sit down, Dan,' Megarry said. 'Dry yourself. What can I get you?'

'I'll have a brandy.'

Megarry waved to catch the barman's attention and waited till he brought the drink. 'Back is a terrible devil,' he said.

'Trouble is, they never can quite put a finger on the problem. What did the doctor say?'

'Oh,' Mulqueen said and waved his hand. 'You know doctors. He told me to rest. He said if the pain isn't gone in a fortnight he'd send me to a specialist. That'll be more money. It's all a racket.'

'Adam Smith said that all professions are a conspiracy against the public.'

'Did he now?' Mulqueen sipped his brandy. 'Well begod he was right. He sure as hell knew what he was talking about.'

Megarry was reminded of their first conversation that day in the Royal Hotel, his complaints about money, making ends meet. He could see now where the temptation had entered in.

He took out his cigarettes and lit a match. 'You know that the case is practically wrapped up. Kelly has charged Paul Byrne and Harry Dempsey. I'm told that the superintendent is delighted. Kelly is a bright young spark. He'll go places.' He waited for the other man's reaction.

'I heard. I got a phone call this morning. Jesus, Cecil, I take so much stick that I hate to be away when things are going well.' He tried to smile. 'But I also hear that Dempsey's out on bail. He's hired the best lawyers. He's going to fight it. He's a powerful bastard. He won't go down easily.'

'We have witnesses,' Megarry said softly. 'People who will testify that he was threatening Harpo Higgins. I think Kelly will nail him in the end.'

'Who?' Mulqueen said.

'I can't tell you that. You know the way witnesses can be intimidated.'

'But I'm the bloody inspector in charge of the case.'

Megarry didn't reply. Instead he said: 'When you talked to the Drugs Squad, they told you that they knew nothing about Higgins?'

'Sure they did.'

'Well, it turns out he had a record.'

He saw something in the other man's face. A brief flicker and then it was gone.

228

'He had several convictions for drugs possession. He served a number of prison sentences.'

'Jesus,' Mulqueen said. 'Is that a fact? Those bastards in the Drugs Squad. You can't trust them as far as you could throw them. I told you that. They're a bunch of prima donnas. They're jealous, they don't like us butting in on their business.' He lifted his glass, finished it off and started to get up. 'Is that what you brought me here to tell me? That Higgins had a record? Is that why you dragged me out into the rain?'

'There's more,' Megarry said.

The other man hesitated, then lowered himself once more into the seat. He tried to avoid Megarry's eyes.

'You knew Higgins had a record, didn't you? You hid it from me. Why did you do that?'

'Excuse me?'

Mulqueen started to protest. Megarry saw that a blood vessel in his neck had begun to pulsate, throbbing violently beneath the skin. He suddenly felt sorry for him. He had felt sorry for him from the first moment he had known.

'For God's sake, Dan. I found the damned thing in your filing cabinet.'

'I can explain it.'

'Don't.'

Megarry thumped the table and the ashtray shivered. 'O'Toole gave it to you. He told me. You withheld it from me. Denied its existence when I asked you. Why did you do that? What did you hope to gain? I was bound to find out in the end.'

He realised that what was hurting him was the stupidity of it all. A promising career in ruins for a stupid bribe.

'You did it to hamper the inquiry. The same way you brought in Eddie Butcher to prevent me interviewing him. You were working against me, undermining me. You went to the superintendent and had me taken off the case.'

'No.'

'Yes. You complained about me. Said I was interfering. An RUC man working on a Garda murder case. And all the time I thought I was helping you. Doing you a favour.'

Mulqueen hung his head.

'How much did Dempsey pay you?'

The other man didn't reply.

'How did he make his approach? Did he offer to make you head of his new security outfit? Was that what it was?'

'No,' Mulqueen said. 'He offered me money. I'm in debt, Cecil. For God's sake. Do you know how much I earn? It's a pittance and I have to knock my ass in, and take all that pressure, all that abuse. Every time something goes wrong I get dumped on. I didn't think it was such a big deal. There's loads of guys taking money.'

'To throw a murder case? I'd say that's a big deal all right.'

Megarry realised that the other man was silently weeping. He took out a handkerchief and passed it across. He looked at Mulqueen, the thinning hair, the dark circles beneath his eyes. He felt his sorrow melt into anger. 'You've a wife and kids, for Christ's sake. Didn't you think of them?'

'Of course. I did it for them.'

Mulqueen blew his nose. A man came in and went to the counter and ordered a glass. He looked around the pub at the handful of drinkers and then he took off his cap and shook the rain out of it.

'What are you going to do?' Mulqueen said at last. 'Are you going to report me?'

Megarry shook his head. 'I'm going to do nothing. It's up to you. You know what you've got to do.'

He stubbed out his cigarette and pointed to Mulqueen's empty glass. 'I'll get you another drink,' he said.

He left the pub and took the bus out to Ballymoss. He watched from the window as the damp city passed by, dreary buildings shrouded in rain. He got off at the shopping centre and went into the butcher's shop and bought a couple of cooked chickens and a ham. Then he called at the supermarket and picked up some small, cheap toys. He got the assistant to wrap them for him.

He climbed the cold, concrete stairs of the tower block and pressed the bell on Annie Nolan's door. She came, tentatively, the way he knew she would, peering out from the cramped little flat, as if wondering what new tragedy he was bringing into their lives.

'I'm going home,' he said. 'I called to say goodbye.'

She brought him in and put the kettle on. He gave her the gifts he'd bought, the food and toys for the children. He thought she might be offended as if it was charity, but she seemed pleased. She put the food in the fridge.

'The kids are at school,' she said. She rattled the parcels. 'What's in them?'

'Nothing much,' Megarry said. 'Only a few small things.'

'They'll be delighted. I'll leave them in the front room and they can open them when they come home.'

She poured the tea and they sat together smoking cigarettes in the kitchen.

'You missed the wake we had for Harpo in the Blackthorn Stick.'

'I couldn't come. Was it good?'

'It was a great night. Great bit of craic. A lot of his old friends turned up. Harpo would have enjoyed it.'

'I'm glad,' Megarry said. 'You know we've charged two people with his murder?'

'Who are they?'

'Paul Byrne. He's a bad person. He killed another man. And Harry Dempsey.'

She looked up. 'That's Harpo's father-in-law.'

'Yes.'

'He should never have got mixed up with those people. They weren't his class.' She shook her head. 'Why did they do it?'

'It's a long story,' Megarry said.

'Will it stick?'

'Yes. I think it will.'

They sat for a while longer. Megarry could see the rain beating against the window, the grey mist stretching away over the roof-tops.

'His wife is trying to get the boy back,' Annie Nolan said. 'Little Henry. She's gone to court.'

'I expected that,' Megarry said.

She reached out and took his hand. 'Harpo loved him. He would have done anything for that kid.'

'I know that,' Megarry said. 'That's why Harpo died.'

They finished the tea and she walked with him to the door. 'You're from the North?'

'Yes. Belfast.'

'It's quiet up there now,' she said. 'Please God it will last.'

'Yes,' Megarry said. 'Please God.'

They left for home the following morning soon after breakfast. It was a beautiful day, a clear sky and the sun filtering through the branches of the trees in the garden.

Andrew took the morning off work and Nancy pottered about the kitchen, wrapping up cakes and boxes of scones. She had been baking for the past two days.

'You shouldn't have done this,' Kathleen said as her sister pressed the packages into her hand.

'They're for Cecil. He likes my scones. Don't you, Cecil?'

'Of course,' Megarry said. He hated farewells, all the fuss.

Andrew helped to carry the suitcases out to the waiting car. 'I'll miss you,' he said. 'Our games of darts. You know you should keep it up. You were really improving. Is there anywhere near you at home where you could play?'

'I'll find somewhere,' Megarry said.

'You should. Even if you only played once a week. It's amazing the progress you would make.'

Megarry stood awkwardly beside the car. Now that the decision had been taken to leave he wanted to get away quickly. Just then he heard a horn beeping and saw Kelly's car come driving up the road. He stopped and got out.

'I've come to see you off.'

'That's very kind of you.'

'Well you've been kind to me.'

He drew Megarry aside and whispered in his ear. 'There's been a development. I just heard this morning. Mulqueen has resigned.'

Megarry raised his eyebrows. 'What reason did he give?'

232

'Pressure of work. Doctor's advice. He'll get part of his pension, I think. He should be able to find another job.'

'He wasn't cut out for it,' Megarry said. 'He didn't have the temperament.' He stroked his chin. 'So that leaves a vacancy for an inspector?'

'Yes.'

'You should apply.'

They all shook hands and Megarry got into the driving seat. He'd got a new radio. He switched it on. There was a band playing traditional Irish music. He remembered the day he had called in to the Cock Tavern and heard the musicians there.

They drove away from the house, down the main street and past the harbour. The sea was peaceful. He could see the sand sparkling on the shore at Ireland's Eye.

'What are you thinking?' Kathleen said as they went past the train station.

Megarry shrugged. 'Nothing much.'

Kathleen punched him playfully on the shoulder. 'C'mon. I know you too well.'

'I was thinking,' Megarry said, 'that I was happy here.'